December Bride

by

Sam Hanna Bell

CAVAN COUNTY LIBRARY

ACC. No. ....

CLASS No. ....

INVOICE No ....

PRICE ....

Belfast

BLACKSTAFF PRESS

1974

First published in 1951 by
Denis Dobson Limited
This Blackstaff Press edition is a photolithographic facsimile of the first edition
printed by Denis Dobson Limited and is unabridged
with the exception of the preliminary pages

This edition published in 1974 by
The Blackstaff Press Limited
3 Galway Park, Dundonald, Belfast BT16 0AN, Northern Ireland
Reprinted 1982, 1983, 1985, 1989

© Sam Hanna Bell, 1951
All rights reserved

Printed by The Guernsey Press Company Limited

ISBN 0-85640-061-0

CAVAN COUNTY LIBRARY

ACC. No. C/29.721

CLASS No. F

INVOICE NO. 6171

PRICE £4.95

To

MILDRED

—'Oh! in brief, they will fade till old,
And their loves grow numbed ere death, by
the cark of care,'
—'But nought see we that asks for portents
there?—
' 'Tis the lot of all'—'Well, no less true is a
portent
That it fits all mortal mould.'

THOMAS HARDY

(This is from the poem 'Honeymoon-Time' in
'Moments of Vision.')

This stanza is quoted by kind permission of
the publishers, Macmillan & Co. Ltd, and the
Trustees of the Hardy Estate.

PART ONE

CAVAN COUNTY LIBRARY

CHAPTER ONE

*

RAVARA MEETING-HOUSE mouldered among its gravestones like a mother surrounded by her spinster children. To-day the winter wind poured across the fields. It flung a handful of starlings over the church and plucked the caps and skirts of the men and women sheltering behind the gravestones. A man, with a billhook in his hand, broke through the hedge that surrounded the churchyard and hurried towards the gravelled path. Along the hedge bordering the road the weak sun glinted on curves and ellipses of bicycle wheels.

In the church, with his back to the communion rail, and the book in his hand open at the marriage service, stood the Reverend Isaac Sorleyson. The man and woman before him, Hamilton Echlin and Sarah Gomartin, were elderly, stooped, huddled together as if for protection. The whimpering wind and the breathless silence of the church heightened the loneliness of the two and gave an impression absurd and pathetic to the ceremony. Behind the bridegroom stood a youth of about nineteen years of age. Throughout the service he had strained to follow the minister's words, only relaxing to glance back into the glimmering church or to reassure himself that the wedding ring was still embedded in his sweating palm.

'Do you, Hamilton, take this woman, Sarah, to be your lawfully wedded wife ...' The responses were given, and

9

at a sign from Sorleyson, the young man dropped the ring into the dark cupped hand of the bridegroom. Echlin took his bride's hand, and with her assistance managed to press the ring over the first gnarled joint of her finger. But the lower knuckle, hard and dented as a chestnut, was too large for the ring and Sarah timorously drew back her hand. Sorleyson caught it abruptly. 'I think we should manage to do it properly,' he said, and tried to press the ring down to the root of her finger. As she winced, he lowered her hand with a look of annoyance, leaving the ring turning loosely in the middle of the fleshless concave finger.

'If you'll follow me to the vestry,' he said, waving his hand towards a door in the shadow of the pulpit. 'You too, Mr Neilly, please!' he called into the empty church. From the darkness of the last pew at the back of the church a man appeared and came trotting down the aisle with a fixed smile on his face, a bunch of keys chattering and tinkling from his hand. 'Right your reverence, right now,' he answered, waving his free hand deprecatingly as he approached them. The bridal party followed Sorleyson into the small room where he unlocked a cupboard, took out a flat black book and opened it on a narrow table. 'You sign here,' and with his firm young fingers he guided the gnarled discoloured hands of the man and woman. 'Now you, Andrew,' and he handed the pen to the youth, 'write your name here, where it says "in the presence of us".' He took the pen, wrote 'Andrew', hesitated for a moment and added 'Echlin'. Sorleyson glanced at the sexton and pointed to the pen. With practised carelessness he scrawled in his signature, laid down the pen, looked at the married couple, and then, without speaking, slithered out of the door and hurried up the aisle.

Sorleyson thrust out his hands and caught those of Hamilton and Sarah. 'Congratulations and may God bless you both!' he cried. He held Sarah's hand for a little longer. 'It wasn't too bad, was it?' 'No,' she replied. 'No, it wasn't. Thank ye, Mr Sorleyson.' 'Aye,' echoed Hamilton fumbling to take the minister's hand again, 'Thank ye, thank ye.'

Sorleyson replaced the register, locked the cupboard, and opened the door leading to the church. 'Now,' he said.

The creak of the varnished door started the sexton from his seat in the last pew. He peered down the shadowy aisle to make sure that Sorleyson and the others were ready to leave the church. Then he slid as quickly and quietly as a ferret round the main door into the porch. When he appeared, the men and women nearest the church rose from the gravestones and shook themselves. The sexton nodded abruptly and glanced over his shoulder. Suddenly he threw up his hand in warning and started back into the shadows.

Hamilton and Sarah came slowly out of the brown dusk of the porch and hesitated uncertainly in the pale sunlight. Behind them came Andrew, his face turned to the minister whose snowy collar gleamed in the shadow. Then the youth looked out towards the churchyard; his face contracted when he saw the waiting country people, and with a word and a touch he urged the newly-married couple forward.

Hamilton, tall and stooped, wore a dark hopsack suit of

old-fashioned cut with all four buttons of the jacket fastened. The arm on which rested Sarah's hand was bent across his chest, holding in its fingers a bowler hat. From his other knotted and discoloured hand hung a pair of gloves, the fingers flat, stiff and unopened. When he left the shelter of the church the wind lifted the strands of hair that had been combed over his bald crown. Sarah was between fifty and fifty-five years of age, erect, with a confident step which became more pronounced as she approached the country people, giving her an air of boldness heightened by the unnatural colour throbbing in her cheeks. She kept her eyes downcast on the gravel as she walked, only raising them for an instant when she felt giddy. Her complexion had the appearance and texture of wax, and the deep and shadowy furrows which ran from each side of her nostrils to the corners of her mouth accentuated the soft, full and fading lips. She wore a tailored coat of fine grey material, open so that the stuff of her wedding-dress was visible, steel-grey in colour, with an ill-cut cameo pinned in the lace yoke. A shallow black hat with a blue and white ornament in front was set straight on top of her mouse-coloured hair, and the hair was so arranged at the temples as to cover, not with complete success, a white streak.

'They make a gladsome couple, eh?' remarked the man with the billhook as he watched Hamilton and Sarah from between two stones.

'Aye, and making his own son follow him as best man —it's a crying shame!' added the woman beside him, drawing her fat arms that were red with the cold, further under her shawl. The man with the billhook shot a lance of tobacco spittle into a cluster of porcelain flowers. '*Whose* son?' he asked, quizzing the woman sardonically. 'He's as bad as the rest—there's bad blood in the whole bloody tribe.'

Andrew, having failed to reply to some question of the minister's or even raise his head, Sorleyson turned his attention to the spectators who had suddenly retreated into the churchyard or made their way out and some distance down the road. After waiting patiently in the chill wind for a glimpse of the newly-married pair, the country-folk were taken aback to find the Reverend Mr Sorleyson escorting them from the church. So now, skulking among the truncated pillars and crumbling doves, they fixed curious eyes on this joyless bridal procession, only withdrawing their glances when they threatened to meet the angry and persistent stare of the minister.

The sexton, who had trotted diagonally through the graveyard winking and grimacing to his neighbours, passed out through a side-gate, and crossing the road, disappeared into the church-house stable. He came out backwards in the shafts of a light trap which he drew on to the road and lowered gingerly until it rested on its step. 'Raḅbie!' he shouted at a little boy in a ragged jersey who stood with crossed legs against the wall, 'away and fetch Mr Echlin's pony!'

The horse being led out, with arched neck and oat husks on his muzzle, Andrew then took charge, and as the bit was being adjusted, a pound note passed into the sexton's hand. A little distance down the road, beyond the church gates, several men still lingered, and in the ditch two or three women, their hands rolled in their aprons, peered through the twigs of a thornbush.

Their scrutiny was short-lived. Mr Sorleyson was seen nodding energetically to a remark of Mrs Echlin's, the sexton flew into the church-house and returned with the minister's overcoat into which he helped him after removing his Geneva strings and billowing gown. The pound note still being warm on his thigh, the sexton, shielding the gesture from the distant observers, endeavoured to shake hands with the party. He secured Sarah's fingertips, touched the closed hand of Hamilton, and found that Andrew had mounted the trap and was now drawing up the reins. The others followed, and the whip being rattled in its cup, the vehicle moved away. The peasants came running towards the sexton who stood cracking his knuckles in glee, his face wreathed in smiles.

The trap stopped about a quarter-of-a-mile from the church at the mouth of a loanen, more dignified than that which led to a farm because of its bevel-clipped hedges. Here Sorleyson dismounted after shaking hands with the occupants of the trap. He held the young man's hand in his for a second and spoke clearly and loudly. 'Why don't you come down some evening and see us, Andrew?' For a moment the strained look left the other's face. He nodded. 'I'll try—some evening.'

The manse which the Sorleysons occupied was visible a short distance along the loanen. It was a pleasant, two-storied, white-washed building, seen through the scattered apple trees on the lawn. The window-panes, crystal clear and bulging outward slightly in their narrow frames, gave an airy appearance to the house. But Mr Sorleyson did not hurry inward. Leaning his arms on the dry yielding hedge, he studied the ploughland on the other side, his eyes running up the curving furrows until they become flattened cogs on the skyline. He felt nothing but satisfaction at what he had done. What weighed most with him, he reflected, was the pleasure that his father would feel in knowing that Hamilton and Sarah were now married. That alone justified the casuistry. Except what his predecessor had told him, he knew very little of their history. From his father he had had only a few disjointed words of concern, and then, on the last time he had questioned him, an agonised pressure of the hand, which had left him in surprise and wondering silence as the old man withdrew to his room. Thinking of it afterwards, he remembered that this had been the old man's first charge, and the son felt again, vicariously and for a moment, the anguish of his father.

As he stood gazing at the pent-in landscape, he thought it no irreverent fancy to interpret as the Divine Will that he should be instrumental in bringing back to the paths of propriety these two souls that must have caused his father so much sorrow. At that moment he raised his eyes to the hill-farm of Rathard. The horse and trap had drawn up in the farm-close and he watched the elderly couple and their son dismount. Echlin and the young man commenced to unyoke the horse, and the woman, drawing her skirts around her, crossed over to the house. Sorleyson's face clouded. He ruffled the hedgetop with his open hand. Yes, I trapped her into it. I failed just as much as my predecessors failed; as much as my father failed. He heard his name called, and turning, saw his father standing under the apple trees.

The elder man came forward, his eyes shining mildly behind his spectacles. His hair turning white, was still full and crisp on the back of his head. He wore a dark suit, a spotless white shirt and collar, and his black tie was loosely twined, the flat knot lying on his shirt-front. He had the benign and silvery aspect of one whose life pre-occupation has been the minutiae of human experience.

He placed his hand on his son's shoulder. 'Are you tired?' he asked. The young minister smiled and shook his head. 'No, not very.' Both men turned and walked slowly across the lawn towards the house. 'And your—most remarkable wedding service, it went smoothly?'

'Yes, oh yes. When I prayed, I asked them to kneel. I think I did right.' The father chose to ignore the note of query in his son's reply. Their feet were sounding on the gravel before the house when he suddenly said, 'If the reasons for most marriages were stated you would be astounded at the ingenuity of your fellow-men—and perhaps appalled at their courage. Fortunately, that is not our business.'

At this remark a look of uneasiness and annoyance came on the young man's face. He shook his father's shoulder gently. 'You old cynic,' he said with a laugh. As Mr Sorleyson was long past the age when the epithet could be considered a compliment he did not smile in reply. In silence the two men mounted the worn steps of the manse.

CHAPTER TWO

*

THE FARM OF RATHARD sat crescent-shaped on a low green hill screened by beech trees from the misty winds that rose from the lough in the winter. On summer evenings the cream-washed homestead, eyed by the setting sun, blushed warmly under the dark foliage. Swelling gently from the shores of Strangford Lough, the hill had borne habitation for centuries. Behind the dwelling-house lay an ancient rath from whence an earlier people had looked down on the sinuous waters of the lough. Now nothing more martial was heard than the cry of a cock, or the low piping of bees from the seven hives which sat in the curve of the bowed earth walls. The house faced inland; to its right, towards the lough, were the barns and byres. To its left, the stackyard, bounded by a delicate file of rowan trees which ended where the rutted loanen, climbing from the road, emptied into the close.

When Margaret Echlin turned her face from her husband and sons, from dung-crusted beasts and hungry fowl and clashing pails, only then did her husband Andrew realise what part she had filled in Rathard. It was as if the whole framework of the farm's daily life had been withdrawn. Hardly a task about the kitchen or the fields but now lacked some essential part. Urgently, Andrew set about finding someone to tend to himself and his sons.

His task was not an easy one, for Rathard was surrounded by prosperous cottiers, the farms of which absorbed all the labour that each family could expend. But in the neighbouring townland of Banyil was a group of labourers' cottages in which lived the old residenters or their children, tenants of a vanished demense. In one of these cottages lived Charlie Gomartin, a thatcher, with his wife and daughter Sarah, now a woman of thirty years. Charlie had travelled the countryside to ply his trade; but as time passed and Sarah grew up, his circuits became wider and his appearances at home more and more infrequent, until at last he disappeared entirely, and a rumour drifted to Banyil that he had died on a Sligo road among tinker people.

Martha Gomartin and her daughter earned their money working in the houses and fields of neighbouring farmers, more often that of Mr Bourke, owner of the cottages. Martha was held in regard for her labour, frugality and honesty. Sarah, like herself, was a fine worker, better in the kitchen than her mother. Some said that she was as simple as a mouse, others that she was a sly lady. But she went her road quietly and didn't meddle with the boys.

Andrew Echlin sent word to Mrs Gomartin that he would have her come up to Rathard at her convenience. Accordingly, the next evening, Martha and her daughter entered the close before the Echlin's farmhouse. A collie rose dustily from a corner of the close and stretching out his neck, barked at the two women. They heard the screech of a chair pushed back on the tiled floor of the kitchen, and Andrew appeared on the threshold, twisting his fingers in his beard. 'Come in, Martha,' he said smiling at his neighbour and her daughter.

The Echlins had worked late at some distance from the farmhouse and were now seated at their evening meal. When Martha had spoken to the two sons, who ducked their heads in answer, she and Sarah took seats along the wall close to the door. Andrew reached down cups and saucers from the dresser and filled them with dark pungent tea. When he added milk the tea turned to a bright unappetising brown. Only the faintest thread of vapour rose from the cups. He watched Martha take one sip and then set her cup aside on the shelf of the sewing-machine. Her daughter held her cup cradled in her lap.

The old man laughed apologetically. 'Ye can see, Martha. There's hands wanted here.'

Mrs Gomartin was cautious. She studied the roughly set table and the choked hearth. 'Things might be redd up a wee-thing, Andra,' she agreed.

'Well, there ye are now,' said Andrew slapping his leg softly.

The young men and the young woman studied each other discreetly in passing glances. The seated men were framed in the long black oak dresser on the shelves of which rested row on row of cottage-blue and willow-pattern plates. The women itched to be at the soot that masked their bright faces. The mother saw them sparkling; the daughter saw them sparkling and ranked in symmetry of size and shape. But not a sign was made. Martha, her hands resting lightly on the arms of her chair listening patiently to the patriarch Andrew speaking for himself and his sons; Sarah listening dutifully to the talk of her elders and only seeming to rest when she glanced casually at the young men. Frank, the younger brother, had stopped eating when the visitors arrived and now pushed crumbs around his plate with the end of his cigarette. He lounged carelessly in his chair, slim and brown, glancing thoughtfully at the girl from below his tumbled fair hair. Hamilton, seated in his father's shadow, had politely suspended his meal until the women had tea. Now he pushed his plate away after mopping up the last of the *mealycreeshy* which had been their evening dish. He spooned honey into the heart of a farl and as the sweet slowly uncoiled from his knife he amused himself with the thought that the hair of Martha's daughter was the same colour, but he turned his dark face stolidly to his father's talk. She's a cold pale one, thought Frank, with no sport in her. Then he caught her calm ever-moving glance, and felt uncertain again.

'Well, Martha, there's room beyont for both of ye,' said Andrew, inclining his head towards the lower part of the house. 'Ye may come as soon as you're free o' the Bourkes. Ye'd be needed here at the harvest, and in the winter it would be a great convenience to have the house tended to.' The old man leaned forward with a smile wrinkling his eyes. 'We dinna often hear a step in the close, but ye can aye go down the road when you're lonely.'

Mrs Gomartin carefully folded her square, work-thickened fingers in her lap. 'It makes no great odds, Andra,' she replied with a quick upward lift of her head. 'A widow's seat is aye a lonely seat.'

'Aye, God knows that's true enough,' answered Andrew, staring sombrely at the wall.

Three days later Mrs Gomartin closed her cottage and came with her daughter to live in the Echlins' house. The women were given the two lower rooms of the house, one as a bedroom and one as a living room. The effect of the Gomartins moving in became quickly evident. In the house, meals were more punctual and a greater variety of dishes appeared on the table. Beds were no longer confused heaps of malodorous clothes. Outside, in the work around the farm, Martha and Sarah took their share of the harvesting. Sarah had an amazing capacity for hard work. She was deft and quick in her movements, and brought her strength to the point where it would have greatest effect. She would have been considered a graceful girl, but she neutralised that by her cold and detached expression.

The Echlins and the Gomartins were members of the same Presbyterian congregation, and on Sundays the five members of the two families drove in the trap to the meeting-house. It had been the custom of the two young men, when the horse was stabled and the trap put away, to join the young men and women in the churchyard where they spent the few minutes before the service began in talking and flirting with each other. On the second Sabbath after they had driven to the church with the Gomartins, Frank was surprised to see his brother hasten into the church with only a nod to his old companions. He sat on a flat gravestone, gazing thoughtfully at the doorway through which Hamilton had disappeared, and quite unmindful of the talk of the young men around him.

The rain and winds which had beaten the corn until it

lay tangled like the hair of a sleeping man, gave way to serene weather and the harvesters eked out each hour of light in the mellow August evening. Andrew opened the fields with his scythe, Hamilton or Frank rode the reaper, while Martha, Sarah and Petie Sampson, a labouring man, gathered and tied. Behind them Andrew stooked the sheaves. Frank's satisfaction at Sarah's indifference to his brother was tempered by the knowledge that it extended to himself. It gave way to chagrin when he saw the growing affection between his father and the young woman. From the first, Sarah had felt drawn towards Andrew, inspired by his kindness, humour and prophetic appearance. She was also impelled by a trait in herself, not uncommon in those who have tasted poverty, which made her prefer the father to the son, the master rather than the steward. But Sarah was a woman incapable of coquetry and none of her attentions to the old man was spoiled by lack of innocence. Only Frank, his mind overcast by his own desires, misinterpreted them.

CHAPTER THREE

*

SARAH MOVED SLOWLY along the hedge that bordered the grazing field sloping from the farm to the brink of the brae over the lough. Occasionally, she knelt and drew out a sere twig from the ditch and put it in her pursed-up apron. She descended the slope until she was approaching the turn of the hedge over the lough. Her gleaning was so small and her steps so listless that it was evident that the gathering of kindling was only the outward sign of an inner preoccupation. But even here, a solitary figure in the dusk, no sign, no smile, no frown or poise of the head betrayed whether her thoughts were pleasant or otherwise.

She had left the kitchen unable any longer to bear the attention of Frank whose eyes she felt fixed on her head as she bent over her flowering, and which he lowered when at last he had forced a response from her. Then, his sunburnt face cupped in his hands, he had returned her gaze boldly, with a look that filled her with apprehension and fear. She rose, folding up her embroidery, and put on her working apron. The tranquil light from the ceiling-lamp fell on the household as she stood with her hand on the latch: her mother, small and bent, tapping her flowering-hoops with her needle; Andrew, following the newsprint with moving lips, his spectacles balanced halfway between light-filled hair and beard; Hamilton, dozing at the fire. Frank stood up, stretching his arms and yawning. But his eyes were alert, bright, questioning her. She had rebuffed him as she lifted the latch and then hesitated on the threshold, half mindful to go in again.

Now she paused with a sharp intake of breath at a gap overlooking the lough. Below her the islands lay like cattle shoulder-deep in dark grass; flank beyond flank down the dull silver of the water until the last merged in the olive underdusk of the peninsula. He had wilfully misunderstood her. She had wanted to deny him and his smile had said, 'I see, I understand, not *now*.' And she had paused and not gone into her mother again. The grass wetted her stockings and she shivered in the chill air.

When she entered the kitchen again Hamilton and Frank had gone to bed, and her mother, dipping their supper cups in a basin of water, was saying to Andrew who sat girning and muttering at the fire, 'Ah, drink up your cocoa like a good man, till we get away t'our beds.' The old man tipped the contents of his cup into the back of the fire.

'Cocoa's the fruit of the Lord as well as bread,' murmured Martha angrily.

'Aye, and so are herring,' returned Andrew, 'but I dinna feed them to a horse. Sarah daughter, wet me a cup o' tea, for my mouth's as grummly as a puddle.'

'What's in the wee shed below the brae?' she asked as she lowered the kettle on the crane.

'A boat that Hami bought nine or ten summers ago,' answered Andrew, watching with pleasure the hot water hiss on the leaves. Sarah thrust the belly of the pot between two turves to simmer, and Echlin continued,

'The three of us were coming home from Downpatrick when the boys heard tell o' a punt selling at Finnebrogue, so they bocht her and rowed her the length o' the lough and were home a round hour afore me and the cart. What do you think of that, now?' The women smiled and nodded.

'Will she swim?' asked Sarah, drawing out the pot.

'Aye, she'll swim! She's as tight as a bottle.'

There was silence as Sarah filled the cups. 'Well, will ye take me for a sail?' Andrew laughed and Martha slopped her cloth noisily on the table. She always felt uneasy when her daughter asked favours like this in such a self-assured way, as if a refusal wasn't to be dreamt of.

'I've an errand over tae the Pentlands o' the Island one of these days,' said Andrew, 'and if we're spared, I'll take ye.' Martha, after waiting for their cups, cast out the dish-water across the dark close, shot the bolt again, and went to her bed in silence.

The rich colouring of the land was shorn away, or beaten down by wind and rain. On the hills the grey fields were like the faces of spent men; the leaves lay in sodden drifts in the loanens, and the water rose brownly in the wells. The men ran new runlets against the equinoctial storms, patched barns and byres, brerded hedges where the falling leaf revealed gaps and listened patiently to the indoor needs of the farmwife. The women felt the breasts of fowls, laid fragrant apples in the loft, and in the comfortable farms drew out again voluminous half-finished embroidered cloths from parlour chests.

The rhythm of life in the countryside moves sluggishly in the winter months, but the insistent note of the coming spring is never unheeded, and one morning Andrew said that he would have to cross over to Pentland's to bring back a prize ram. His idea was that all five of them should go, but Martha was against putting her foot in a wee husk of a boat, as she called it. By midday the sky had darkened, and Mrs Gomartin tried to dissuade Sarah from going with the men. But the girl insisted, and after some bickering with her mother, left the farmhouse with Andrew, Hamilton and Frank. As they descended the brae to the beach Andrew pointed out to the girl Pentland's island which lay about a mile and a half down the lough and beyond several smaller islands. From the top of the hill the house could be seen shining in a shaft of sunlight which fell for a moment through the mounting clouds.

Before the boathouse lay bleached rollers, half-buried in the shingle. Andrew unearthed them, and the others ran the boat down to the water, where it rocked gently, with an eager kissing sound. Hamilton lifted Sarah in his arms and placed her in the stern. She thanked him, ignoring the shadow on his brother's face. Andrew pushed off and passed the oar forward to Hamilton, and the two brothers sent the little boat dancing over the shallow leaden waters. Above them to the east, a cloud rose up, spreading rapidly on either hand like a sheaf shaken loose. A blue light played swiftly over the low hills of Ards, followed by a distant brattle of thunder. The boat threaded its way between the intervening islets, crept across the sound, and grated on the shingle beach of Pentland's island. They left the boat and crossed the loose stones. Beyond a belt of coarse grass and shrivelled hare-bells they came upon the path leading up to the farm.

The island was less than half a mile long, and the Echlins and Sarah had arrived on the highest point so that they could look down the whole length of it. Except for two cultivated fields to the east the ground was given over to sheep-grazing, and the animals could be seen moving about in little grey drifts among the knowes and rocks that burst through the close-cropped turf. At the beach nearest the mainland was the shell of a monastic settlement surrounded by smooth grassy mounds, which, Andrew told Sarah, were 'the graves of ould kings'. The farm sat in the middle of the island, and from it, as the travellers paused on the skyline, came the barking of a dog.

Beyond the island, black clouds were mounting on each other's shoulders. 'It's raining down the lough,' said Hamilton, pointing to where a ragged curtain of light fell across the water. A puff of wind lifted their hair. 'Will the boat be all right?' asked Andrew looking back at the beach. When the two young men had satisfied him on this, they moved down towards the farm.

A skift of rain struck their faces as they hurried into Pentland's close, and the sound of their feet on the paving-stones set the dog barking again from whatever outhouse he sheltered in. Fergus Pentland met them at the door-way. He was a man of about thirty, with a brick-red complexion and lank black hair that kept falling down into his eyes. He wore a fine white shirt, a tweed vest and riding breeches, and the porch in which he stood, with its shot-horns and churn of corn hanging on the varnished walls, indicated a genteel and prosperous farmer.

He greeted his visitors affably, but his uncle Andrew's

response was as curt as decency would allow, and he would have pushed past Pentland had the other not retreated before him, which surprised Sarah, who thought him a very well-set-up and pleasant young man. The noise of their arrival had been heard by someone inside the house, for a high quavering voice was heard calling on Andrew's name. Hamilton and Frank beckoned Sarah to follow their father and they entered a large red-flagged kitchen where an old woman sat knitting before the fire.

'Aye, its me, Mother Pentland,' said Andrew, in answer to the old woman's question. 'And who's that wi' ye?' asked the old woman peering beyond the men to Sarah. 'It's Martha Gomartin's daughter. They're gi'ing us a hand up at Rathard now. Come forrit, Sarah, till Mrs Pentland sees ye.'

While Mrs Pentland was shaking hands with Sarah, her grandson was setting forward chairs for the visitors. A young servant appeared, her arms still freckled with meal, and lifting the rings on the range, set the kettle on the fire. When she went to spread the cloth Fergus Pentland rose lazily from the table-corner on which he had seated himself to lean against the firecheek, from where, brown arms folded, he kept up a stream of good-humoured banter with his cousins, occasionally glancing into Sarah's face to see if he had her attention. The girl, seated between Andrew and the old lady who had their heads together and Frank, Hamilton and Pentland, tried to remain slightly withdrawn from both conversations. On the one side old age and low voices; on the other youth, and laughter, and the invitation in Pentland's eye. She smiled, then she laughed and moved her chair a degree towards Pentland. She decided that she had never seen such an elegant good-natured young man before.

The meal was almost finished when the storm broke in the lough. The farmhouse quivered under the first impact and the windows chattered in their frames. Then there was a momentary relief in gushing rain. Unable to see through the streaming panes, Andrew went to the door. Beyond the ken of the island everything was blotted out, and the rolling knowes and farm loomed and disappeared in the driven fog. The hiss and whine of the rain filled the air, but when the wind lifted its bow the roaring of the lough in its thousand holes and rocks came to the old man's ears.

'Is it wild, Andra?' asked Mrs Pentland as he came in.

'There's a bit av a blow on, but that's no newance in these parts,' he answered.

'Ye may bide a while then,' said the old lady.

'We'll bide till it clears a bit, but we'll have to be on the move afore dark. Could the ram be got ready?' Andrew addressed himself to Mrs Pentland as if reluctant to speak to her grandson.

'Fergus, will ye fetch the ram and halter him? Ye can get Geordie tae lead him down tae your uncle's boat.'

'Peh!' cried Andrew. 'Aren't there three of us in each other's road already, to fetch a bit o' a ram across!'

But when the rain and wind offered a moment of escape, it was found that the ram, a powerful and thick-coated Border Leicester, had been so enraged by the tethering that he hung back on the rope as intractable as a donkey, and had to be dragged up the close. Now as he slithered and danced angrily outside the door, his bellows, penetrating the storm, were answered by his plaintive dams as they stood heads buried in the whins and tails out to the rain. Pentland came stamping into the kitchen and it seemed to Sarah that some of his good-nature had worn away. 'Sorra take it for a bad beast, that!' he declared, slapping his chafed hands on his soaked sleeves. The farm-hand standing in the doorway declared that it would be folly to attempt to drag the ram over the island and suggested throwing him on the slipe and hauling him down to the boat.

Hamilton agreed with this, but Andrew seemed determined to oppose any suggestions of Pentland's, and declared that a man could carry the beast round the island, and going out he caught the ram by his woolly pow and with the unwilling help of his sons raised it on his shoulders. But his triumph was short-lived. The muscular arm could not hold the writhing animal, and after a few staggering steps the ram slithered out of his grasp and would have been away into the mist had not the servingman caught the tether and Hamilton thrown himself on the animal's fleecy back. 'That's enough o' this foolishness,' said Hamilton sharply, taking the rope in his hands. 'Away and fetch the slipe, Geordie,' he said to the man, and when it was dragged out the ram was tied and laid upon it.

By this time the Echlins were soaked and Mrs Pentland would have delayed them further to dry themselves, but they were determined to go. Fergus returned to the kitchen with an armful of oilskins. As he unknotted the strings of Sarah's sou'wester he bent his mouth to her ear,

'Let's hope there's warmth and sunshine when ye come back,' he said.

She looked up at him from under the hood. 'Then it's the summer ye want to see us again?' she asked with a smile on her lips.

'Ah, I didn't mean that, at all!' he protested laughingly. 'Leave me to find an errand soon in Rathard!'

They went out into the mist and rain again. The wind had died away and did not impede the men as they dragged the slipe and the silent ram along the tracks or lifted it like a hurdle over the ditches. As they reached the highest point of the island below which their boat lay, Sarah looked back on the road they had come. The wind had come up again and driven the mist from the high points, the crumbling monastery, the farm and the scattered knowes where the sheep moved like detached fragments of mist that had been shaken off. Suddenly she cried out. To the south, upon the Mournes, a fantastic cloud-formation leaned, and from a fissure in the topmost billow a ray of sun poured down balor-like upon the earth. The beam, fire-tinged, and the looming mass behind, struck a chill of fear into the tired and buffeted group on the headland. Then, as though a lid swam sleepily, the eye diminished and the head seemed to nod forward. The farmhand turned with an oath and clattered down the path leading to the beach, the slipe bumping behind him, and the others hurrying on his heels. Had they delayed a moment they would have seen the cloud decapitated by the straining wind and the malignant glow appear diffused, opalescent and harmless.

At the beach Hamilton and Frank tilted the boat to run

off the rainwater. Andrew and the farmhand released the ram from the slipe and it now scrambled to its feet looking very dejected and sorry for itself. At least Sarah seemed to think so, for she stood over it, crooning and scratching its drooping head, but she moved away lightly from Pentland as he approached her.

'Let us be going now,' said Andrew. The ram was urged to the water's edge and hoisted into the boat. Sarah was snatched up by Frank, and as he stood thigh-deep in the water he turned a little towards Pentland with his burden before he seated her in the stern. Already the two men on the beach were vague and indistinct, and their shouts of farewell came torn and disjointed to those afloat. 'He's a crabbit ould blirt, too,' grumbled the servingman, referring to Andrew, as he and Pentland turned away. But his master only grunted. He was preoccupied with the image of the sturdy, pale, smooth-haired woman in whose company he had been for the past three hours. He remembered Frank Echlin's fingers sunk in her thigh and waist and a tremor ran through him. The slipe caught on a stone, and Pentland turned round to look down on the lough. The boat had vanished and the grey fretted water was hardly distinguishable from the rain and mist that swept across it.

CHAPTER FOUR

★

SARAH STUDIED ANDREW'S face before she spoke. 'Why do ye no like Mr Pentland?' she asked. The old man, whose eyes had been fixed on the rowers, turned to her. He dashed the drops vigorously from his brow and mouth. 'Pah! That pachel—he's only an ould jinny of a man!' When she did not respond he added without taking his attention from the boat's course: 'When ye see mair o' him, you'll heed what I say.'

The nose of the punt was set below Rathard so that the rowers could get what ease they might by running with the race down the lough and pulling up again in the calmer waters under the hill. Andrew now crept forward and took a third oar, so that he and Frank were pulling on the starboard side and Hamilton, the most powerful rower of the three, was rowing on the port. Slowly the boat began to move obliquely across the channel-race. The wind was rising again, and it became evident to the three men that they were being carried down at such a pace that it would be impossible to make the passage between the small islands which lay between them and home. Hamilton decided that they should give up the idea of landing at Rathard and let themselves be carried further down and round the shelter of a third island from where they could pull across into Dufferin Bay, two miles below Rathard. He shouted this in disjointed sentences as he bent and straightened to his oar. With a rusty tin Sarah bailed the rain water and spume that gurgled and slopped at her feet. She was drenched to the skin but long past caring. When she looked up she saw the heads and bodies of the three men approaching and receding as they combed the tumbling waves.

Impeded by hundreds of islands, the waves never mounted to the fury of those of the sea, the menace lying in the currents that raced through the passages between island and island. The punt was now crawling across such a passage and approaching the deep channel where a swift racing band of water, broken and wind-blown, raised itself like the ruff of an angry dog. Then, as they neared mid-channel, Sarah felt a sudden exhilaration and a surge of kinship and love for her three companions. Her fear was subdued and lost in this feeling of kinship, of nearness to men who recognised the danger, accepted it, and were battling with it. Unconsciously, her body moved in sympathy with the rowers. The bow entered the frothing race, Andrew and Frank strained on their oars, the boat shuddered madly and was straightened by Hamilton. Then they were across safely into the choppy broken lea-water of the island. Frank threw back his head and laughed aloud.

They were coming up under the lea of the island. At a hoarse word from Andrew, Hamilton pulled the nose of the punt from a patch of water that revolved with sinister glassiness in the midst of the spume and fret. But in the end they came too close. A shaggy rock suddenly loured above them. As Andrew shouted, a sheep scrambled up in fear and brayed at the passing boat. Frank felt the ram

34

writhe under his feet. He beat down savagely with his fist on its iron-hard head. The animal scrambled up until its forelegs lay over the gunwhale. Hamilton, raised high above the water, dragged his oar in a flurry of broken foam and fell back over his father. The boat dropped down drinking deeply, and sank. The four people lay in the tumbling water.

The punt rose sluggishly among them, keel uppermost. Sarah lay for a moment with her face to the sky, then fingers of iron, sinking agonisingly into her flesh, lifted her and hurled her across the shelving keel. Shaking the water from her nose and mouth, she raised her face and saw the three men riding the waves, their arms stretched over the curving belly of the boat. 'Pull yourself forrit, Sarah, and lie on our hands!' shouted Hamilton, gripping the ridge of the keel. The girl dragged herself forward and laid her body on the hands of the brothers. She stretched out and caught Andrew's hand and forearm. The boat guttered and her head was plunged underwater. She felt Andrew's hand to which she clung deliberately shake itself free and draw away. Choked, and with streaming eyes, she saw him slip away, his head visible for a moment in the spume and mist. The boat sprang up at the bows, and under her belly she felt the two brothers grasp convulsively to retain their hold. She moved her head from side to side of the keel: 'He's gone! Your father's gone!' she screamed, and looked into the eyes of drowning men.

The boat was drawn into the broken race below the mainland, and circled down and across it, like a bruised fly in a gutter. Sarah, her face beaten and bruised by the plunging keel, lay like wax across the hands of the brothers. With a plunge and stumble Hamilton touched ground. He dragged his brother ashore and lifted the girl from the boat and laid her on the shingle beside Frank. Above him, on the hill, he heard the shrill cry of a boy and saw him running, zig-zag, down the shadowy slope. With a groan he fell on his knees between his brother and the girl.

CHAPTER FIVE

*

A N OLD WOMAN, gathering wrack after the
storm, found Andrew on the beach. Sarah
stooped over him as he lay in his coffin in the
parlour of Rathard. His beard, washed and combed, lay
like a sheaf of silver threads on his linen gown. The
shining plum-red life had gone from his lips. His nostrils
and eyelids had become delicate, waxen, translucent like
shells. She heard a step at the door and drew back as
Hamilton entered, bending his head at the low doorway.
'The neighbours are coming in,' he said. He laid his hand
gently on her shoulder, turning her to the light. 'Is it wise
for ye to be on your feet?'

She passed her hand across her bruised forehead. 'I'm
bravely now,' she answered. 'Are the people in the
close?'

'Aye, but rest yourself. I bade Agnes Sampson come up
and help your mother make what little meat there'll be.'
He seated himself on a chair near the door and laid his
hands on his knees. 'Sarah,' he began, 'now that he's
gone,' he nodded towards the coffin, 'I would like you
and your mother to bide here for a while till Frank and
me get settled. You're in no hurry away, are ye?' He
rose and walked to the coffin and placed his hand lightly
on his father's brow. 'He was a good man,' he said, 'and
he was gey fond of you.' Sarah rose swiftly and stood with

her face to the window. From the kitchen came the low murmur of voices and a rhythmic beat like a tiny drum as some farmhand rocked his sparbled boots on the tiled floor. Hamilton stood watching her silently. 'If my mother wants to stay, I'll stay,' she said. Without looking at him again, she turned and left the room.

She went up into the kitchen where the mourners were ranged around the walls, some seated, some standing, and each with a cup of tea in his hand or on his knee, while Mrs Gomartin and Agnes Sampson moved among them, offering plates of slim scones and boiled ham on bread. The murmur of voices dropped as the girl entered the kitchen, and a few of the dark-clad men, mostly strangers to her, smiled and jerked their heads while the others looked at her furtively, as one who had been in danger of death. Stewartie Purdie, Echlin's oldest neighbour and friend, rose and took her hand. 'We're thankful to see that you're able to be about, lass,' he said, and as he retreated to his chair the others looked up, cleared their throats, and nodded. Then their heads clustered together in twos and threes and again the murmurous talk of crops and cattle arose.

When the old man released her hand Sarah walked to the half-door, where she stood with her back to the room looking out over the close. Her hands grasped the top of the low door in a fit of anger. She hated the people in the kitchen for their interrupted talk, their sly curious stare, and for the use of the word 'lass' by old Purdie. Then most humiliating of all, her mother's smile of gratitude, almost fawning, which had rested on Purdie as he took her hand. Her eyes filled with tears of self-pity as she thought of the old man who now lay silent in the parlour. She would show them all that she was more than a servant in this house! But as she stood there, disregarding her mother's voice at her shoulder, caution, like a tardy sentinel, took up its position again in her mind. Her eyes hardened, her full lips lifted again at the corners and she would have turned unconcernedly and cheerfully to her mother, had not the sound of a step in the close drawn her attention.

Two men were approaching the house. One of them, a clergyman, paused at the top of the loanen to wait on the other who was coming in by the gate over the lough. A thrill of pleasure ran through the girl as she recognised the figure and long abrupt stride of Pentland. She thought she saw him raise his hand to her but fled back into the kitchen. 'The minister!' she said in a low voice to her mother, tossing the words like coins to placate the old woman. She swept on, looking neither to right nor left, down to the parlour to tell the eldest son of the minister's arrival.

Hamilton was screwing his reflection sideways in the narrow plush-bound mirror over the fireboard as he pulled up his tie. 'Mr Sorleyson's here,' she said. He adjusted his tie before he turned. She noticed that he had placed the lid loosely on the coffin. 'I'll go up now and speak to him. I want you and your mother to be here when the prayer's said.' They heard the kitchen door open and the footsteps of someone coming down the passage. The steps faltered as the intruder realised that he was approaching the death-room. Pentland appeared in the doorway.

He came into the room and took his cousin's hand. 'I'm right and sorry to hear what happened, Hami. It's a terrible thing that it should have happened crossing from our place, too.'

Hamilton nodded and returned the pressure of the other's hand. 'It was a sore blow tae us all, Fergus, but its well it wasn't worse. I'll leave ye now, for I've to go up and speak tae the neighbours. Frank's in bed wi' a bad fever.'

When Hamilton had gone Pentland stood gazing down at the coffin but he did not make a move to raise the lid. 'I'll never forgive myself for letting you go that day,' he said at last.

'Oh, don't talk like that!' cried Sarah. 'Sure, Andra was as set on going as anybody was. There's no blame lies wi' you, Mr Pentland.'

'Ye think not?' He turned and looked anxiously into her face. Sarah shook her head. 'It was ill-chance, that's what it was.'

'Did ye cry?' asked Pentland suddenly, leaning over her. 'Did ye shout in the water?'

'No,' answered Sarah, unwinding her clasped fingers and stepping back a little.

'The sound mightn't have carried to me wi' the wind, anyway. But it's terrible to think o't! Ye might have been drowned!' Then Pentland recognised the effect his words had on Sarah. Colour glowed in her pale face and her eyes moved shyly and restlessly as if she was about to fly from him. He turned away a little, endeavouring to compose his mouth and hands and voice. He glowed inwardly, and at the same moment a shadow of fear darkened his mind.

In the silence that followed Sarah had overcome her confusion which was much more simple and direct. 'Well, I wasn't, that's all,' she said, shrugging her shoulders.

'Surely that was not all, Miss Gomartin,' said a voice behind them. Startled, the girl turned to see Mr Sorleyson regarding her from the doorway. The minister came farther into the room, nodding to Pentland whom he had met in the close. Sorleyson's complexion was fair and his eyes, brown and smiling, were magnified a little by his spectacles. His voice although commonplace, was clear, and everything he said was marked by an upward inflexion which gave it a note of diffidence and willingness to please. 'Surely you won't dismiss your escape from drowning in such a casual manner, Miss Gomartin? I've heard the whole tragic story from Hamilton, and its a matter of deep thankfulness to our Heavenly Father that you and Hamilton and Frank are here to-day, although we grieve for the loss of our brother, Andrew.' As he finished, Hamilton entered the room and seeing that the minister did not require him, turned to the window.

Sarah would not have answered Sorleyson's mild reproof had he not mentioned Andrew's name. Now it brought up again, in vivid and painful detail, her last sight of the old man as he struck out from the overladen boat. 'And why should God have let Andrew drown? He was a good man, Mr Sorleyson.' Hamilton turned impatiently from the window. 'Mr Sorleyson,' he said, 'the carriages are here.'

'In a moment, Hamilton,' replied the clergyman: 'God moves in strange ways, Sarah. The old were taken and the young, we hope, will profit by this experience.' He would

41

have gone across to Hamilton, but Sarah laid her hand on his arm. 'I've something to tell you, Mr Sorleyson. Andrew wasn't taken because he was old, and we weren't spared because we were young. I saw him leave go of the boat and swim into the fog. If he hadn't done that, there's no telling but all four of us would have gone.'

Sorleyson was about to reply but Hamilton spoke first. 'Away and bring your mother down, Sarah, and open Frank's door so that he can hear the prayer.' His face was dark and scowling and she knew that he was angry at all this chatter round the dead body of his father. Even as she left the room the words rose unbidden ... and if it hadn't been for you, Frank and me would have drowned. ... She felt full of remorse, and an urgent desire to please him.

When she had brought her mother down to the parlour Sorleyson prayed. Sarah silently ran her nail over the worn plush on the arm of the chair at which she knelt, as Sorleyson's words filtered through to her: ' ... my son, despise not the chastening of the Lord, nor faint when thou art rebuked of Him. For whom the Lord loveth he chasteneth, and scourgeth every son whom he receiveth.'

She had ventured a little too far, having words with the minister before Hamilton. Until the funeral left she would stay in the background behind her mother and Agnes, silent, only coming forward when she was needed. That was her place as a servant in the house. In the meantime, anyway, until her false step had been forgotten. Sorleyson cleared his throat before he launched into his special prayer for the occasion: O God, Who hast in Thy great mercy spared the green and taken the ripe; teach, we beseech Thee, thy sons and daughters gathered here, that Nature framed by Thy almighty hand can never be tamed to man's will. That storms and tempests will continue to brush aside man as a housewife brushes aside a cobweb. And when Thy inexorable processes run counter to man's hopes and desires, help them, O Lord, to humble themselves under the mighty hand of God. May their sorrows yield the peaceable fruit of righteousness, so that each of them shall be able to say: It is good for me that I have been afflicted. And mercifully grant unto all of us here present, and to as many as mourn with us in this sorrow, that we may hear the voice of Thy Spirit saying to us, Be ye also ready, for in such an hour as ye think not, the Son of Man cometh …

They remained for a moment in silence on their knees. Then they rose, Mrs Gomartin helping herself up slowly from the chair at which she knelt. Hamilton and Sarah looked at the face of the dead man, then they went up into the kitchen.

The undertaker's men slipped unobtrusively into the parlour and closed the door. Once there was the shrill scringe of a screw driven into wood. The mourners had shuffled out into the close where they stood under the rowans in the pearly afternoon light. Hamilton came to the door and beckoned silently to two or three of them. He chose elderly men and close neighbours. These were the first bearers of the coffin.

As they came up from the parlour their laden unsteady steps passed over the brain of the sick man like great lurching wheels. They carried the coffin round the gable of the house to pass his window. While the indistinct shadow of their passage moved slowly across his room he lay with closed eyes and twitching fingers, murmuring to himself.

Pentland had spoken to Sarah before he took his place at the coffin. 'I'll be back this way for my boat,' he said. 'You'll stop and have your tea?' the girl asked. He smiled and nodded then followed the other men into the house. Behind him stood Sorleyson, brushing the nap of his hat on his arm. 'Be comforted,' he said to Sarah. 'I hope to see you at church on Sunday.' He included both women in his glance, then he hurried away to take his place at the head of the mourners beside Hamilton.

Sarah stood with the other women at the head of the loanen watching the funeral procession wind slowly among the fields and vanish in a fold of the road. But she followed it unseeingly as she brooded over Sorleyson's remarks. And the more she thought on them, so anger and revolt stirred in her. To her simple mind, the idea of a vast overleaning spirit, ever present, which with infinite patience followed the coming-in and going-out of a human being for eighty years, and then, at a pre-ordained time plucked him from the world, bore the signs of an ultimate responsibility. But now she suspected, and her anger rose at the thought, that Sorleyson had bent a fortuitous and tragic occurrence to buttress his own beliefs and teachings, and had in some way robbed the lustre of Andrew's self-sacrifice.

When the last trap had disappeared Agnes Sampson went back across the close. 'We'd better be getting redd up, for they'll be coming back soon,' she said. Martha and Sarah followed her back to the farm.

44

As they were about to enter the house Martha turned to her daughter and said in a low voice 'I was wondering what they'll dae about us, now the old man's gone. Did Hamilton say anything?'

'He wants us tae bide on, he says.'

'Well, we could dae that. I don't doubt but one or t'other of them will get married soon.'

Her daughter turned on her in a blaze of anger. 'What makes ye say that!' she cried, striking her hand on the doorpost. 'You're talking daft, mother!' She strode ahead into the kitchen while Martha gazed after her in amazement.

CHAPTER SIX

*

AFTER THE DEATH of Andrew there was no further talk as to whether Sarah and her mother would remain at Rathard. Once the fever had passed its crisis, Frank came into the kitchen and sat crouched at the fire, while the women went about their work, indoors and outdoors. His fever had been broken by some concoction brewed by Agnes Sampson, and she came up each day with more brews in which the herbs had changed their proportions, or to which fresh ingredients had been added. The Echlins had a great regard for Agnes, and soon Sarah also was looking forward with pleasure to the visits of this laughter-loving old woman with the heavy bosom and slim ankles. When her light dancing step was heard in the close and she came into the kitchen, talk sprang on people's lips, and the fire which had been nodding in the hearth drew up vigorously under the lowered kettle, as though it felt the eye of its mistress. It was during one of these visits that Sarah learned that Fergus Pentland had the gift of charming sick animals and people suffering from erysipelas. 'A lock of ungodly nonsense!' cried Martha angrily, and Frank threw back his head and laughed for the first time since his illness. Let him be better and get about his work again, prayed Sarah, as she heard his laugh.

For in each of those few days she could almost feel the

springs of vitality and desire rise again in the man at the fireside. His eyes rarely left her as she moved about the kitchen. He answered Martha from the corner of his mouth as he gazed at her daughter.

She had been kneading bread at the table when suddenly he got up and came towards her, his blanket dropping from his shoulders on to the chair. His eyes were ardent, and there was a gleam of triumphant laughter on his face as though some obstacle between them had been removed. He stretched out his hand to touch her. She moved round the table from him, watching him wide-eyed. Her elbow knocked over the flour-mug which starred out with a little explosion on the floor. In the silence that followed they heard the steps of Martha in the upper room. 'Hae ye broke the bowl, Sarah?' she called. The girl laughed silently in his face. 'No, mother, I knocked over the wee mug.' Frank went back to the fire and sat down with his back to her, cowling his head in the blanket. After a moment she ran down to her room where she gazed into the mirror for a long time, clapping her hand swiftly over her mouth when her breath came in a crow of excitement.

In November, as was their yearly custom, the Pentlands moved across to a little farm on the mainland to winter. Fergus had come up twice to Rathard during Frank's illness, and then when Frank was better the visits continued. He would come into the kitchen in the evenings with his head lowered and his eyes blinking in the lamplight. At first Hamilton had put aside whatever paper he was reading, or whatever work he had in hand, to talk to his cousin. But now, when Pentland called once or twice

47

a week he would only look up from his work to wish him good-evening. Frank greeted his cousin with a slow secretive smile that lingered on his face as he gazed into the fire. And Pentland, having found a seat close to Sarah, and laid some little parcel of honey or sweets in the shadows behind her, would watch the grin on his cousin's face, and fall into a vexed silence, unconscious of the stolen glances of the girl at his side.

So are misunderstandings born; and Pentland as he stumbled down the dark rutted loanen, swore once more that he would never enter Rathard again. He became convinced that Frank was the girl's lover, and that they, and Hamilton, and perhaps even old Martha, were laughing at him. The first time the idea entered his head, anger soon gave way to a peculiar pleasure in the thought, and he lay in bed and tortured himself, imagining words and actions between the two. Yet every time that he swore passionately never to see her again, the sincerity and warmth of her embrace came flooding back, and his turmoil waxed and waned like the shadows that crowded round and fled from his swinging lantern.

Sarah, the blood throbbing in her lips, her breast still tingling from his embrace, watched Pentland's light till it was swallowed below the brae. She crossed the rath behind the house and mounting the ancient wall picked out his lantern as it pricked its way slowly through the darkness. Then it disappeared for the last time and she returned slowly to the house, downcast and dissatisfied.

Some weeks after the funeral, Mr Sorleyson called again at Rathard. He remained with Hamilton in the lower room for a time, before he came up into the kitchen where Martha and Sarah were working. 'So you intend staying with Mr Echlin for a while, Martha?' he asked.

The old woman nodded. 'Aye, they want Sarah and me here.'

The minister glanced round the trim kitchen. 'I can see that,' he said. 'I didn't see you in church after all,' he added, turning to Sarah.

Mrs Gomartin put aside the brush with which she was blacking the crane. 'I'm wearied talking to all three of them, Mr Sorleyson,' she interjected. 'But not one of them will go a step wi' me.'

The clergyman looked down at the floor with a grave expression. 'It's your duty to go with your mother, you know, Sarah.'

The girl turned away with a slight shrug. The red sun pierced the kitchen and gleamed on her fair hair. Sorleyson considered her figure as she stood in the roseate light. He regretted the shapeless apron that hung from her waist.

The minister picked up his hat from the dresser. 'Well, I must be away,' he said. 'I hope to see you all on the Sabbath.' He shook hands with both women, and they heard him salute Frank as he crossed the close.

'Ye heard what the minister said, Sarah?' asked Martha when they were alone again.

'I did—I heard him rightly,' answered the girl irritably.

Martha straightened herself and turned round. 'Aye, but did ye heed him?'

'Why should I heed him? What has he to do wi' me?'

'He's your clergyman.'

'I didn't ask for him! Why does he come here interfering in my concern?'

In her fumbling way Martha tried to explain what she meant. 'It isn't Mr Sorleyson, daughter. It's what he stands for. He's the servant o' the Church o' God—the Church that ye were reared in—and your folks afore ye. Ye can't prosper, Sarah, if ye forget your duty to God.'

Her daughter turned on her with strident voice. 'Aye! Our folks prospered, didn't they, with their running tae Church on a Sunday! My father died on the roads, and ever since I can mind my life has been nothing else but slaving for other folk. And always (here she mimicked her mother cruelly) its "be humble, Sarah, God will reward ye." Well, I'm tired o' it! My ways are my own. I get up in the morn tae my work, and at night I lie down in my bed, and if I fall dead in the midst o' it, there'll be little talk and less weeping!'

'God, what have I done tae hear my own daughter talk like this! Mark my words, Sarah, ye'll see the day when you'll regret on your bended knees that ye scorned the words of your mother and your minister! For its pain and evil you'll bring on yourself if your hard heart isn't changed!'

'There's pain and evil in me now!' cried the girl, the tears springing to her eyes. 'But I'll thole it—and it won't be on my knees!' and snatching up a basin she ran out of the kitchen.

Frank, lying below a cart and driving nails into a floorboard, saw her run across the close into the mealshed. After she had disappeared his strokes became slow and erratic. At last he laid his hammer down, and crawling out walked over to the shed. Sarah, her eyes blinded with tears, was plucking feverishly at the fastenings of a meal bag. He laid his hands on her shoulders and turned her towards him. Under his gaze her brimming eyes dried like summer pools under a noonday sun. For a moment, but only for a moment, his lust wavered under her look of supplication. He took the basin from her nerveless fingers and laid it on the sill. The straw motes circled lazily upward in the red sunlight.

CHAPTER SEVEN

*

AGNES SAMPSON and her husband, Petie, lived in one of two small thatched cottages which sat on top of Knocknadreemally, so called because here the fringes of Ravara, Banyil and Lusky Woods touched. The visitors entering the cottage set swinging clusters and strings of herbs and roots hanging from the dark rafters. On the mantelpiece and deep window-ledge sat jars filled with tormentil, tansy and golden rod, and many other dried pods, flowers, barks and roots. From time to time there arose murmurs among the wealthier farmers of an inquiry into the old woman's traffic, and a possible prosecution. But as it was never proven that she had injured any of her poor patients, but on the contrary had dispelled innumerable fevers, bruises and domestic upsets, nothing was ever done about it.

Her humour, energy and skill, and the many wild nights when she had clung to the back of a frantic man as he whipped his horse along the roads, so that she might be in time to wipe the lips and catch the last words of some dying crone, or deliver safely a whimpering child had further endeared her in the affection and respect of the country folk.

Her husband, Petie, was a small soft-spoken man who only put on a jacket when he was going to meeting-house. He had a remarkable collection of parti-coloured waistcoats which he wore three at a time, winter and summer. Thus he had twelve pockets in which to mislay his chewing roll, opportunities of which he took full advantage. But as he was a gentle humorous creature, the search was calm and leisured.

Having neither chick nor child, as the country folk say, Petie and Agnes had worked for many years in the fields of their neighbours, particularly the Echlins and their cousins the Pentlands. Agnes had been present at the birth of Hamilton, Frank and Fergus; and having watched them grow from childhood to manhood, fed them when their childish wanderings brought them over Knocknadreemally, and consoled them when they had been punished at home, she looked on them almost as her own sons.

Knowing that he would receive good advice, and possibly sympathy, Pentland climbed the road one afternoon to Sampson's cottage. When he entered, he found Petie seated on one side of the fire with his dog Kipper which rested its head on its master's outstretched legs and communed silently with him through half-closed golden eyes. On the other side sat Agnes knitting, her skirt gathered into her lap and her woollen petticoat kilted to her knees.

'Good-day to ye,' said the young man pausing in the doorway. Agnes narrowed her eyes to see who it was that stood silhouetted in the bright doorway, while Petie, too indolent to turn around, scanned her face as if hoping to see reflected there the identity of the visitor. 'Ah, Fergus, ye scairt us!' cried Agnes when she recognised who it was. 'Come in, son, and don't stand there like a bagman. Put

53

that animal away from ye, Petie, and let Fergus sit down.'
She enquired after the young man's grandmother, and
then Pentland fell to stroking the dog's head and there
was silence for a time.

'And are ye bravely yourself?' enquired Agnes at last.

Fergus paused long enough to give his answer the
proper note of doubt and despondency. 'Ah, I suppose
I'm rightly,' he answered with a slight nod that implied
exactly the opposite.

Agnes glanced quickly at him over her knitting. 'Petie,'
she said, 'take that animal away out and hae a dander
t'yoursel' '. Obediently the old man pushed Kipper towards the door and left the house.

'You're looking rightly, too,' ventured Agnes tenta-
tively, when her husband's steps had died away.

Fergus gave the short bitter laugh of a man who could
reveal untold agony within if he had a mind to. 'I was
thinking of putting an end to myself in the lough,' he
said, gazing straight into the fire.

'Were ye now?' queried Agnes looking up from her
knitting. 'Aye, maybe you're not as well as ye look—
come, tell ould Agnes.'

Her remark had the desired effect. Pentland's reserve
went down like a flimsy barrier before the trouble he had
been nursing for so long. Springing up from his chair, he
thrust his hands into his pockets and strode distractedly
up and down the kitchen. 'To tell ye the God's truth,
Agnes, I'm a verry worrit man, and I don't know what
way to turn, at all!' He came back to her and the crisp
bulbs dangled and swung behind his head.

'Sit down, son,' said Agnes, 'and tell me what's putting

these wild thoughts in your head.' But the little outburst had eased him, and as he sat down he felt his trouble to be unreal after all, and he regretted that he had come.

He sat gazing gloomily at the dancing flames, his head sunk in his shoulders. 'Ach, it's nothing,' he said at last. 'My mind's aye chasing mice.'

'Ah, it's something, or ye wudna carry on like that,' returned Agnes, jerking her knitting back into her lap. 'Hae ye got yourself into trouble wi' a girl, or something o' that sort?'

'In a manner o' speaking—yes.'

'Is it Stewartie Purdie's lass?'

'It is not!' he declared emphatically, looking sharply at her.

'Aye. Well then, is it Martha Gomartin's girl?'

He smirked painfully. 'How did ye guess her?' he asked.

'Are ye simple, Fergus? Sure you're never away from about the place!'

'Well then, it's her,' he replied in an offended tone.

'And what's wrong between her and you?' persisted the old woman, the click of her needles never ceasing.

Pentland seemed at a loss to reply. 'Well, there's nothing wrong between me and her,' he commenced at last, 'but she seems to be changing every day she's up there. She's changed a lot since the day ould Andrew was drownded, I can tell ye.'

'That's no to be wondered at, considering where she sprung from,' said Agnes. 'It's wonderful what happens tae black-clocks when they get intae long grass,' she added with malice.

55

'Ah, there's nothing wrong wi' the girl!' declared Fergus, stung into defence of his sweetheart.

'No, no—there's no a ha-porth wrong wi' her,' agreed Agnes soothingly. 'And her mother's as honest a woman as ye'd find in a day's walk. Tell me then, what's got intae ye?'

Pentland stood up and threw the hair back out of his eyes. 'I can't abide her being near that crature, Frank Echlin!' he burst out. 'Sitting there wi' that sneer on his face when I come in! I declare to m'God I could lift the throat out of him for it!'

Agnes stiffened. Fond as she was of Fergus, she had always been fonder and closer to the Echlin brothers and Frank had been her special favourite. Petie and she, getting old, were now dependent on the Echlins for their livelihood and the cottage in which she sat was owned by the family at Rathard. Again, she was too old and wise in the ways of her neighbours to get caught up in any quarrel between the cousins. So she drew in her lips, raised her knitting, and remained silent.

But Pentland also realised his mistake and now he was intent on justifying his remarks. He came and sat down, drawing his chair closer so that he could look into Agnes's face. 'Tell me, Agnes, how would *you* feel if ye had to sit, night after night, beside a man that's sneering and smirking at every word ye say?'

'What makes ye think Frankie would be sneering at ye?' asked the old woman coldly.

'God in Heaven! don't I see it on his face, every time I look at him?'

'For why?'

Pentland relapsed back into his chair. 'I think he's carrying on wi' Sarah,' he said in a low hard voice.

Agnes stirred uneasily. But she laid down her knitting and laughed. 'Ye sit there and tell me the girl favours ye and you're worrying about Frank Echlin girning and cracking his fingers at ye over the fire? D'ye think if he was prospering wi' her that ye'd be let in sight o' the close o' Rathard? If ye believe that you're no long frae your mother's teat!'

'D'ye think there's nothing in it, then?' asked Pentland unable to stifle the relief in his voice.

'I know there's nothing in it,' declared the woman stoutly. 'If ye want the girl don't go footerin' at her as if ye didna. And for Frankie's sneers, pay nae heed to him. Remember the ould saying that the bee leaves a sting where he sooks nae honey.'

'You're right, no doubt,' said Pentland springing up with a smile. He seemed to be as much pleased with himself now as previously he had been downcast and gloomy. His wish gratified, he did not delay any longer in the Sampson's cottage but set off with a cheery word to Petie who was shivering on a stone outside the door, his walk long accomplished. As Petie hastened gladly to the fire he saw his wife standing at the gable-window gazing after the young man. 'God forgive me if I'm a liar, and I don't doubt I am,' he heard her say. Then, as she turned from the window she exclaimed 'the bad hussy!' and looked broodingly at her husband's peaked and questioning face.

CHAPTER EIGHT

★

WITH THAT URGENCY with which religious old age invests such matters, Martha still endeavoured to make the younger members of the household return to church. Hamilton had continued to go for a few Sabbaths after his father's death. Then one Sabbath morning he had gone out into the fields and from thence his attendance became more desultory, until now he and Frank contented themselves with driving Martha to the church and returning for her after the service. As time passed they did not even trouble to dress or shave themselves for these journeys.

On the homeward way the churchgoers would watch the Echlin trap pass, and pull down their mouths and say 'changed times at Rathard since ould Andra died,' and others would maliciously add 'or since the Gomartins went up.' But most of her neighbours sympathised with Martha.

These whispers and glances did not escape the notice of the old woman, but the final humiliation was delivered by the Reverend Mr Sorleyson. One Sunday morning as she left the church, he drew her aside and asked her, kindly enough, to prevail on the Echlins to come back to the congregation. 'Aye, and my Sarah?' 'Of course,' exclaimed Mr Sorleyson after the faintest pause. 'Sarah, as well.' But the momentary hesitation in Sorleyson's voice went to the mother's heart like a knife.

When he left her she stood in the shelter of the hedge endeavouring to still the trembling in her legs. A dull burning pulsed in her cheeks and as she looked after the departing minister bitter tears flooded her eyes. 'Ah, Mr Sorleyson,' she whispered, 'could ye no leave the ninety and nine and go after that which is lost until ye find it! Sarah, Sarah, your mother's heart's sore for ye this day.' She dabbed her eyes with her black cotton gloves and walked slowly towards the church coach-house. The broad road before the coach-house was empty now, and when she looked into the Echlin's box in the stable two or three sparrows were quarrelling on the floor of it. 'They hae forgotten me,' she said, sitting down on the bench that ran along the wall. After a little while she arose and set out on the homeward road.

Hamilton, coming from the byre, saw the trap sitting in the close, its shafts in the air. An uneasy feeling made him hasten into the house. The hands of the clock pointed to twenty minutes past one. He hurried out to the stable and pushed open the top-door. Both horses stood in their stalls. 'Hell roast his sowl,' he muttered, 'he's forgotten the ould woman.' He went to the middle of the close and putting his hands to his mouth hallooed on his brother's name. He paused, expectant, as his shout rang over the empty fields. A few birds rose from the ridge of the stable and whirred away. Then he called on Sarah's name and as he listened he thought he heard a faint distant sound of laughter. He led out a horse, pulling cruelly on its mouth, and yoked it, single-handed, in the trap.

About two miles along the road he came on Martha seated on the ditch. He had to dismount and help her over to the trap. When she left the church she had vowed to herself that she would refuse to ride with them if they came to meet her. But now all her pride was gone; she had lost a glove somewhere and her fine buttoned boots, of which she was so proud, were coated with mud. Her face was drawn with weariness, and she had to press her lips together to keep from bursting outright into tears of misery and loneliness.

In a halting manner, and keeping his eyes fixed on the horse's ears, Hamilton tried to apologise for his brother's lapse. The old woman gathered from his remarks that Frank and Sarah had disappeared from the house.

'Did she lay the table?' Martha asked.

'I didna pay any heed,' answered Hamilton, touching up the horse.

'If it had been set you'd have noticed it,' she said briefly.

As they turned off the road into the loanen they saw the blue smoke of a replenished fire rise from the chimney of the farmhouse.

Frank stood leaning over the half-door of the stable with his back to them as they drew up in the close. Hamilton unloosed the horse and led it out of the shafts, slipping the brichen over his arm. As he heard his brother approach Frank unbolted the stable door and held it open, but Hamilton checked the horse on the threshold. 'What came intae ye?' he demanded, scowling at the other. Frank smiled, 'I forgot all about the ould one,' he answered. Although he smiled, his eyes were alert and he rocked gently on the balls of his feet. Hamilton stared at him for a moment than he spat contemptuously on the ground and led the horse into the stable. Frank loitered in the close until his brother appeared again, then without looking up or speaking, followed him into the house.

They sat down to the meal in silence. Frank, carefully watching the old woman, noted with apprehension that Sarah was doing the same. He had hoped that the two women would have had it out before he and Hamilton came in. As Sarah rose to bring the rennet dish to the table he suddenly turned to Martha and opening his lips was about to speak. At his gesture she looked up at him coldly and silently. At the sight of her faded eyes and in-drawn lips the words died in his throat. He felt a sudden hatred for Sarah's mother with her cold reproachful look. As if he were bound to go when she said, go; and come when she said, come. To hell with ye, he said inwardly, you're nothing to me.

But his gesture stirred the old woman. Not content with knowing that her silence filled both the young people with remorse and anger she turned to her daughter. 'Where were ye, when I was at church?' she asked.

'We went over the fields to the head o' the brae,' answered the girl without raising her eyes from her plate.

'Weren't ye left tae look after the house?' demanded Martha.

'There now, Martha,' interrupted Frank angrily, 'the house didna run away.'

Martha ignored him. Her whole attention was fixed on her daughter. 'Since when hae ye taken to skiltin the fields on a Sabbath? Look at yourself—you're as tossed

61

and through-other as if you'd been doing a day's work. What way's that to behave on the Sabbath?'

Sarah sprang up from the table. 'Lay me alone!' she cried. 'I'll go out in the fields when I want, Sunday or any other day!'

Martha had risen to her feet also, her face flushed and fingers plucking at her apron. Hamilton, who had been eating stolidly during all this talk, now rapped the table irritably with his spoon. 'Sit down, Martha,' he said, 'and let us get on wi' our dinner.'

Martha turned on him. 'Listen to me, Hamilton Echlin, and you Sarah, and you Frank. If there's not a change in this house I'm going tae leave it and go back tae Banyil God forgive me—I should ha' spoken out before. But I'm no going to see my daughter run about a heathen. If the memory o' your father won't send yous t'church, at least I'll see that *she* goes!'

'Don't meddle with me, Martha!' exclaimed Frank angrily. 'I can look after my own affairs. Hae ye forgotten already what my father brought ye here for?'

The old woman raised her hands to her head as if she had been struck. 'Wilt thou afflict the widow or fatherless child? If thou afflict them in any wise, and they cry at all unto me, I will surely hear their cry—' she intoned in a dull voice.

'Ah, give me none of your biblical cant!' cried Frank, beside himself with anger and shame at what he had said.

Hamilton struck the table with his open hand. 'That's mair than enough!' he shouted. He turned to Martha who had seated herself at the fire and was rocking backwards and forwards in her chair. 'Ye canna interfere wi' us,

Martha. If you're no happy here, I'm sorry. It seems a wee thing tae leave us for. Nobody hinders ye going to church and after to-day I'll warrant ye that you'll no walk home again.' As he said this he looked at his brother, but Frank stood gazing sullenly out of the door. The younger brother's anger was really not so much at Martha's presumption as at the fear of being haltered again. Andrew had not been a tyrannical father but he had always commanded implicit obedience from his sons. In doing so he had been strengthened by affection and usage. But at his death, Frank had felt himself a free man, his own master. Without anything having been said between them, his word was as good as Hamilton's on the farm. And he possessed an undisputed delight which he hugged in secret glee, the enjoyment of Sarah. So when Martha, a stranger and a servant, upbraided him, it was like a stranger's hand on the neck of a wicked and restive horse.

Sarah stood with her hands clenched agonisingly together. She had never dreamt that her mother would jeopardise her comfortable life at Rathard for principles. She had forgotten easily and too soon that her mother was a spiritual and racial descendant of the two Margarets who, choking at their stakes in the rising waters of Solway, saw Christ and He wrestling. Martha's God was a terrible but hearkening God. Her every word and thought was weighed on His fingertip. Before a faith such as that, comfort and a hearth and a little folding of the hands burned away like so much dross. But to Sarah the novelty of her new position in life was too fresh for her not to appreciate the change for the better in her fortunes. They had come as servants and labourers to Rathard, and now

63

she at least, had attained the position of mistress in the Echlin household. It was not avarice, but the fear of returning ᴐ a life of drudgery that filled her with hatred as she stood between the brothers, listening to the old woman.

'Will ye change your ways o' going, Sarah?' her mother asked.

'There's nothing wrong wi' my ways o' going,' the girl answered sullenly.

'Are ye going to do as your betters bid ye, and return to your church?' persisted Martha.

The girl raised her head sharply. 'My betters!' she exclaimed, her face flushing in anger. 'So that's it! Mr Sorleyson has been at ye—now isn't that the truth!'

'Aye, that's the truth. Your minister came down from his pulpit to beg wi' me that my daughter would come back. That's what I had to endure in my own church.' The old woman's voice grew bitter. 'He said that Frank and Hami would remember their father. God forgive them, they hae forgotten before the sod's healed over him.'

'Let us be, Martha,' said Hamilton uneasily, turning a cup in his hands. Frank stirred in the doorway but stood with his back to them, listening.

'It's your own affair,' said the old woman, rising. 'But I'll see to it that Sarah doesn't go that road.'

'Quit it!' shouted Sarah. 'Ye keep on talking o' me as if I was a helpless wean! Ye can go to your church if ye will, but you're no taking me!'

'Very well, then,' said her mother. 'We're leaving this house as soon as we can gather our wheen o' things thegither.'

64

The girl turned and clutched Hamilton's arm. 'Hami, will ye give me a job here?' she cried. Her eyes searched his face, and the man winced in her grasp.

He released his arm from her fingers and crossed to the fireplace. 'It's not for me tae interfere between you and your daughter, Martha. You're welcome tae bide here as long as ye wish, and I can't hinder ye if ye want to go, for you're neither blood nor kin tae us. You've done your work well, and if ye go we maun get another. But go or stay, singly or together, you're as free as the birds o' the air. That's my word.'

For a long time mother and daughter looked at each other. The girl's pale lips scarcely moved. 'I'm staying,' she said. The old woman turned away to the door of the lower room, leaning faintly for a moment on the handle.

She set about collecting her belongings with silent diligence. She accepted Frank's shame-faced offer of a wooden case for her linens. Of every three pieces she left one aside for Sarah, and the girl going down into her room in the dusk found them lying across the bed.

Martha's quiet determination to abide by her resolve with neither recrimination nor bitterness, succeeded in reducing her daughter to an anguish of spirit which in moments of weakness she thought almost too much to pay for her new life. Neither encouraged by an air of martyrdom on her mother's part, nor possessing herself that characteristic which in revolt and despair casts the whole burden of shame on the person who occasioned it, the girl was tormented by a superstitious belief that some day she would have to pay for her actions. She was fortified only by a secret stubborn shame and a hatred of subordination and its drudgery. Yet when at last Mrs Gomartin, with her few goods boxed and basketed, sat in the springcart, one backward glance would have brought her daughter into her arms. The old woman never looked round, and Sarah, through tear-blinded eyes, watched the small bowed figure nod and lurch beside Hamilton as they drove away.

CHAPTER NINE

*

WHEN THE APPLE trees shed their leaves on the lawn of Ravara Manse, the house could be seen from the road with its pouting door-way and tall blue-black windows, the alabaster lion in the fanlight and chairs at every window, broad splatbacks and the cupid bows of country hepplewhite. By the time the road had ceased to ring under the heel, the thin branches bristled with splitting buds. In May the blossom frothed to the eaves of the house. In August the green globes of fruit nodded in the warm air. Every year Master Herriot sent his pupils to gather them in for the minister. By October the leaves lay tattered at the feet of the trees and the house gleamed again through the thin arms of the branches.

The manse itself was a commodious and well-planned house. It held a remarkable collection of chairs clustered in hall, landings and odd corners. Brought there by succeeding young matrons of the manse, they had their day and as prosperity increased, or an urban flock called, were discarded by the departing shepherd.

Mrs Sorleyson, the present mistress, had been the daughter of a prosperous Belfast merchant and had gathered round her husband and herself household goods unusual in a country manse. This affluence had even added a lustre to the books in her husband's library. She was a slight pretty woman, the hue of whose eyes, hair and skin was a little too light, trembling on the edge of faded love. She had brought to her marriage an un-questioning admiration and respect for her husband. If any doubts had arisen in her mind during those six years of married life, she had attributed them to her own unworthiness rather than to any flaws in her husband's character. Unfortunately for Edwin Sorleyson's peace of mind, he was only too well aware of his selfishness, his boredom with his life, his inability to return his wife's affection. He had honestly tried in the first years of their life together to be a loving husband, and it was with both a knowledge of failure and a sense of relief that he watched their relationship change to that of strangers, bound for a lifelong duress to stifle the fruitless blaze of anger, and perform all the little acts that convention expected.

Sorleyson was a creature of habit and he went into his study every Thursday afternoon to refurbish his sermons. He took down one of his favourite poets, Pollok or Heber or James Montgomery, and began to read, pausing only to make notes. Then his pencil fell, his notes were for-gotten and he slipped the volume forward on the table and leant back with a lover's smile on his lips. At this point he sighed, lifted his pencil, adjusted his spectacles and set himself again at his macabre task. On the follow-ing Sabbath evening the congregation of Ravara would be edified by a discourse liberally sprinkled with quotations from the lesser nineteenth-century poets, or listen again with drowsy loyalty to 'God, Nature and Robbie Burns.'

He was seated at his study table when the sound of a

springcart passing on the road below made him glance out of the window. He saw the figures of old Mrs Gomartin and Hamilton Echlin nod along above the level of the hedge. His interest in the Rathard household still being active he rose and looked down at the departing cart. In the back of it he saw various bundles and baskets and after deciding that they were on their way to market glanced idly around the sombre countryside before again sitting down to work. It was not until they were seated at their evening meal that he turned to his wife, 'Do you know of any markets on Thursday, in this part of the world, Victoria?'

The woman seated across from him shook her head. 'No, not on Thursday, dear. Why do you ask?'

'Nothing,' he said. 'It's of no significance.' And he forgot the matter.

Meanwhile Martha and Hamilton jogged on in silence until they reached the old woman's cottage. Dismounting, Martha crossed to the door where she kicked away the drift of leaves that had blown into the doorway. She took a large iron key from under her shawl and turned it with a grating noise in the lock. As she lifted the shutter from the little sunken window, Hamilton looked morosely round the little room before turning away to bring in her belongings. The last article to be brought in, a lidded basket with a sally-rod through its wicker hoops, he laid on the table. He was on his knees breaking twigs and placing them in the hearth when Martha came up again from the bedroom. She had taken off her boots and her bare feet slapped on the polished earth floor. She was about to speak when she saw the unfamiliar basket on the table. Opening it, she drew out a dressed chicken and a cake. 'Who put this in?' she demanded, turning to Hamilton who lay with his cheek to the floor nursing the fire with his breath. He stood up and rubbed his eyes. 'Sarah,' he replied, 'I saw her putting it in.'

The old woman slammed the lid down angrily. 'I didna bring it—ye may take it back.' Hamilton rubbed his chin slowly, gazing round the bare little cabin. 'Martha,' he said, 'don't be harsh on the girl. She's gey sad at ye leaving. Look,' he raised his boot over the pulsing heart of fire, 'let me put it out an' we'll go back.' She followed his glance and shivered. Hamilton's face lit up with a slow unfamiliar smile. She turned her eyes away and pulled the cowl of her shawl over her face. The young farmer's boot clumped down on the floor and he walked slowly towards the door. 'Is there ocht else ye want before I go? Water? Kindling?'

'Thank ye kindly, Hamilton. All's in now.'

He turned again at the door. 'I'll come over tae see ye, maybe?'

Martha hastened forward both hands outstretched, her face glowing with affection. 'You'll aye be welcome.' She caught his hand between her thin hard palms.

Hamilton clambered up into the cart and wheeled the horse to the road. 'Good night tae ye, Martha,' he said. The old woman was an indistinct figure in the gloom of the cottage. The flesh of her head and her hands and her feet shone palely in the glow of the fire.

At the top of the hill he checked the horse and looked back at the cottage. The light suddenly grew stronger in the window. Martha had lit her lamp.

CHAPTER TEN

★

ENCOURAGED BY AGNES'S advice Pentland overcame his doubts and went back to Rathard a few evenings later. He went determined not to be irritated by Frank, repeating to himself, as he climbed the loanen, Agnes's saying about the honey and the sting. But he was perplexed to find that his cousin's demeanour had changed. The tolerant scorn had gone from his voice and he gave Fergus a brief and sullen answer to his greeting. Fergus was perplexed and yet, at first, a hope rose in him. Perhaps the issue had been joined between Frank and the girl and the verdict had gone in his favour, and against his cousin. But nothing in Sarah's manner encouraged him in this hope. At every whispered word from Fergus she glanced fearfully across at Frank before she responded. When the young man asked her to put away her work and come out, as they always did on dry evenings, she pleaded that the night air was raw and cold. Yet she did not seem to be afraid of Echlin. Her eyes were hard, when she looked at him as if challenging him. Perhaps, thought Pentland, and the hair bristled on his neck, perhaps he said he would thrash me if I came back. He leaned back out of the circle of lamplight the better to see his cousin. He gripped the seat of his chair. In a few seconds his scalp itched with sweat as if he had been running under the sun, and his eyes felt as if they were bursting. But Echlin sat brooding over the fire, only moving his lips when he shot long slivers of spittle into the flame, or lifted an eyebrow to gaze at the outline of Sarah's legs in the firelight.

The girl stood up to lower the kettle on the crane. For the first time Pentland realised that Mrs Gomartin was absent. 'Is your mother ailing?' he asked, looking behind him into the shadows as if expecting to see her seated there. Sarah, who had been lifting cups off the dresser, started at his question. 'My mother?' she repeated, and then after the faintest hesitation: 'Did ye not know? She went back t'Banyil last week.'

'Ah.' There was such a note of comprehension in Pentland's voice that Echlin raised his head sharply, and Sarah paused, her hand on a cup on the dresser. Pentland's eyes moved unseeingly over the objects on the mantelpiece. On his mouth was a bitter triumphant smile. He rose abruptly, buttoning his jacket. 'I'll go now,' he said, without looking at the girl. 'The kettle's near singing,' she said in a small despairing voice.

His heart smote him and he looked at her. But even as he looked he was smothered in hatred and a desire to hurt her. Without moving his eye a hairsbreadth he could see Echlin seated at the fire. There they were, both of them in the same vision, close together, waiting for him to go. And in her greed she wanted him too. In her insatiable childish greed she wanted everybody. Me, *him* and Hamilton, if she hasn't got him. 'I don't think I'll wait' he said, with as much malice and contempt in his voice as he could summon. He saw her wince and her eyes darken. He turned away to the door almost choking with joy.

God, if there was no end to the suffering he could make her go through! Then he became cunning. There was the faintest droop to his shoulders as he lifted the latch. 'Good night,' he said without raising his head. He went out and drew the door after him. When he had rounded the rowan bushes, he stepped silently like a cat, glancing back over his shoulder. He saw the light from the open door and Sarah's figure in the bright gap. To the man standing in the hedge she seemed to peer out for a moment and then the door closed softly and slowly. Pentland waited for a few seconds, then he hurried away without a backward glance.

When Sarah closed the door she crossed the floor to the hearth. She had been throwing the drains of the teapot across the close. She knelt down and brewed fresh tea. When it had bubbled a little at the hearth-cheek she brought it over to the table. She drew up a chair and sat down. 'Are ye coming over now?' she asked. Frank rose and dragged his warm chair across. They were silent during the meal. Several times he was about to speak but when he saw the soft brooding mouth the words died in him. When she was finished the girl rose and poured fresh water into the pot and placed it close to the fire. She turned to Frank. 'If the tea's too long infused when Hamilton comes in, tell him he may make some more for himself.' Frank nodded. He knew that she did not want to sit alone with him to-night. He watched her as she stood covering the butter at the dresser. He trembled to steal up behind her and slip his hands round her, under her armpits. But the way she stood with her back to him, not looking round, warned him. Before she left the

73

kitchen she let down her hair, combing it back with her fingers, and letting it fall loosely over her shoulders.

With the departure of Martha from Rathard the brothers and Sarah became secretive and restrained and self-absorbed. To Sarah, who spent most of her waking hours in the kitchen, the house seemed empty and re-sounding. When a timber creaked or a mouse stirred in the lower rooms her heart raced and she lifted her face, listening. The sense of emptiness rushed in on her and she would have to go out into the close and listen to the muted drumming from the barn where Hamilton seeded potatoes. Nor did the presence of Hamilton and Frank in the house soothe her. The tiled floor that had sounded all day to the tap and shuffle of her mother's feet now clashed harshly under the feet of the men.

The absence of Martha brought back with acute poignancy the death of Andrew. Although all three of them felt this in varying degrees, the feeling of restraint prevented them from talking about it to each other. The older woman had absorbed into herself, silently and un-obtrusively, the void and bitter longing left by Echlin's death. The illusion of youth seemed nurtured and pro-longed by the presence of familiar old age. But now Martha was gone and there was no one to stand between them and the passing days. Sometimes, as the three of them sat at their evening meal, safe inside the circle of lamplight with the night pressing against the window, the keening of a dog across the fields made the familiar place strange and hostile to Sarah, and they seemed lifted up in the hollow of the ancient rath, adrift without guid-ance on a dark and desolate sea.

They were now passing through the short glimmering days of the year, days of drenched storm-driven twilight. Every day from horizon to horizon the sky was filled with matted clouds creeping to the east. At noon for an hour, an unearthly pearly light fell on the walls and fields, a light that pressed on the head and hurt the brain, and those who had to be out at that time did so with averted heads, hurrying quickly from doorway to doorway. Then the baffled sun drew away and the countryside slid back again into dripping icy darkness.

There was little that the men could do in this weather, so they stayed indoors and sat about in Sarah's road. Hamilton nursed the fire in his lap, as Sarah said crossly, whittling eternally with his knife. He cut teeth for the new-fangled horse rake and then he made a butter-print for the girl, a cow in relief on a shamrock. She scoffed at the crude figures, but he was content for he saw that she was pleased. Frank lay smoking all day, turning the yellowed leaves of a natural history book. Sometimes he threw himself fully clothed on his bed, and Sarah found rinds of mud on the blankets. When she scolded him he threw the book away, fluttering and shedding leaves, and went outside. He came back in a few minutes and lounged about in a hangdog way. 'I'm going down tae Sampson's—is there anything ye want?' he asked at last. Sarah lifted the paraffin jar and shook it. 'There is,' she answered, thrusting it into his hand. 'And ask Agnes tae get me half a dozen candles and a loaf o' baker's bread from Skillen's shop.' He put on his hat and drew a sack over his shoulders and went out.

They were seated at their evening meal when he came

back. Sarah rose when she heard his feet on the close, and lifting his plate from the hearth, blew the embers from the rim with her breath. They heard him fumbling at the latch, and then he came in with a little rush. Regaining his balance, he stared at them foolishly for a moment, blinking his eyes in the light. He lurched again as he set the oil-jar in the corner. Skimming his sodden hat across the room where it left a mark on the crocus-yellow wall, he crossed over to the table and sat down. His lips were wet and quivering, and his hair, darkened with the rain, tumbled on his brow so that Sarah's heart suddenly yearned to him. 'Fetch us down a couple o' glasses, Sarah!' he shouted and drew a half-pint of whiskey from his pocket. He set the bottle down with a thump among the tea-things and little trills of laughter ran through him as he peered at the bright amber liquor. Then he raised it between his eyes and the lamp. Shaken thus, the liquid released whorls of light that rose slowly up the bottle, melting and reforming again in spirals and flecks of golden fire. The light penetrating the liquid cast an aureate glow on the drunken face held close to the bottle. He sucked a great breath into his mouth. 'God, but it's a wonderful lovely thing,' he said. The sober awe in his voice startled and shocked Sarah. 'Ye drunken crature!' she cried, 'did ye ask Agnes tae get the groceries?' He stared at her dumb and outraged, then waved her impatiently aside. He turned to his brother. 'Hami, will ye have a wee drop?' There was a pleading note in his voice. Hamilton shook his head without looking up. 'Noan for me,' he mumbled.

The young man stared angrily at the other two bent

over their plates. The cork squealed as he drew it from the bottle. Still they did not look up. He tilted the bottle over his cup and looked at them again. Their heads were low over their plates and their lips were scarcely moving. To his drunken mind they seemed to be saying grace. He drove the cork back again with his fist and set it down with a crash on the dresser. His actions were wanton, violent; he wanted the others to look up and speak to him. The meal finished in silence and towards the end of it Hamilton stole a glance at his brother. His face was sober and sullenly turned away. He looked at the bottle on the dresser. The golden liquor glowed like an idol. He was uneasy and perplexed. It was the first time that strong drink had ever been in Rathard.

The whiskey bottle sat on the dresser for some days and Sarah lifted it to dust under it each day. Then by that inexplicable process that activates household articles it was moved to the window ledge behind the bowl of shamrock. After a time it was carried down to the parlour and at last it came to rest, still untouched, in the darkest corner of the camphor-scented press in the sideboard.

The relationship between Sarah and the younger brother changed imperceptibly but vitally during those few days. They still came together in furtive moments when Hamilton was about his work or when he had gone out in the evenings. But Frank sensed the growing antagonism in the girl. There was nothing said between them, but Sarah felt a great need to retract and be free again. The wave of frustration and rebellion that had torn her from her early cautious way of going had carried her out too far. Now she wanted to find her feet again and weigh her chances for her own future advantage. And she felt, always present, an overhanging guilt at the separation from her mother. She had a deep superstitious fear that she was casting off too many ties and that she would be punished. She thought calmly on the matter. In the first days of her liaison with Frank they had been recklessly impulsive; how reckless, she shivered in recalling. As she lay in bed at night, sleepless, she could scarcely believe that her mother or Hamilton could have failed to see what was going on. Frank with his crude passionate gestures outraged her, until he touched her again: but she, self-centred and independent, had treated him coolly before the others, never betraying herself. She remembered, with a wry smile, how furious she had been when he mimicked her one evening, as she lay spent and warm in his arms. Now her unmerited chance must have recognition. She retracted and drew away from Frank a little, watching Hamilton all the time.

The weather released them. Sarah opened the door one morning to find the world bathed in cold vibrating light. The snared raindrops quivered like jewels on the thatch; a prodigal starling, trembling with ecstasy on the stable ridge, mimicked the song learnt last Spring from a merle in the apple trees. Looking out on such a morning, with the birdsong in her ears, the girl felt a great cloud lifting from her heart. Hamilton came down into the kitchen behind her. He put his head out over her shoulder and sniffed, turning his sleep-heavy eyes up to the washed lofty sky. 'Isn't it fine to see it!' she cried, smiling at his dark unshaven face. 'You'll get a bit o' ploughing done afore Christmas.'

'It's like Royal Charlie. But better late nor never,' he answered going back to the fire. When he had beaten his socks against the hearth-cheek and put them on, he said: 'Make me up a piece for the fields.'

As they sat at breakfast Hamilton turned to Frank. 'There's a wheen potatoes not seeded yet. Ye may finish them, for I'll be ploughing while the weather holds.'

'I've tae bring the mare up frae Burke's, but I'll dash them off after that,' answered Frank. He spoke with zest, smiling at Hamilton and Sarah. When they had finished Sarah washed the dishes. She could hear Frank whistling to the starling, and Hamilton stamping amiably at the hearth as he thrust his feet into his boots. The rain had gone and the sun was shining on the fields. The farmhouses and the little roads of their neighbours could be seen again. The three of them were happy and looked into each other's eyes when they spoke.

Hamilton ploughed in the field running down to the road. The earth laid bare would be cleansed by the winter's frost. As his day's work went forward, the light-heartedness of the morning left him. He was perplexed and brooding again as he bent to the plough. At last the light began to go and he pulled the plough into the side. As he shaved the dry soil from his hands he spoke aloud to the horse, 'Damn-it-skin, what affair is it o' mine if she marries him?' The animal turned its head in mild wonder. He caught the horse by the mane and mounted. At the head of the field he turned to look down on his day's work. The furrows gleamed in the brittle evening light like fresh-combed hair.

CHAPTER ELEVEN

*

THE ROADS HAD been deserted except by a
few hard-pressed travellers, but now that the
weather had hardened the countryfolk appeared
in ones and twos on errands to which the storm had given
a little urgency; some to the shoemaker, the smithy, the
thatcher or Skillen's grocery shop. Among them appeared
Mr Sorleyson, eager to finish his visiting-round before
Christmas. He came up to Rathard one afternoon. Sarah,
who was busying herself at the fireside with meal for the
fowl, heard his tap at the open door and bade him come
in. He approached her holding out his hand and then he
looked at hers, all meal-daubed, and smiled. Sarah
laughed and brushed the hair from her eyes with the back
of her hand. 'We're in a right pickle here,' she said,
cleaning her hand on her apron and pulling forward a
chair.

'Well, I know better than to interrupt,' said Mr
Sorleyson as he sat down. 'Tell me, is Hamilton in?'
'No,' answered Sarah stepping a shade too quickly to the
door. 'But I'll call him.'

The minister raised his hand to stop her. 'To tell the
truth, Sarah, it's yourself I want to speak to.'

'Oh?' The sound was no more than an audible breath
laden with misgiving. She did not come back to the fire
again but stood as if ready to fly. There was silence

between them: she, standing there, poised, her eyes on the defensive; Sorleyson, his head sunk, turning his shallow black hat slowly on his fingers. He sensed in her attitude a need for care in his words. He wondered, not for the first time, why this country girl demanded from him such a pondering and weighing of words. With a bland, slightly unreal smile he looked at her. 'Can you spare me a moment? Will you sit down, please?'

She turned a chair slowly out from under the table and sat down on the edge of it. The reassuring smile deepened a trifle on Mr Sorleyson's face. He nodded his head gently, hung his hat on his knee, and placed the tips of his fingers together. 'I believe your mother has left Rathard. Is that so?' and he nodded again, so winningly, as if all he sought was kindly confidence.

But all this, far from calming the girl, made her more hostile and fearful. She nodded stiffly in reply. 'She has,' she said.

'Does she intend to stay away for long?' queried Mr Sorleyson leaning forward, his fingers outstretched on the crown of his hat.

'She's gone for good. Did she send ye here?'

'No, no,' said Mr Sorleyson hastily. 'No: Mr Burke told me that your mother had occupied his cottage again. I was surprised to hear that she'd gone back alone,' he added looking at Sarah closely.

'What's surprising about that?' she demanded. 'Isn't it her own home?'

'And yours?'

'And mine too, if ye want to know, Mr Sorleyson. But poor folk have tae work—and the breaking up of poor folks' homes is a small matter.' What's a lie at this time and day, thought Sarah.

But it seemed to have convinced Mr Sorleyson. 'Well, I see by your remarks that you accept the responsibility of your mother. I'm sure she'll come to no want.'

'Of course she'll come to no want!' said the girl sharply.

The minister stood up. 'Don't misunderstand me, Sarah. Your mother is an old member of the congregation, and it was only to satisfy myself that she was being well looked after that I came up here.'

Sarah was rather taken aback. So that's what they think of me already, she thought. 'Thank ye for calling, Mr Sorleyson. There, now I never offered ye a cup o' tea!'

'It's no matter,' he answered. 'I've other calls to make before dark.' He turned to her before he left the house. 'You'll give my regards to Hamilton and Frank?'

'I will indeed. Are ye sure ye wouldn't like me to call them?'

'No, please don't trouble them. I must go now, before dark.' He shook hands with her and left the farm.

CHAPTER TWELVE

*

S HE DID NOT go down to her mother's house on the next day nor the next. But on the third morning after Sorleyson's visit, immediately after breakfast, she tidied herself and made ready to go. She was alone in the house; Frank had left early to go down to Purdie's farm, and as it was Friday, market-day, Hamilton was preparing to go into Belfast. When he came into the kitchen he noticed that she had her outdoor dress on. 'I'm going down to my mother's,' she explained, pinning up her hair at the little mirror.

'H'm,' he said and loitered about for a while before he went out. He was back again before she was finished. 'I'll be passing your mother's house in a while,' he said in a strange hurried way. 'Would ye like tae come on into Belfast wi' me?'

The girl's eyes lit up. 'Yes—yes, I would like that fine.' Then her mouth dropped. 'But, oh no, there's the fowl and Frank's dinner.' Hamilton waved his hand. 'Never mind that. Frank'll be staying on at Purdie's for a while and Petie Sampson can come up tae the fowl.'

'D'ye think it'll be all right, then?' Hamilton nodded and she smiled at him, pleased and strangely shy.

It was still early morning when she set out for her mother's house but the ice on the puddles was already starred by early market-carts. On her left hand the sun drove up a herd of coral-red clouds and drab little winter birds fled from the horse-droppings as she approached.

The kitchen of her old home was empty when she reached it, but the floor was swept and the fire newly-made, little pouts of smoke rising between the turves. It was all as she had left it. The small window sunk in the wall, the warped glass of which made the briar stem out-side now thin as a rush now swollen as a bough. The scrubbed table still stood there, scooped out by the hundreds of earthernware dishes it had borne. The spotted dogs on the mantelshelf still stared disdainfully over her head. The earth floor glowed warmly as a flame lapped up.

Her mother stood on the threshold of the lower room. Martha felt a thrill of triumph run through her as she saw her daughter stand uncertainly between the doorway and the fire. But the mother was old, full of painfully-gazed wisdom and the scrupulous regard for the dignity of others inherent in her race. She came across with her little tripping step and laying her hands on her daughter's shoulders, pressed her lips to the girl's wind-cool cheek. Sarah felt the dried lips quiver as they touched her, and the doubt that had held her rigid and watchful melted away in the embrace. She clasped the other woman in her arms and they stood locked in bliss, mother and daughter once more.

The fire was broken up, the kettle lowered and tea brewed. They sat one on each side of the hearth, with their cups in their hands, talking. They talked about the hard winter, and how Martha's turf stock was going down, and the bog in winter flood. Sarah described how her boiling of winter apples had jellied. 'Look,' she said, and taking a pot from the basket she had brought held it out to her mother. It was a delicate moment, the first interchange of gifts. Martha accepted it critically, held it against the light, shook it, praised its colour and firmness. Then she rose and lifted the lid of the earthenware crock on the dresser. She came back with an oatmeal pudding in her hands. 'Oh!' cried Sarah, her face alight with surprise and pleasure. 'Where in the world did ye get the pig's bag at this time o' the year?'

'The Burkes slaughtered one on Monday,' replied Martha in an off-hand way, but it was easy to see that she was gratified.

'Look—there is money. It's part o' my wages,' said Sarah abruptly, laying some silver wrapped in a one-pound note in her mother's lap. Mrs Gomartin raised her hands away from the money, looked at it and then at her daughter. Then, after a moment, she took it between her finger and thumb and pushed it on to the mantelboard. Sarah was satisfied.

They pulled their chairs closer to the fire and drank more tea. But when Martha heard wheels on the road she said, 'There, that might be Hamilton now. Go and see who it is,' and as Sarah looked out her mother stood close behind her so that the passers-by could see them together. Once it was Mr Burke's housekeeper and Martha was so pleased and called out 'good morning' so brightly and loudly, that the hard-faced woman in the trap looked back in surprise. After that Sarah went back to the fire and sat down.

Then they heard the prance and clatter of a horse, and

Hamilton's voice. The shadow of his cart fell on the door and darkened the little kitchen.

Sarah rose and pulled on her coat hurriedly. 'I'll not keep him waiting,' she said and went out. Hamilton got down and helped her on to the seat. He tucked the rug around her feet before he got up himself. 'If the frost's no too hard we may be back this way home,' he called to Martha. He rattled the whip in its cup and the cart moved off up the hill to the main road.

It was pleasant, thought Sarah, to sit up here beside Hamilton, a strong farmer going to market. Pleasant to watch the rhythmic plunge of the glossy haunches before her and listen to the subdued dash of the harness. There was a richness in the twinkling of the grass-green spokes and glittering hubs against the sullen hedges. There seemed even to be a richness in the soft yielding of the springs to the road.

And she had made peace with her mother. Her heart quickened as she remembered the touch of those withered lips on her cheek. Ah, it warmed the heart to know that she could go to her mother again with her troubles. A shadow stirred deep down in her soul at the thought and she turned resolutely to the present. Slowly, like a late spring in her life, her desires were budding to fulfilment. A hearth, a home to preside over, the daily life of cattle and fowl in her hands, the desires of her own body—she winced and turned away again from that impalpable shadow that hung in the depths of her mind.

They passed heavy orange-coloured carts, lurching and clanging, but Hamilton and she rushed swiftly past, swaying gently in their seats. They overtook the children

86

going to school and Sarah laughed when they raced the cart, *peep-peeping* at the turkeys that craned their naked ridiculous heads from the basket under the seat. She laughed again when the children fell behind and threw themselves with smoking breath on the roadside banks. Hamilton smiled at her pleasure, his eyes watchful on the road, the reins moving in his strong alert hands.

The horse's stride lengthened on the thawing road and soon they were passing through the little clachan of Moneyrea, and the haze of Belfast rose before them, above the tree tops. They wound carefully down the long hill into the city, the people on the road became more numerous, and the hedges gave way to the heavy grey walls of an estate. Then came a row of white-washed cottages, once the village of Castlereagh but now chained to the city by row upon row of red-brick houses. Hamilton reined the horse down to walking pace as they joined the long jolting cavalcade of carts arriving in from the townlands lying to the south and east. Towering among them the horse-trams lurched slowly towards the city centre.

Hamilton, unlike the majority of his fellow-farmers, sold his butter, eggs, fowl and garden crops direct to a grocer situated near the market district. In return he bought nails, paraffin and whatever household goods were required in Rathard. In the old days his father had come with a list in his vest pocket, but now he had Sarah to help him. She bought cheese and rice and currants and raisins and barley, and a side of dried ling for their own needs. She asked for a feeding bucket and a score of coloured leg-rings for the spring poultry. 'I couldna have

87

carried a better list to market,' said Hamilton as she passed from counter to counter. She laughed and coloured a little. She watched him as he made his purchases for the outdoor life of Rathard. He was taller and bulkier in his homespun clothes than the people around him, and as he lifted, talked and moved about he seemed to overshadow the dark crowded shop. All their purchases made, Hamilton arranged to call for them on the way home and Sarah and he went out to the cart. There was a warm pride and pleasure towards each other as they mounted again and drove further into the heart of the city.

Although living only twenty miles from Belfast, Sarah had never been in the city before. Now she sat high in the cart, turning her head from side to side as she watched the teeming crowds of oil-stained men crossing the road, some under the horse's very nose, and some waiting impatiently until the traffic slackened.

'Where would they be coming from?' she asked, her eyes wide with surprise. 'They're shipyard workers,' Hamilton explained, pointing with his whip to where a mass of slender gantries like a piece of jagged lace stood at the bottom of a hill with a sliver of grey water at their feet, 'and this is their dinner-hour.'

She stared in wonder at a woman who shot out of a low doorway, like a cork out of a bottle, with a rabble of laughing dirty children tumbling behind her on to the pavement. A man in a tweed cap stood in the doorway shouting and shaking his fist. As the woman passed close to the cart Sarah saw that she was weeping.

They passed over the bridges leading into the town and Hamilton left the horse and cart in Cromac Square. He led Sarah to the variety market where old women, surrounded by piles of bedsteads, clothes, pictures, boxes of fruit and tottering columns of books, paused only in their monotonous cries to blow on their numbed fingers. Sarah bought a lustre jug and a worn paisley shawl for her mother. When Hamilton saw her eyeing two highly glazed and warty figures of a highland girl and her lover on whose delph plaid a tartan was daubed, he fished with finger and thumb in the slit pocket close to his waistband.

They carried their purchases back to the Square and laid the figures, wrapped in straw, at the bottom of the cart. When Hamilton had shaken up the horse's nosebag they went to a little eating-house close to the markets. The warm steaming air of the place was filled with the noise of voices and the clatter of knives and forks. The heat of the food and the rank smoke of their husbands' pipes had brought a dew on the faces of the women, as they sat with their dresses open at the neck, and their thick flushed wrists, toiling away at their plates.

After the meal Hamilton had to fetch some harrow teeth from an implement shop. Sarah walked slowly round the Square, pausing now and then to glance into the low shop windows. Tiring of this she stopped to look at the hurrying people. A man who had been approaching her slackened his pace as he neared her, and catching her eye, winked broadly. The girl started in surprise and confusion. Turning, she started to walk rapidly away, but as she passed through the crowds she became aware of bold friendly glances from the men. Gradually a feeling of pleasure came over her. She paused to look at her reflection in a shop window and the innate peasant appreciation of harmonious colour and line in living things was satisfied. The hat of brown velvet enriched her smooth ripe hair. Her ready-made coat failed to muffle the lines of her strong shapely body. Her eyes darkened with pride. Amongst the city women, with their strained hurrying faces and their arms torn down with baskets, she moved with ease, her movements a promise of warmth and desire. Three young shipyard workers, walking arm-in-arm, smiled at her, their teeth shining in their oil-smudged faces. She turned her head away, her lips quivering with pleasure.

Suddenly she realised that she had been away from the cart for a long time. Hurrying fearfully through the traffic she crossed the Square and found the cart still there, untended. Hamilton arrived a few minutes later and dropped a small sack with a chinking thud into the cart. They climbed up and Hamilton rounded the horse's head into the homeward traffic. Sarah, gazing down from her high seat thought the people strange and hostile again. The shawled women hurried by unseeing, the men whistled and stamped their feet impatiently, waiting a chance to duck under the horse's head or swing through by the tailboard. When they looked up their glance was curt, indifferent, like men who had tired of the sight of human faces. The holiday was over. She shivered and wound her hands in the rug, longing for home.

Their cart was one in a long procession of carts, moving back through the dusk of the winter evening towards the townlands. They overtook great country carts laden to the brim with bags of feeding meal on which the driver lay, and perhaps one or two others, smoking and singing.

On the quiet verge of the road tramped men and women carrying baskets of city purchases. At the loanen-heads, sleepy numb little children, silenced by the cold and stars, were gathered under greatcoats in clusters of two or three, waiting for the return of their parents. Then the thin golden cries ringing over quiet fields as a cart lantern halted on the road and the great tufted horse set his feet carefully on the loanen. The youngest child was hauled up by his braces and crouched, shuddering with joy, under the warmth of his father's jacket.

Hamilton's light cart bowled on through the cold green twilight, overtaking carts and people on foot. He drew up outside Ardpatrick and lighted his lamp. A man whom he had just passed came running out of the dusk, calling on his name. 'I thocht I saw ye going past,' he said, leaning breathlessly against the wheel. He carried a large hamper on his arm. Echlin, dazzled by the candle flame, peered down into the stranger's face. His breath smelt of whiskey. 'It's me,' he said, stepping out into the light. Hamilton's face lit up. 'Eh, is it you, Shuey? Sarah,' he said, 'ye know Shuey Carspindle of Lusky Woods?' The man ducked and touched his forehead. 'I hope you're well, ma'am,' he said. 'Get up, Shuey,' continued Hamilton, lifting the man's basket into the cart. 'I'll leave ye down at your loanen.' The man hesitated; then, 'I'm much obliged t'ye,' he replied, and climbed up by the wheelhub and sat down on the floor of the cart behind them.

'And had ye a brave day at Belfast, ma'am?' he enquired when he had found his basket again.

'I had indeed,' answered Sarah, 'and had you, Mr Carspindle?'

The man behind them smacked his lips. 'Fair enough, ma'am, fair enough. But going to Belfast is no newance to me. Sure I've been going to Belfast market ever since I was the height av two peats. I went first wi' my da, God rest him, five-and-forty years ago. My da was a very wicked wee man and told the daftest tales. Did ye take notice av all the church steeples sticking up out av the town, ma'am?' he asked, prodding Sarah in the ribs.

'I did that.'

'Well, the ould boy told me that God and St Peter were travelling over Ireland on a cloud onct, and God dandered out to the edge and peeped over. "Where would that be now," says God, pulling at his beard and looking by the way he was mystified. St Peter takes a keek down. "Oh-ho," says he, not to be taken in, "sure ye know rightly that's Belfast." "Is it now," says God, "so that's where they're all coming from? By-my-name!" says he, "wi' all them sharp points sticking up I thought it was a harrow, cowped on its back in the rain." Ye see, ma'am?' cried Carspindle, 'God was lettin' on he didn't know what the steeples were!' The girl nodded violently, and now Hamilton was laughing outright. 'Oh, he was the harey boy for the stories, was my ould da,' said Carspindle, relapsing back on the floor of the cart.

They were passing through the single street of Ardpatrick. It was an oasis of light in the dark countryside. Through the flitting windows Sarah could see the lamplight fall on old pictures, halters, clocks and the heads of men and women gathered round the supper tables. The last light in the street had a ruddy glow as if from the open door of a furnace. Carspindle plucked Hamilton's sleeve. 'I'll light down here for a while, Hami,' he said. Sarah looked through the window from where the glow came and saw a row of warm brown barrel-ends, grained and varnished, with a brass spigot in each. The head and shoulders of a ruddy-faced man could be seen; by his movements he appeared to be mopping the bar-counter, and all the time he kept talking and nodding to some invisible audience. Carspindle paused with one leg over the wing of the cart. 'Will ye come in?' he asked. He lowered himself on to the ground and pulled his hamper after him. ' "Will ye" is a bad fellow, come on in and keep me company.' There was no reply from the people in the cart. 'Come on in,' the man continued wheedlingly, 'I'll no detain ye a minute.'

'Well, that's fair enough,' said Hamilton suddenly, looking at Sarah. The girl sat silent, not knowing what to do. She had never been in a public-house before. Since she was a child she had had the evils of drink dinned into her, she had seen the example of her father. Yet the excitement of the city was on her, and Hamilton, whom she had expected to drive on, was waiting for her word. Carspindle, on the road, leered up at her. 'Come, ma'am,' he said, 'it's not often ye grace the market. Don't kill the day for a thimbleful o' fun.' Sarah laughed and stretching down her hand to Carspindle, leapt lightly to the ground.

When she entered the tavern she saw the men to whom the publican had been speaking. They were three labourers, the first of the evening's company. They sat with their backs to the wall on a long form, dressed in their evening best, with shaven faces, bright cloth caps and gleaming brass studs in the necks of their collarless twist-tweed shirts.

The publican nodded familiarly to Carspindle and moving swiftly down the bar, threw open the door leading to the kitchen. Hamilton hesitated on the threshold. 'Maybe it's too much trouble—we aren't stopping over long,' he said.

Carspindle caught him by the arm. 'Damn-it-skin,' he said in a low voice, 'ye can't have the lady sitting there!' nodding to the bar and its three interested occupants.

'Ah!' said Hamilton, and plunged down the dark passage after the publican. The man ushered them into the empty kitchen and there Carspindle took charge. In the light of the hanging-lamp Sarah saw her fellow-traveller more closely. He was about sixty years of age, sturdily built, his shoulders already bowed and his hands hanging down, knuckles out, on the front of his thighs. He had no hat and his thin hair and naked scalp filled the girl with pity and distaste. He wore a leather waistcoat and had bundled himself into three threadbare overcoats of varying length and colour. The knot of his wollen scarf, damp with drunken spittle and condensed breath, had chafed his throat and was now twisted behind his ear. Some whiskey drinkers achieve a pale, almost ascetic appearance, but with Carspindle the irregular temples, the cheeks, the pouches below the eyes, the nose itself and the moist and quivering chin were composed of little sacks of reddish flesh, the whole held together in the shape of a face, as it were, by a web of fine dark veins radiating from the root of his nose. He snuffed the odours of the bar, swaying a little on his feet; a vessel crammed and

94

running over with folly, fecklessness and good-humour.

Hamilton, who had caught the look of repugnance on Sarah's face, shuffled his feet uneasily. 'Maybe we'd better wait outside for ye, Shuey. The pony'll be getting restless.' He made as if to step to the door. Carspindle woke out of his trance. 'Damn the fears av him!' he said, jumping forward. He hurried to the wall and dragged out a chair. 'Here, ma'am, sit down and rest your legs. Paddy!' he shouted, turning his head to the door, 'what's detaining ye?' As he heard the feet of the publican in the passage he thrust his hand into his pocket and brought it out with notes and coins peeping from the crevices of his fist. A florin slipped from his hand and ran tinkling across the tiles. The man stood crouched under the lamp watching the coin until it wobbled and fell at the feet of Paddy as he came in. 'A good dog aye knows its own master,' he said with a wry laugh as the publican lifted the coin. 'What'll the lady have, Hami?' he asked, holding his finger and thumb suggestively apart. Echlin looked in a helpless manner at Sarah as she sat at the fire.

'Port, maybe?' he said.

Paddy shook his head. 'No port.'

'There's only one drink for a night like this,' declared Carspindle, 'and bring it in a bottle and no in wee drops ye can snuff up your nose—and I'll have a pint o' porther.'

The publican returned with a pint of porter, a bottle half full of whiskey and three whiskey glasses. Carspindle pushed Hamilton's outstretched hand away. 'It was me that arst ye in, wasn't it?' He poured out whiskey for the others and handed it to them. As Sarah raised her glass to her lips she recoiled a little from the sweetly pungent smell of the liquor. Her eyes met Carspindle's. 'It's fine stuff, that,' he said. She put the glass to her mouth and tilted it back. 'Aaah,' she said and shuddered. The level of the whiskey in the bottle dropped steadily downward.

Carspindle, with his funny bald head and his mouth drawn down as he told his story. … She had never known such good company before. She knew that she looked beautiful at this moment. Delicately she touched her cheeks and upward curving lips. And oh! the movements of her hands. Like a swan or an osier beside the stream. She threw out her hand in a queenly way to the man opposite her. A glass shivered on the floor. A sudden panic ran through her. She saw Hamilton sitting rigid in his chair. Carspindle's moist red face swooped down on her as he kicked the pieces under the table.

With a great effort she fixed her eyes precisely on the latch of the door. The floor rose and fell beneath her feet as she went forward, her hand raised. Behind her, Hamilton scrambled up, pushing the table from him. Carspindle steadied the bottle and glared after his companions. He heard the snick of the latch, and a cold blast of air struck him. Echlin ran out, clashing the door violently at his heels. 'Damn ye for a bitch!' Carspindle shouted, forcing the cork into the bottle and staggering upward.

Sarah ran blindly through the public saloon looking to neither right nor left. She saw the glow of the cart lamp at the gable of the house. The bitter cold of the night made her draw breath with a hiss. On the white-washed wall across the street a man lay spreadeagled. 'D'ye know the Three Curses av Ireland, ma'am?' he bellowed,

'Priests, Parsons an' Porther!' She reached the cart and fumbled at the step with her foot. She found it and raised herself up, kneeling on the shaft, then on the lip of the cart. With a sob she tumbled forward on the seat. The heavy footsteps behind her stopped and she saw Hamilton climbing up by the wheel. He forced his way past her and sat down heavily. 'In the name of God, Sarah!' he shouted angrily. She put her hands to her face and sobbed outright. The horse, feeling the reins tighten on his mouth, stirred gladly and clicked his hooves on the stones. The door of the public-house flew open again and Carspindle stood on the step. 'Damn your sowls—don't go off wi' my basket!' he shouted running towards them. The horse did not move and he ran heavily against the side of the cart. 'Hold him, Hami,' he said, groping with his foot for the spokes. 'I thocht ye were away wi'out me,' he said in an apologetic voice, worming himself down into the bags behind them.

The echo of the horse's feet grew and fell away as they passed the last irregular walls of the village. Then they were out in the silence again, running swiftly through the fields, and the gleam and sound of their passage was swallowed by the black hedges. The homing horse, feeling a lax hand on the reins, opened his stride on the hard ringing road. His breath came back in coloured vapour around the lamp, and where the hedges stooped the light shot in swift arrows across the fields.

Sarah, crouching in her seat, nodded weakly to the movements of the cart. Her mouth was full of a sticky aromatic taste and she had a sensation like a hard fiery ball in her chest. At that moment she thought she knew the truth of her mother's words 'Like a leper smits you with leprosy, a drunkard smits you with misery.' She heard the squeak of a cork behind her and after a pause felt Carspindle push the bottle between her and Hamilton. She did not even trouble to look down but she saw the glint of the bottle as Hamilton raised it to his mouth. Then there was the rasp of a match as the man behind them lit his pipe, and in a low unsteady voice, to the drumming of Carspindle's bottle, Hamilton began to sing:

> I will gie ye fine beavers
> And a fine silken goon:
> I will gie ye smart petticoats
> Flounced tae the groon'
> I will gie ye fair jewels,
> And live but for thee,
> If ye leave your ain true love
> And marry wi' me.

Carspindle ceased his drumming and leaned over the side of the cart. Ahead, a light gleamed frostily at the side of the road. Carspindle straightened his muffler. 'Pull up, Hami boy,' he said, 'I'll light down here.' The door of the cottage at which they had stopped opened a little and they saw a woman standing in the crevice of light. She held back a struggling dog between her leg and the door. 'Is that you, Shuey?' she called in a thin plaintive voice. The dog wriggled past her and shot out, shaking and cringing with joy around Carspindle as he lowered himself to the ground.

'Have ye got your basket now?' Hamilton asked.

'I have, and I'm much obliged to ye. Here, hold hard a minute.' He came round to the front of the cart and held up his bottle. 'Old friends, Hami, old friends,' he urged, seeing the man in the cart hesitate.

'H'm. Give me the hold of it,' said Echlin, grasping the bottle. He tilted it to his mouth and was seized with a violent fit of coughing. Carspindle reached up and took the bottle from his hand. 'Are ye rightly, Hami?' he asked.

'Damn it!' shouted Echlin, whooping for breath, 'it near choked me.' He shook the reins. 'Good night.'

'Good night, Hami. Good night, ma'am, and I'm much obliged again.'

'You're welcome,' said Echlin as the horse moved off.

High above them the stars glittered, chill and remote. Streams fell silent, stones and trees cracked in the grip of the frost, and the earth resounded like a bell under the horse's feet. They were entering the townland of Lusky Woods and the road, gleaming faintly in the starlight, undulated onward through boglands checkered with crisped heather and black peat banks. Echlin's body was lapped in a warm stupor. From his shoulders downward he felt relaxed and drooping. His legs were relaxed and bowed so that his feet lay sole to sole on the floor of the cart. But his neck and head were rigid, balanced between the knifepoints of the bitter air.

On his loin and thigh he could feel the woman nestling into his warmth. He gave his warmth prodigally and his whole body was aware of her. She was insistently bearing into the glow of his body, and at the realisation of this a warm flood ran down him to the pit of his stomach. He released a hand from the reins and put his arm deliberately around her. His heart gave a great beat as he felt her respond and come closer into him. He pressed his arm up under her armpit and his hand closed on a curve of her body. At the touch of his hand cradling her breast the hard pain broke in the girl and ran through her in tingling fiery jets. She raised her head and drew in a deep shuddering breath. Below her side she could feel the man's thigh quivering uncontrollably. They hesitated, silent, scarcely breathing. She gave willingly to the pressure of his hand, sliding her hand under his coat until it lay over his heart. The beaded rime on her smooth hair pricked his lips, and he gently edged her face upward. His mouth closed down on the warm hollow of her eye and the reins dropped from his hands. She lay back on his arm, her eyes closed and her lips a little parted. The horse stumbled and stood trembling on the road. The man was stooped over the woman, his mouth pressing down on hers. At the horse's stumble they slipped downward amongst the bags, silently, without laughter. The patient beast lowered his head to nuzzle the stiff tracery of the hedge …

Presently Sarah stirred and sat up. 'Listen.' In the distance they heard the ringing beat of steps. When they had gained the seat, needles of light were rising over a hill in front of them. A man carrying a lamp came nearer. He raised it and hailed them. 'It's a hardy one, that,' he said. They saw the face of Fergus Pentland in the light. He stared at them for a moment, then lowered his lamp and went on without speaking again.

Echlin and the girl drove on in silence. They sat apart, deep in silence. Once or twice he glanced at her, but her face was hidden in the scarf that she had drawn over her head. Her gloveless hands hung forward on her knees, swaying listlessly to the motion of the cart. Around her, the earth in cold purity turned its face to the stars, but neither wind nor frost could purify her hands. There was something uncanny in the way she sat, her cowled head sunk in her shoulders, her hands jerking listlessly. The horse slithered on an icy rut. Echlin lashed it with the whip. 'Damn ye, have ye gone dumb!' he shouted to Sarah. She neither moved nor spoke, staring ahead into the darkness. It was the first time that he had ever spoken to her like that. Something stirred in her, rebellious yet strangely comforting.

The tired beast came to a halt in the close. The door opened and Frank stood silhouetted in the light. He stared out at them without speaking, eating something from his hand. He came forward without a word and started to move the purchases from the cart. As Hamilton led the horse out of the shafts something came tinkling down the floor of the cart and shattered into fragments at Sarah's feet. She picked up a piece that gleamed in the light of the window. It was her mother's lustre jug.

CHAPTER THIRTEEN

*

NEXT MORNING, as usual, Sarah had the fire kindled and the kettle singing before she heard the clump of feet in the room behind the hearth. Frank came down first and without speaking passed through the kitchen on his way out to the 'ditch', a stone wall under the rowan bushes, on which sat buckets and basins, filled, if it had been raining, with soft rainwater. In the crevices between the stones were slips of fiery red and white soaps, the toilet preparations of the Echlins. The young man cracked the ice on the butt and filled his basin from it.

When he came back into the kitchen again, fumbling behind the door for the towel, Hamilton was seated at the fire, pulling on his heavy grey socks which had been hanging on the crane. Frank, red and glowing, came over to the fire, and sat down on the opposite side of the hearth. Between them, Sarah bent over the frying-pan, cooking the breakfast.

'I brought teeth for the harrow,' said Hamilton, without looking up, 'will ye have time to knock them in the day?' Frank sat rolling down his sleeves, his eyes fixed on his brother. Getting no answer Hamilton looked up, his face unshadowed and questioning. He did not repeat his question but jerked his head in interrogation, 'Will ye?'

The younger brother was angered at the simplicity of

the question. 'No,' he growled, 'I've to go down to Stewartie Purdie's the day again.' Sarah rose with their breakfast plates in her hands and in silence they followed her to the table and drew in their chairs.

Frank sat tense and suspicious at the meal. He felt himself hang over the table like a hawk, heart and brain stilled and narrowed for a look or gesture between his brother and the girl. No one spoke and he sensed somewhere a strain, vibrating and tense as his own. He examined Sarah covertly as she ate. Her face was calm and detached as ever. What thoughts were passing behind that broad calm forehead? His brother's arms or the feeding of hens? Perhaps she was sitting tense with laughter knowing that she could always outwit him and knowing that he knew it too. And because he could not break her with his silence and read what she tried to conceal, his knife clattered on his plate with rage.

There was Hamilton left. Slow and powerful as the animals he worked among. Hamilton set his life by the sun and seasons and moved as irresistibly. As long as he could remember Frank had jeered at him and turned to him in moments of fear. He grew out of the soil and a man and a bush and a beast kept their appointed places in his world. The swift accidental things of life did not exist for him. He never kicked or swore at inanimate things but bent patiently and saw where the beam had been rotten, the rope frayed, the wheel caught on a stone.

But nothing was to be learnt from Hamilton. He hung his head low over his plate and shovelled the food into his mouth. Then he raised his head and chewed meditatively, gazing at the wall. Then down went his head again to meet his loaded fork. Twice Frank stole a glance at the dark placid face. The second time Hamilton caught his eye and held him.

'That harrow'll have tae be fixed afore long.'

'Ah,' said Frank.

'Will Stewartie soon be redd up, down there?'

'The day should finish it,' answered Frank shortly.

'Well, see if ye can put a hand to the harrow, afore Sunday.'

Frank rose without answering and Hamilton cocked his chair back and fell to picking his teeth with a match.

As he stumbled down the path to Purdie's, Frank asked himself angrily if they thought that they had fooled him. Suddenly he stopped with a question trembling on his lips. Why did he suspect them and did he care a damn anyway? His angry mind proffered a thousand reasons for suspicion. Their slipping away to market together. His astonishment at smelling drink on his brother. The flushed face and heavy eyes of the woman that he knew too well to misinterpret. And now this hard silence hanging over them. And Hamilton, the simple one. Perhaps there were depths in a man only uncovered by such a thing as this? He kicked a stone from under his foot and watched it go bounding down the hill. He descended more slowly now, thinking over the second part of his question. Did he love Sarah Gomartin? It was difficult to lay out the threads of that problem. Against every firm thread of regard a rotten one snapped in his hand. To touch her, yes. But then she was herself so quickly again, like a pool you lash into foam with a branch and in a twinkling the ripples die and it stares up cold and impersonal, mirroring your still hot and tremulous face. To enjoy her food and attention and skill in the house, yes. But then in unguarded moments to catch the calculating glance in her eye that turned all her little attentions to mockery and her own presence to that of a stranger and a trespasser.

But now his pride would not let him give her up so easily to his brother. Somewhere perhaps, and he could not even take his oath on that, was a woman with the qualities Sarah lacked. But the girl had satisfied his greatest hunger and these finicking imperfections had only been revealed later.

When he knocked at Purdie's door it was opened by Eileen, Stewartie's daughter. She was a heavy, red-faced girl with dank coils of hair slipping untidily over her neck. At school Frank and his companions had made her life a misery. She giggled sheepishly when she saw the young man and drew the opening of her dress over the roughened reddish skin of her chest. Below the flushed skin, Frank caught a glimpse of her white breasts. He wrinkled his lips and the image of Sarah came into his mind again. The young woman turned and shuffled back into the warm, red-flagged kitchen and then Frank noticed that she was wearing a pair of unlaced men's boots. On the hearth stood Stewartie in long, red, woollen underpants, balancing himself on one leg as he drew on a pair of breeches. The knee bands were tight for his swollen calves and when he had pulled them up he stood breathless, the front of his breeches gaping open. An old woman and two younger children still sat at the breakfast table. Eileen stood behind her father and stole glances at the young man, exchanging little tittering laughs with the elder of the two children, a girl.

'Ye must ha' rose at the skraik o' dawn!' shouted Purdie, his arms hanging loose.

Echlin smiled and shook his head abruptly. 'It's past nine, man. Get yourself ready, and I'll wait outside.' He refused a cup of tea and left the house walking across the close and into the field where Purdie and he had been working. He turned up along the hedge until he stood at the back wall of a barn against which ranks of stinging nettles clung stubbornly. The field in which he stood was fringed by the waters of the lough that lapped grey and chill under the winter sky. On the bottom of the hill, which sloped down from Rathard, Purdie and he had opened a trench and now water was gushing down it, still discoloured with raw clay. At the end of the trench where it passed close to the barn a square pit had been dug and beside it lay the axle and blades of a waterwheel.

One evening in the autumn, Purdie had come up to Rathard and asked permission to turn a little stream which ran along the bottom of the hill into the lough, so that it would pass behind the wall of his barn. When Hamilton heard that Purdie meant to turn his barn machinery with the water power, he laughed. He took Purdie out and showed him the rivulet where it ran on the hillside below the rath. 'There's not enough power in that trinket tae drive a turnip-cutter let alone fans. Stick tae your horse on the horse-walk, Stewartie.' But the old man was obstinate, Frank backed him up for the novelty of the waterwheel, and Hamilton shrugged, laughed, and gave permission.

Purdie came through the gate with two axle-sockets of stone in his arms. 'We'll set these first, Frank, put on the wheel an' couple her up wi' the shaft.' He dropped the sockets and indicated a driving-shaft protruding from the wall of the barn.

They set to work and in a short time the sockets were secured and the wheel lowered under the falling water. Both men stood back, their eyes glistening with pleasure and excitement as the bladed wheel gathered speed until it hummed on its axle.

'Quick now, the shaft. Couple her up, man, couple her up!' shouted Purdie. The teeth meshed and a significant groan came from the arrested wheel. Purdie turned and ran clumsily towards the gate with Frank on his heels. When they arrived at the barn they heard a muted clanking noise. The shaft was spinning slowly at the base of the wall.

'Would ye just look at that now!' said Purdie, squatting down beside it and grinning with pride. Frank placed the palm of his hand firmly on the shaft and the contraption stopped with a jerk. 'God damn ye!' roared Purdie, knocking down his arm violently, 'd'ye want tae ruin my waterwheel!' Frank sat back on his heels roaring with laughter at the old man's angry face. The shaft took up its load again and started to revolve slowly.

Purdie stamped up and down the barn once or twice. His face brightened. 'I'll clear the burn further up and lighten the cogs. That should settle it,' he said. He turned to Frank, 'Come on in tae the house for a drop o' tea.'

As they crossed the close Purdie raised his hand and pointed to the hillside. 'There's a boyo for ye,' he said.

Frank saw his brother swinging the plough to a fresh furrow. The colter glinted once in the light. Suddenly the young man stiffened. He saw the gleam of Sarah's apron as she came from the farmhouse. She stopped at the gate of the field where Hamilton was working and slipped a can and a small parcel through the bars. Frank watched his brother raise his hand, draw in a coil of rein, and his clear 'hup now!' came faintly through the air. Horse, plough and man crawled slowly down the face of the hill again. Frank felt a feeling of shame as if he had been caught eavesdropping. He turned and followed Purdie into the house.

PART II

CHAPTER ONE

*

THE DAYS THAT followed in Rathard were tense and silent. Hamilton proved fiercely adamant, determined to give up nothing: yet he lacked the courage to ask the woman to give up Frank. There was nothing further to be hidden now from any one of them. The brothers moved warily in each other's presence, knowing that a sudden action was fraught with violence. And Sarah went about the house, eyes and ears strained to catch every word and gesture. Sometimes when her mind became tired and numb, she felt that she was watching a scene and she had neither sympathy nor blame for the woman she saw. Yet when she was nakedly conscious of what was happening to her she never wavered in her calm attention to the men, never setting one above the other. And all the time her fear was being dissipated by a mounting pride fed by all the humiliating years when she was a girl. She had two men.

Frank quickly realised that this new relationship with Sarah meant very much to his brother, and though he called on jealousy, he called in vain, and his anger weakened. At times as he thought of himself, he felt a desire to laugh. There was something insanely comic that this should have come about where his father and mother had lived and moved a few months ago.

Of the three of them Hamilton was the least disturbed.

He saw clearly that his brother's relationship with the woman was a chancy thing, rooted in pride and appetite. He himself asked nothing from her that she was not prepared to give, but he had raised crops on stony soil before.

Although there was sufficient passion and confusion present, which, in a more inactive and leisured household might have broken out in violence, the insistent demands of the farm took them away from each other for long periods. The Echlins had a few sheep on the slope overlooking the lough and several of the ewes dropped lambs prematurely. A sudden squall of snow followed by a bitter frost killed several of the feeble creatures, and Hamilton spent a day and a night tending the survivors in an outhouse. The store of coal ran low and twice Frank had to turn back on the frozen roads to Killyleagh. Trees had to be cut down, hauled to the farm-close and sawn into firewood. These communal activities made it necessary for decisions to be taken in the evenings, at the fireside, and advice offered and considered. And as the outside world thawed and the sound of running water was heard once more in the dykes, so speech began to move again, sluggishly at first, between the brothers.

Yet, in the end, Frank and Hamilton fought. They had left the house after the midday meal and as Sarah went to the door to empty a basin, she heard the heavy breathing of men. There was something evil and deliberate about the sound. Then there came a hoarse grunt and the thud of a falling body. She flew to the byre and saw them on the ground between the stalls. The animals were tossing their heads in fear and crowding away from the struggling men. Hamilton knelt on his brother's chest, his fist raised like a hammer and his head nodding patiently as he timed his blow on the face jerking from side to side beneath him. The woman screamed and lifting a graip, struck Hamilton on the back. The brothers rose slowly, picking the filth from their clothes. They stared at each other like men who had wakened from a nightmare. 'You fools!' shouted Sarah. They did not even turn to look at her. They stood there, their hands moving mechanically over their bodies, gazing into each other's faces. Hamilton closed his fist and stared at it dumbly. Is this the fist I meant to smash you with, brother? his eyes asked. Slowly the woman felt their hurt bewilderment: she knew that at that moment she did not exist. She was alien, barred, shut away from them. And the knowledge of her own guilt quelled any rebellion in her. She turned away, her head lowered, and left them. Yet before she had reached the house, her instinct was stirring in revolt against this bond between the men.

CHAPTER TWO

*

SPRING CAME, WARM and turbulent. The drab sheets on the hillsides were torn under the ploughman's heel and a tawny light rose from the soil. The sower came, scattering wisely from his sheet, then the plunging harrow driving the hard silver grain underground, and lastly the roller, clanging like a bell as it wheeled, and leaving, for all the boulders piled upon it, faint pock-marks of hooves in the smooth soil. Rainshowers came leaping through the hills and were gone before the sun had time to shadow. Five times a lean cat stole across the close of Rathard carrying a kitten in her jaws. She went straight as an arrow, her head close to the ground and the proud cock trotted out of her way.

In the house, Sarah sat at her bedroom window overlooking the rath in the wrinkles of whose broken walls primroses were already gleaming. The men were out and there was a deep silence in the house. Nothing stirred and the beat of the kitchen clock did not penetrate through the closed door. The shawl that she had drawn over her head to go out had fallen down on her shoulders. She put her hand swiftly to her body feeling the movement below her heart again. No need now to go down to Agnes Sampson. She was to have a child. A stunned look came into her eyes. 'I am having a child,' she said aloud, impatiently, as if upbraiding herself for her lack of understanding. She put her hands over her face, and sat like this for a long time, staring through her fingers. A wag-tail, bobbing and dipping on the sill, took fright and flew off.

She rose slowly, as if very weary and went up to the kitchen. The untended fire fell in a cloud of ash and flames. She built it up again and lowered the kettle to the turves. As she carried dishes from the dresser to the table, laying the evening meal, she moved as if she were in a dream, and her face was grey and haggard.

A plate slipped from her fingers and shattered on the floor. She started and looked round her sharply as if she had been rudely awakened. After that she moved deftly and carefully about her task in her usual way but the haunted look was still on her face and she would stop suddenly and stand for long moments, gazing before her, unseeing.

That night when she lay in her bed alone, all the pos-sible and impossible consequences of her guilt that a heated brain could imagine were drawn to her pillow. She saw herself thrown out by the Echlins, scorned by the countryside and hunted by her neighbours. Echoes of such old stories sounded like spoken words in her ear. She started up in bed, the sweat running down her body. The voices fled and she lay down again. She thought of her mother and saw that small lean woman trembling when she told her and heard the passionate outburst of anger as she was driven from the house. She recoiled from the thought. Years of living in the one house, of sharing food and labour, of tending each other in sickness were not to be set aside so easily. There was a grain of comfort in the thought, and at last, as the darkness thinned in the east, she fell asleep. Not once, in that long sleepless night, had she thought of the child.

In the cool light of morning with the simple familiar things at hand to be taken up, she smiled briefly and bitterly at her midnight fears, yet the comfort that the memory of her mother had given her, echoed in her mind. When her work was done, she put a shawl over her head, drew the door and started for her mother's cottage. As she walked along the road, stumbling blindly over the rough places, she kept turning in her mind what she would say. But as the end of her journey grew nearer her pace slackened, and she stopped irresolute in the road. Slowly, with lagging steps, she approached the top of the hill looking down on her old home. She saw her mother come out and gather peat from the stack at the corner of the house. When she had filled her basket, the old woman raised her head and looked up the road, shading her eyes with her hand. The woman on the hilltop stole into the shadow of the hedge and leaned her arms on the curved bough of an ash tree. She saw her mother raise the basket and go indoors and in a second a fresh puff of smoke leaned away from the chimney and trailed like an azure veil over the fields. Tears ran down the face of the woman standing in the hedge. She turned away, walking slowly on the road she had come.

Down in the cottage, Martha had lowered the kettle on the crane and set out two cups and a sugar basin and a milk jug on the table. She hurried to the door to see again the figure she had seen below the trees. There was no one there and the road was empty as far as the eye could see.

She stood in the doorway till she grew cold, but no one came. At last she turned and went back into the house. She sat down in her chair before the fire. The kettle sang and at last spluttered up, rocking its lid. She sat there for a long time staring numbly into the fire. Occasionally she rubbed her hands down her legs which had a strange burning feeling in them now, when she sat too near the heat.

CHAPTER THREE

*

FRANK WAS CLEANING the bee-hives. Sarah could see him standing in the blue shadow of the thorn-trees, his veiled head bent over the frames. Over the wall of the rath between the roots of the thorns the white blossomed fairy lint broke in foam as though a sea of flowers tossed outside. A field of young corn lay beyond the rath, the grey cracked earth still showing through the pale shoots. The air was filled with small humming sounds as if someone were plucking a slack fiddle-string. The sound awoke a longing for sunshine and ripe nodding grass. Because something was lacking Sarah felt ill at ease, and sensed a note of panic in the flight of the bees. She had laughed when she saw Frank come out of the barn, a veil drawn over an old straw hat, his trouser-legs tied at the bottom, and gloves on his hands. He had given her cord to tie his cuffs. Then he had lighted his smoker at the fire and the acrid smell of burnt paper hung in the air.

A small rusty bee landed clumsily on the window-sill. It crawled along the frame until it reached the corner. Unable to go any further, it turned out towards the edge. It tried to rise and then fell over the edge, landing on a dusty cobweb which shook under its weight. She saw the delicate flexing of the spider's legs in the hole above the web. The bee struggled in the web, stabbing down with its pointed body. In a few seconds it hung motionless and silent. The spider came out with slow cautious steps. The wings of the snared bee fluttered weakly. The spider drew back. The bee lay motionless and again the spider approached. Slowly, under the fascinated eyes of the woman, it drew across the web. Then, at the end, with a little rush it was on the bee. The insects clung together as in some sort of communion. Then the spider moved back a little, carefully and delicately cleaning the web from the bee. As the little mass of life and death moved upwards to the hole, the woman lifted a duster, and opening the door, ran outside to the window. She beat down the spider and its burden to the ground and trod them under her foot.

Frank looked up as he heard the clack of the latch. 'Keep inside, Sarah,' he called, 'and keep the door closed. I think the bastes'll swarm.' He puffed with his smoker until a blue cloud drifted across the rath and Sarah could only see him indistinctly as he worked at the hive.

The bees swarmed, clustering in an angry confused mass around the queen. Carefully, Frank worked among them with his fingers in an effort to release the hapless female. The insects hung like a mass of ripe fruit from his gloves and arms.

'Sarah! Are ye there?' he shouted. The woman rapped loudly on the pane to show that she was attentive. 'Fetch a basin of water and lay it on the ground, here,' he called. She went out to the ditch and filled the basin. Stray bees were humming like gnats over the soapy stagnant water in the runlet behind the wall.

'Stay your distance, now,' said Frank when he heard her steps behind him. 'Set the water down and go back in.' She crouched down, pushing the basin as near him as she could. A bee danced angrily round her yellow hair as she ran back.

When she got back to the window Frank had lifted the swarm clear of the hive. The bees dripped down from his hands like wet vibrating sea-weed. He lowered the mass slowly over the basin. A high-pitched whine penetrated into the house. The bees streamed out from the man's grasp as if they were lifted by a wind. He held his hands out as they lifted into the tree overhead where they bent a bough with their dark murmurous weight.

She saw Frank turn sharply and nod to someone in the loanen. Peering round the side of the window she saw the flat-brimmed hat of the Reverend Mr Sorleyson. 'Most inadvisable,' she heard him say, 'much too drastic, Frank. Even if you get them back, they won't settle down for days.' The reverend gentleman was flapping his hand aimlessly round his head as he looked over the hedge. 'Did you get the queen?' he asked. Frank shrugged his shoulders and turned away.

A few moments later the minister tapped at the kitchen door and came in. 'Good afternoon,' he said, 'I see you're having trouble with your honey-makers.'

'Sit down, Mr Sorleyson,' said the woman pushing forward a chair. 'It's Frank that's having the trouble—I know nothing about them.'

'H'm, well,' said Mr Sorleyson, brushing the subject aside, 'I came up to tell you that your mother is poorly. Not *tell* you,' he added drily, glancing up at Sarah, 'you must have noticed that when you visited her. I wanted to discuss with you what is the best thing to do.'

'Best thing to do?' she echoed weakly.

Mr Sorleyson's irony gave way very quickly. 'Yes,' he exclaimed irritably, 'the best thing to do with your mother who is alone and ill. I've spoken to you before, about your duties to her. I did it because it was *my* duty to her, but I'm not going to reopen the matter again. I know quite well that, for some reason, you've stopped going down to see her.' He had been speaking rapidly, and he paused for breath. 'But if you think, Sarah, that by sending your mother some money every week you have discharged your obligations, then I can only hope that you'll be treated differently by your own children.' Sarah was about to speak, but the minister waved his hand fretfully to stop her. 'Let us consider what's to be done. Her legs and arms are badly swollen and she can fend for herself no longer. Now what do you mean to do about it? Will you go back and stay with her for a while?' Mr Sorleyson thrust his head forward aggressively. His round bespectacled face, usually so mild, was pink, and a frown creased his forehead with unaccustomed wrinkles.

'I'll go down to her, Mr Sorleyson. If she's fit to move, I'll bring her back here with me.'

'Oh,' exclaimed Mr Sorleyson, rather taken aback. He felt like a man who had thrust violently against a door only to find it ajar. 'Well—well, that would be very satisfactory. But will she be happy here?' he demanded with some of his former brusqueness.

'I'll see that she's well looked after,' answered Sarah in the same flat tone.

It was only when Mr Sorleyson was on the road home

that the significance of Sarah's promise to take her mother back to the Echlins struck him. Was that a strange thing for a servant girl in her master's farmhouse to say? Mr Sorleyson wasn't quite sure. He had tried very hard ever since he had come to this congregation to understand the ways of the country people. He had learned by trial and error, and because he was a kindly man, eager to help, he had learned quickly. There had been the occasion (he had only been in the manse a few weeks) when he called into the little National School in Ravara. Only a dozen or so of the smallest boys and girls were present. The old schoolmaster had explained that the elder children were kept at home to make the best of that one dry day in the fields. 'But their schooling!' exclaimed Mr Sorleyson. The old man smiled and looked at him strangely. He had tried to dissuade Mr Sorleyson from calling on the parents of the children. The very first man he had spoken to, one of his own elders, after listening to his remonstrances, had laid down his scythe and coming over to the hedge told him in as many words to attend to his own affairs and not hinder their work under the drying sun that God had granted them. Afterwards, when his resentment had gone, he laughed ruefully at the memory of the scowls on the faces of the two young urchins tying sheaves behind their father. But he learned that the most important thing in the lives of farm people is saving their crops. As he turned into the manse drive he paused to look up at the farm of Rathard and tried to understand the attitude of the woman there. Maybe she, too, was caught up in the relentless cycle of farm-work. It was a deceptive life, he thought, seemingly so slow and laborious and yet so all-consuming that people must at times forego their duties to themselves and others.

Sarah sat thinking when Sorleyson had gone. The minister's charge that she should return to her mother, found her, in a certain sense, prepared. It was an eventuality that she had already considered and now that it could no longer be avoided she proceeded, calmly and carefully, to reflect in what way it could be used to the least disadvantage. She did not give a second thought to the suggestion that she should leave Rathard, even for a time. If she did that there was no way of telling how long she would be away. Three months, maybe, and three months would be too long. The brothers would know about her then. Already she imagined that Frank was watching her with dislike and suspicion. Hamilton was different, considerate and kindly for all his dullness. But the risk was too great to leave them. Frank would be at his brother's ear the moment her shadow had gone. There was nothing to do but bring her mother back to Rathard and keep her own foot in the house.

Frank came in, in a bad temper. He had lost his swarm of bees and had been stung twice on the wrist. In his annoyance he forgot to ask the reason for Sorleyson's visit and Sarah carefully avoided the minister's name.

Hamilton came in from his ploughing and they sat down to their evening meal. 'How did ye get on wi' the bees, Frank?' he asked.

'Eh, don't talk to me. I made a bad hand at them.'

Sarah leaned across the table. 'Did Mr Sorleyson say the right thing?' she asked.

'Aye, at the wrong time,' answered the young man shortly.

'What fetched him up?' asked Hamilton glancing at Sarah.

The woman paused a moment, keeping her head lowered. 'My mother's ill,' she said. 'He wants me to go down and tend her. I may go back and forrit to Banyil till she's mended.' She closed Frank out with a steady gaze while she waited for Hamilton to speak.

'It's a long road to Banyil,' he said thoughtfully. He was silent for a moment and then he spoke again. 'Is there ocht been changed in the lower room?'

'Nothing since she left.'

'Then bring her back here and tend her. Ye won't have to leave the house then.'

'I could look after ye all, if she was here,' agreed Sarah in a flat matter-of-fact voice.

'Well, then, fetch her up,' said Hamilton wiping his mouth. 'Can ye manage the pony and trap yerself?'

'I'll go for her now, when I've redd up,' answered Sarah, rising.

And so it was settled. The old woman offered no opposition to her daughter and she was brought back and given her old room in the Echlins' house. For a time she made an effort, when the men were out, to follow Sarah round the house. But she could do very little work now and somehow she felt that her daughter didn't want her in the kitchen any more. Her legs were swollen; and sometimes, when there was a longer pause than usual in the irregular thumping of her heart, she drew herself upright on her pillow, gasping hungrily for breath.

Each day she stayed a little longer in bed, until the time came when she was content to hear the men go out in the morning, and let the day pass as she slept or lay with her eyes closed, thinking of the past, until she was roused again by the clatter of the milking pails and the low voices of the men gathered at the evening fire. She was very grateful for the peace that she was enjoying, and when Hamilton came down to see her in the evening she took his hand in hers and held it against her breast, and they sat for a time in silence, until he bade her good-night and went away again.

As the time passed Sarah grew more careful in her mother's presence. Every little while during the day she took her milk or broth or tea, setting them at her bedside and going back to the kitchen. Only in the dusk she lit the small lamp in her mother's room and read to her from the Bible or sat talking a little and sewing.

One evening, as Sarah was about to go to bed, she heard her mother call. 'What is it, mother?' she asked, when she got to the old woman's side.

'Open the window a wee bit, daughter. I'm near choking.' Sarah lowered the upper part of the window and stood looking out. Away beyond a ridge of night-black trees the sky was inlaid with shafts of green. A star twinkled in the pale sky above the house and the mournful cry of a whaup came from the lough. There was a sense of melancholy and peace in the scene, and the woman, silhouetted against the window, unconsciously drew her hands over her full body. Even as she did so there was a choking inarticulate cry from the bed. She saw her mother rising in bed and caught the gleam in her distended eyes. 'Sarah!' she cried, lifting her arm till the sleeve fell back on her shrivelled shoulder. The daughter stood there, stupid with fright, her hands still laid on her belly. In the indistinct light the woman on the bed seemed to rise on to her knees. Her grey hair fell down over her face, veiling her eyes. She clawed it back and her mouth worked as she tried to cry out again. Then with a horrible rattling noise in her throat she pitched face forward on the bed. Weeping with terror, the girl ran forward and lifted her mother in her arms. The old woman's head lifted a little and a long shuddering breath came from her lips. Martha lay dead in her daughter's embrace.

CHAPTER FOUR

★

TO THE DESULTORY traveller, the passage
of a few weeks works a silent and unobtrusive
change in the countryside and never so much as
in those months that ripen from spring to summer.
Without a stick or stone displaced, the face of the land
seems to have changed. On that hillside where the green
down of young grass failed to hide the cracked earth, the
hedges now restrain a lake of ripened hay whose bronze
waves ripple and break against the thorn blossom.

The loanens, which the winter's rain had laid bare to
the whinstone, are patched and the patches are softened
by the dappled gloom of the tall trees. Everywhere grass
and weed attack man's handiwork. Nettles climb to the
roofs of barns, grasses sprout between worn stones, rag-
weed nods in the hay. Even in Ravara churchyard
Martha's raw swollen grave sinks under the rain, and
yellow-blossomed saxifrage crosses and re-crosses the
withered wreaths.

In the evenings, the people of the townlands heard the
rumble of the drums as the Orangemen practised for the
July walk. Petie Sampson and his fife were the pride of
Ravara's Loyal Sons, and the little man had led his Lodge
to the Field and back for many years. Now as they
marched and counter-marched on the country road to
the patterned thunder of their drums, Petie skipped ahead

of them, blowing vigorously on his instrument. For years the drumming had been held some distance from Knocknadreemally, at Petie's request, because of his regard for his neighbour, Owen Dineen.

Andrew Echlin had never joined with the Orangemen. He was too deeply a man of his faith and race not to sympathise with their aspirations. Yet he had never joined them nor asked his sons to join them. Twice in his lifetime he had left his church for long periods. A few years before his death, when he was an elder of the congregation, the minister had installed an organ in the church. Andrew had protested. His protest had been unheeded. The organ had been installed and the old precentor, whose bass voice had led the praise as long as anyone could remember, had been driven out to a pew in the church. That Sunday morning, on the first note of the instrument, Andrew and several of the elders had risen and left the building. Many years before that, as a young man, he had wanted to join the Orangemen. He went to the Field on the Twelfth of July with the men of Ravara. 'You'll hear powerful speeches' promised the companion who took him. He heard and saw the powerful speech-makers.

Some he already knew by name and sight, but he recognised them all for what they were: landlords, politicians and clergy. Not once did he hear a simple man like himself speak from a platform or a longcar. The final revulsion came when he saw a mill-owner whom he knew by repute, stand up. His gorge rose as he watched the creature's face redden and the veins of his neck swell as he ranted. It was for this man that women blinded themselves working embroidery at ha'pence a dozen. He saw him lift up his hands as if he bore aloft, visible, like sacred relics, the shrivelled and relinquished liberties that he and his kind had bought and bled for.

Andrew came home, angry with himself and the men from Ravara. From that day there was planted in him a hatred of 'political clargy', whether they wore Geneva bands or chasuble. Then, in time, being a good-natured young man and fond of gaiety, he went to the dances and soirees in the Orange Hall. It was there that he met his future wife, Margaret Pentland. But he left to his neighbours the July walk, the bouncing fife and the braggadocio of the belly-drum.

The hay was ready for harvesting at Rathard. Early in the morning Hamilton went down to the field and 'opened' it with his scythe. The sun was well up and a few laggard clouds were hurrying across the hot flawless sky when Frank brought the reaper in, with a merry jingle of harness and the leisured purr of meshing wheels.

The binders came trickling in, one by one—Petie and Agnes and Sarah, the women with their hair tied up in bright cloths. A can of buttermilk sat in the shadow of the hedge, and the men fished out little green insects with their fingers before they drank. Frank sat on the reaper, his sunburnt face and chest beaded with sweat. He sang as he swung his rake, doling out the hay in loose sheaves. Slowly, patiently, crouching to the earth, the women moved behind the machine.

Sarah worked on in a blindness of pain. As every sheaf dropped from her hand, she raised her open mouth to the air, as if she were choking. Then, at the corner of the field nearest the house, she cried out and fell to the ground. 'Is it my time, Agnes?' she asked, as the old woman drew her up. Agnes nodded, 'Now,' she said. They passed through the cool shadow of the rowans and onwards into the house. Agnes undressed her and laid her in bed. ...

Someone spoke at a great distance. Through the deep small window came the sounds of the harvesting field, the bustle of bees, and a tapping noise close by. 'Chase the hens from the garden, Agnes,' said the woman on the bed, opening her eyes. Her neighbour still leaned over her waiting on an answer to her question. 'Sarah, who's the wean's father?' she asked again.

The woman on the bed lay silent, her suspicious brooding face mirrored in the midwife's eyes. Suddenly the old woman understood. Stupefaction, incredulity and a trace of lecherous glee struggled on her face. The young woman stared at her with hard and defiant eyes. Then her gaze wavered and dropped and she turned her face away to the face of her infant son.

CHAPTER FIVE

*

THE YEAR RIPENED into August and early autumn. In a few days Sarah appeared in the outside world with her son. The hay had been cut, and the weather being good, the stacks sat in the haggard. Hamilton knelt at the base of a stack, half hidden in the hay, feeding, with dexterous hands, the strands of a sugan rope twisted by Frank who backed across the close as the rope lengthened.

Sarah crossed the close to Hamilton and kneeling down, held up the child to him. The baby's eyes moved with solemn indifference over leafy branches, man's face, and bleached hay. Suddenly his nose wrinkled, his face reddened, his mouth opened and his eyes closed. He sneezed. Hamilton laughed and caught the child's bare foot between his finger and thumb.

The sugan rope sagged and dropped to the ground as Frank ceased to wind. He stood watching the group at the stack. Sarah rose and came towards him. She turned the boy in her arms so that he could see his face. A little smile kept coming and going on the man's lips. He put a crooked dark finger up and pulled away the shawl from the infant's head. 'Husha, you're a bould boy,' he laughed. 'He's a brave one, that,' called Hamilton behind them. 'He's a brave one, indeed,' said his brother pressing back the shawl.

The people of Rathard, sitting high over the surrounding countryside in this mellow afternoon, seemed to be out of the world. Below lay the fields drenched in sunshine and every extraneous sound that came through the quivering air seemed distilled till it was less than the tiny chinks and rings of the insect world. A great golden bee bumbling across the close, drowned, in his passage, the distant clatter of a cart.

Frank detached the thrawhook from the rope and walked slowly towards Hamilton, rolling the rope into a large prickly ball. At the barn door three hens were industriously scooping out hollows in the warm dust for their bodies. Sarah glanced upward at the sun, measuring with her eye when the shadow of the rowan trees would fall across the boy and her. He lay, tired of the sun, turned into her bosom, asleep. The woman had never known contentment like this before.

The men were in the fields the following day when Mr Sorleyson came up to Rathard. Sarah was seated at the door when he came into the close, and she retreated before him into the house as he came towards her. 'May I come in?' he asked, darkening the threshold. The woman nodded silently. He came in, and with only a fleeting glance at the child in its crib, took the chair she offered. 'You are better?' he asked.

Sarah nodded again, a flush rising on her face.

'I wanted so much to speak to you,' he continued and then was silent, agitatedly turning his circular hat in his hands.

Sarah did not help him. She was hostile and wary. His appearance reminded her that outside the familiar circle of the farm was a world of strangers, moving about, whispering among themselves as they looked up at Rathard.

Sorleyson placed his hat on the table and folded his hands. 'Sarah,' he said, gazing straight into her face, 'will you look upon me as a friend? Don't think—oh, I know you do!—that I'm going to reprove you, No, rather—can't we think of some way to right this terrible thing that's happened?' The woman was picking at the child's blanket, her head lowered so that he could see only the curve of her sullen mouth.

'Tell me,' he put the question delicately, in a low voice, 'tell me, is the parentage of your poor child uncertain?'

She looked at him, not understanding.

'Do you know who the father of the—eh—child is?'

'No.'

'Oh, Sarah, Sarah, what darkness has fallen on this house!' he cried bitterly. And then because she was silent, he said 'Which of the men will you marry?'

'I'll marry noan of them,' she returned, looking at him in sudden anger.

'Oh!' exclaimed Mr Sorleyson springing up in amazement. 'But, Sarah, this is inconceivable! Think of your good name!'

'What ails my name?' demanded the girl, thoroughly aroused.

'Ails your name!' he repeated, wheeling on her. 'It—' But his words were checked by the baby's cry, which came in protest to their shouting.

The interruption gave them time to collect their thoughts. As Sorleyson watched her soothing the child, his arguments became completely unreal for a moment. What detail in the picture of this mother crooning over her child was evil? Was this not the very thing that he himself had pictured in his most secret thoughts? Ah, no, life was not so simple as that. One had obligations to God and one's fellow-men. Of what avail was virtue if lust and irresponsibility were to be crowned with contentment?

The child made signs that it wanted to be fed, and Sarah looked questioningly at the minister. Sorleyson started back uneasily, feeling that in some way he was being cheated.

'Can't you put the child somewhere, until we've finished talking?' he asked irritably.

'No,' she answered. 'It's past his feeding time anyway.'

In his annoyance, Sorleyson said something that he had already considered and rejected, as being contemptible and cruel.

'Sarah, tell me, what do you think your mother would have felt about this?'

He saw her wince and immediately regretted his question. The young mother looked at him calmly for a moment. 'Well, you said you came as a friend, Mr Sorleyson. I hope you're satisfied now. What you've said to me is no different from what the people of the townland would say. You're a man who's supposed to know better. Everything should be a kind of a way for you to be right. Nothing ever is. It was the same when—'

'When what?' asked Sorleyson, leaning forward.

'When Andrew died. I don't know how ye did it, but ye stole something away from that too!'

'Surely, surely I didn't!' cried Sorleyson.

'Yes, ye did!' cried the woman springing up in passion. 'I told ye he left go of the boat for us, and ye said something about a sacrifice that should teach us something. It was like as if he had done nothing more than throw a pound note on the collection plate. He gave his life for his sons and me, and all the time you were thinking how it could be made to prove something else. My God, Mr Sorleyson, things *happen* to people!'

'Yes, Sarah,' answered the minister, 'but there is a guidance that helps us to combat the temptations of life, and a Divine help which supports us in those evil hours that none of us can avoid. Have you availed yourself fully of that?'

'Here's your answer,' said the woman smiling bitterly and holding out the infant. 'And what was it ye said? To marry one of the men. To bend and contrive things so that all would be smooth from the outside, like the way a lazy workman finishes a creel.'

'I was thinking of the child's future,' answered Mr Sorleyson coldly, stung at her bitter tone.

'Were you?' she asked, looking at him keenly.

'Like a picture off a grocer's calendar,' said a voice behind them, and Frank came into the kitchen. He threw his hat against the wall and rested one thigh on the table-corner. 'Well, Mr Sorleyson, have ye blessed the wean?' he continued insolently.

The minister frowned at him, as he sat there, his head thrust forward truculently. 'Is your brother about?' he asked, lifting his hat.

'You'll pass him in the loanen,' said Frank.

Sorleyson nodded to them both and went out. Frank moved to the door and watched him until he disappeared beyond the rowan bushes. 'Is he gone?' asked Sarah at last.

The young man turned and walked quickly towards the door leading to his bedroom. 'Aye, he's gone!' he shouted. 'The way all decent people will be from Rathard!' Before she could speak he had left the kitchen, slamming the door behind him.

Sorleyson found Hamilton working in the loanen. The farmer touched his cap to the minister as he approached. 'Will ye not bide till suppertime, Mr Sorleyson?' he asked.

Sorleyson started at the question. For an instant he wondered if these were the simple people he had known so long. He stood looking silently at Echlin.

'Hamilton,' he said at last, 'this is a sad day for me to come to Rathard.'

'Is it?' asked the other stolidly. Then, as if ashamed, he lowered his head. 'Aye,' he added.

'Tell me, Hamilton, what do you intend to do about Sarah Gomartin?'

'Do about her?' repeated Echlin in a puzzled tone.

'Surely you must see that the girl will have to marry either one of you,' said Sorleyson wearily. 'Will you not marry her?'

Echlin looked him up and down with a cunning expression in his eyes. He examined his round hat, his questioning face, his spotless collar, his slightly protruding vest, his black mud-smeared boots. 'To tell ye the God's truth,

Mr Sorleyson,' he exclaimed looking up suddenly and frankly, 'I'd marry her flying. But she won't have me.'

'H'm,' grunted the minister, breaking a twig from the hedge. 'What about Frank, then?'

The other man made a gesture of impatience. 'Frank'll no settle down to marry anyone.' He stood looking at the ground for a moment. 'But she'll no marry me,' he repeated.

'But what hope is there for her otherwise?' demanded Sorleyson. 'If she doesn't marry one of you, where else can she go?'

Echlin stood scratching his nose and looking at the minister. A frown gathered on his face. 'Who's talking about her going anywhere? She'll bide here, this is her home now.'

'But good heavens, man, that's impossible! How long can this unnatural arrangement last?'

The other man shrugged his shoulders. 'D'you know, Mr Sorleyson? No? Well, no more do I.'

'But I know that you can either make or break it. Can't you put it to her that she either marries you, or leaves the child and goes?'

'No! There's to be no more talk of her going. What sort of a creature would I be to turn the girl out now?'

'And what will the countryside think?'

'I'm not feard of what the countryside thinks. Thank God, there's little chance o' us falling into *their* hands,' added Echlin, turning to look across the fields that lay on each side of the loanen.

Sorleyson followed his gaze. 'There's no happiness that way, Hamilton.'

'Maybe, maybe not. But I'll no force her to marry me, all the same.'

Mr Sorleyson paid no more visits that day. He walked home very slowly thinking of the people of Rathard. He was ashamed to find that he no longer felt any indignation against them. This is impossible! he exclaimed angrily. These people have deliberately sinned! But he couldn't recapture his mood of righteous disapproval. He recalled Hamilton with his dour loyalty, not to be budged by fear of censure. And Sarah with the child in her arms. She had seemed so natural, so essentially right. How futile it was to appeal to a woman like that for convention's sake! He had felt a strange languor as he spoke to her. And now, in a moment, he realised that he did not want to blame them. He envied them. These people had grasped what he had always secretly longed for—in a proper way, of course! He stopped for a moment, leaning on the upper bar of a gate. The image of Sarah came before him, her smooth hair, her full bosom, her rebellious mouth. He closed his eyes and clung to the gate, feeling suddenly weak.

When he was almost home he stopped in the middle of the road. 'I should have offered to baptise the child!' he exclaimed aloud. The thought kept nagging at him during dinner so that he failed to attend to his wife's remarks. When he did look at her, his face wore such a preoccupied expression, as though he were looking at a stranger, that she ceased any further efforts at conversation.

CHAPTER SIX

★

THE BROTHERS HAD been lifting their potato crop in 'dribs and drabs', as they say in the townlands, but now, with the ripening of the Mourne Banners, Stars of Down and other early breeds, they set about the work in earnest.

It was impossible for Sarah to go into the fields so Agnes Sampson brought her neighbour, Bridie Dineen, to help with the lifting. Bridie was a thin, autumn-faced woman, with a crest of red hair pinned up that gave her the look of a hen. She had another henlike quality, for even when she was alone, she walked with a short hesitant step as if she were afraid of trampling one of her many children. Outside her own house she spoke to her neighbours with that courteous but evasive briefness that marks the Catholic in a Protestant district. Before she had set her foot in the kitchen of Rathard Sarah disliked her.

When the dinner was ready Sarah went down to the rowans and called on the potato-pickers. Agnes and the woman Dineen were bent over the same creel. At the sound of her cry Sarah saw the red-haired stranger look up and lay her hand on Agnes's arm. The old woman straightened her back painfully and nodded. As Sarah turned back to the house she saw the woman staring after her.

The harvesters came up from the field, their boots

shapeless masses of clay. Hamilton led the horse, Frank came with Petie and Agnes with Bridie. They stopped at the ditch to wash hands and scrape their boots, and Sarah took them out a towel. One by one they dried their hands and came in, all but Bridie. Not wanting to leave the stranger alone, Sarah went to the door. She saw the woman shaking her wet hands and staring at the house, then, before Sarah's eyes, she crossed herself. Sarah threw the towel across the halfdoor. 'Ye may dry your hands on that,' she said loudly. The woman looked at her with startled suspicious eyes. 'Thank ye,' she said.

Then, as Sarah set their plates before them, she saw Bridie flush and gaze at her curiously. Her sensitive conscience rankled. There could only be one reason why the woman stared at her like that. The others started to eat hungrily but Bridie sat with her hands in her lap, and as Sarah stole a glance at her she saw her look pleadingly at Agnes. The old woman understood in a moment what was wrong. She lifted the bacon from Bridie's plate and put it on Hamilton's, then she drained the gravy off and set it before her again. 'What ails ye?' asked Hamilton, looking at the woman.

'Nothing ava,' she replied, smiling and glad to be at her meal.

'The day's a Friday,' explained Agnes.

Hamilton struck the table. 'It is indeed. I'm right and sorry, Mrs Dineen. Sarah, is there anything else in the house?'

'There's a bit o' ling,' answered Sarah, without raising her head. An awkward silence fell on the table, broken only by Bridie's assurance that she was content.

'Well, if there's fish in the house get up and cook the woman a bit!' said Hamilton loudly and angrily.

Sarah sprang from her chair, and rushing round the table snatched the plate from before the embarrassed woman. 'I'll get ye a clean plate, too,' she said, girning in fury at her.

Bit by bit, as they started to talk again, Sarah pieced together their morning's work. She learned that Agnes and Petie were picking behind Frank, driving the potato-digger. But Hamilton, who had two or three drills of a long golden potato that he didn't want broken by the horse, was digging them with a fork, and Bridie Dineen was picking for him. She sat there, listening to them, her face burning with anger and humiliation.

When the others had trooped out of the kitchen Hamilton spoke to her before he left for the field. 'That was a sore way ye had wi' that woman,' he said abruptly.

Sarah turned her back on him and went on scraping dishes.

'Are ye heeding me?'

'Aye, I'm heeding ye.'

'Well, listen to what I'm saying.' He put his hand under her chin and drew her round, and at the touch of her face in his fingers, his resentment weakened. 'There's been a power o' harvesters come and gone here in my father's and his father's time. Not one of them but couldn't say he got good kitchen and the right money in his hand at the end o' the day. It'll be the same in our time. Heed that now, like a good woman.' Her soft petulant face was framed in his fingers. He bent and kissed her on the mouth.

141

She stood motionless in the kitchen, watching him through the window as he crossed to the stable. The dishcloth had fallen from her hand to the floor. The words 'in our time' went singing through her like strong wine. But the image of Bridie Dineen came back to her mind, and she hardened her heart in anger against the red-haired woman.

CHAPTER SEVEN

*

MR SORLEYSON WAS lifting his potatoes, too. He had had a few drills planted and was working among them now, gathering sufficient for dinner in a little shopping-basket. He had never been quite happy about this potato-patch. In the lawn beside it grew clove-lilies, mignonette, sweet-william and verbena, and these, in their turn, carried on a scented pageantry from spring till autumn. To his city mind there was something peculiarly distasteful in this proximity of flowers to vegetables. In the spring the knifesharp symmetrical drills seemed uncouth beside the delicate blossoms, and even in the summer, when the dark heavy leaves of the vegetables hid the soil, they remained blatantly potato leaves.

He had often walked through his neighbours' gardens. None was so well kept nor so neat as the Manse garden. There he saw dog-roses growing among beans and carnations stretching their indolent silver stems over shive-beds. On the whole, he had to admit, there was a pleasing harmony in these gardens. But without being quite able to explain why, Mr Sorleyson felt a strong aversion to this mingling of the orderly with the arbitrary. Perhaps it was because it ran counter to the attitude to which he clung so strenuously. Perhaps it was because it resembled too closely the lives of many of his congregation. He had discovered that these men and women who, from child-hood, had been taught to esteem righteousness, could, without any feeling of inconsistency, show a deplorable tolerance to things that were far from righteous or seemly. He had come to the conclusion that Nature, with her continual and invariably indiscreet fertility, was a bad example to simple folk.

How could he explain the grievous conduct of the Echlin brothers and Sarah Gomartin? Such a catastrophe and such men and women had never before entered into Mr Sorleyson's experience. Since the last time he had spoken to Sarah he had set out determinedly for Rathard on two occasions. And then, when he had got to the head of Echlin's loanen he had hung about not certain as to why he was there. Was it to appeal to her again to marry one of the brothers? Or had he intended to offer to baptise the infant? Or was it because he was tormented now with an insatiable interest in her and wanted to speak to her again?

Without waiting to lever the roots clear of the earth he snatched the plant so violently that the fat purple potatoes were scattered widespread. He raked them up and flung them so forcibly into the little basket that it leaped on the ground. 'I will go!' he said aloud and stabbed the potato-fork into the soil.

He carried the potatoes into the house and set them on the kitchen floor. He changed his boots, scrubbed his nails and carefully brushed his hair. As he was picking up his hat in the hall he heard the light step of his wife on the stairs above. 'Are you going out, dear?' she called.

'I have a few calls to make—not far away.'

144

'You'll be back for dinner?'

'Yes, yes. Of course I'll be back for dinner.'

He rushed down the steps of the Manse and out on to the road. He was filled with an unreasonable anger against his wife. Why had she to see him going out now? And why must she always be so gentle and attentive?

An unpleasant feeling of pricking sweat and breathlessness made him stop on a hill under some great beech trees. He looked around him in a distracted manner. With an effort he calmed himself, and sitting down, took out his handkerchief and mopped his brow. 'It's my duty to insist that the child is baptised!' he exclaimed, striking one hand on the other. He sprang up and pressed onward to the top of the hill.

In Rathard Sarah stood in a little shed open to the close, beetling grain for the fowl. Hamilton and Frank had gone to a timber auction in a nearby plantation and the boy was asleep in the bedbox in the kitchen. She was startled to hear a step at the corner of the shed, and looking up she saw the Reverend Mr Sorleyson.

'Good afternoon,' said the minister, taking off his hat and fanning his face with it. 'It's very warm to-day.'

The woman looked at him suspiciously. 'It is. Did ye want to speak to Hamilton?'

'No, no. It was about the boy. Have you decided on a name for him yet?'

'The men have a liking for the name of Ben.'

'Benjamin. That is a very noble name. Do you know what it means, Sarah?'

'What it means?' She laughed. 'Names are things you're bid by, Mr Sorleyson.'

'Yes, but they've meanings too. Your name means "a princess." '

She let the beetle drop from her hands, and laughed, colouring a little. 'A princess? And has your name a meaning, too?'

'My name means—well, Edwin means "a conqueror." ' They looked at each other for a moment, and then Sarah said, 'And the name—Ben?'

'Benjamin means the "son of a right hand." '

He saw her stiffen, and she bent lower over the crock in which she was kneading the grain. 'Why did ye ask for the child's name?' she demanded suddenly.

'That is really why I came to-day. Would you like me to christen him?'

She shook her head. 'I don't know. I would have to hear what the men say.'

Sorleyson came a little closer. 'Sarah, your boy will be called Ben Echlin when he grows up. Will he have to be ashamed of one of his names? He won't, if you marry Frank or Hamilton.'

'Isn't it just because of that, that I can't marry either of them? God in Heaven, Mr Sorleyson, don't make it harder for me nor ye can!'

'I'm not making it difficult for you. I'm showing you a way out of your difficulty. It's my duty to advise on these difficulties, Sarah. I tell you that you're mistaken to think that you can't marry either of them!'

'If I did what ye bid me, it would only be putting a scab on a sore. What right have I to give myself and the child to one man over the other?'

'Do you not lean towards one of them yourself?'

She straightened and looked angrily at him, her lips drawn closely together, and Sorleyson did not press the question.

'And are you content?'

'I'm content.'

Sorleyson withdrew to the corner of the shed and stood gazing gloomily over the lough. Sarah glanced at him once and then went on with her work. It had been a defeat, and yet Sorleyson found himself strangely indifferent to the outcome of the conversation. When he thought of Sarah and when he talked with her he felt himself oppressed with apathy towards the very course that he urged on her. All his subterfuges were falling, one by one. His insistence that she should marry one of the men was only a nod to the world. His offer to christen the child only an excuse to bring him back again. For the first time in his life Sorleyson really knew that there were two separate and antagonistic beings in him: his spiritual self on which all his studies and hopes had been concentrated for the past twenty years, and which now, when put to the trial, proved puny and impoverished, and his natural carnal curiosity in men and women which he had tried to stifle for so long in pious ready-made explanations and half-fulfilments such as his own tepid marriage. And Mr Sorleyson, standing at the corner of the shed, listened in fearful pleasure and did not stop his ears.

Attracted by the rhythmic movements of the woman, he shifted his gaze to her. She had forgotten him and was completely absorbed in her work. Small damp tendrils had loosened from her smooth head and curled on her brow. He saw the firm smooth flesh of her upperarm quiver at every plunge of the beetle. As she withdrew the stick on its upward stroke her face was visible for a moment, her eyes blank as if her thoughts were far away, and her moist lips open a little as she breathed. Sorleyson quivered and turned in towards her. As she bent again he had a glimpse of her body through the open neck of her dress. With silent fascinated steps he approached and then he bent down, and gently, as though he were clasping a bird, he stretched out his hand and touched her bosom.

She did not recoil faster than he did. As though an electric shock had passed through their bodies and hurled them apart the minister and the woman stood wide-eyed, shocked and breathless, gazing at each other in silence. Sorleyson stood with his back pressed to the wall of the shed, his eyes full of horror, his hands clasped in a gesture of supplication. 'Forgive me,' he whispered, 'I don't know what I've done. Some evil power came over me.'

Sarah closed the neck of her dress with her hand. 'It would be better if you went away now, Mr Sorleyson,' she said. Nothing more than that. She didn't scream or cry out or run away from him. He saw she was shocked and that she pitied him, and he was ashamed of the pity he saw. Very timidly he came towards her. 'Sarah—I can say no more. God forgive us both. I'll go now.' The woman nodded gravely and he turned and hurried from the farm.

As he stumbled down the loanen, the roughness of the track and the stubborn little hills in his path slowed him, and he became less agitated. He paused at a spot in the lane sheltered from both the house and the road, and sat down on a grassy bank. For the first time he thought of his wife. To have had a wife with whom he was in love, what a safe anchorage that would have been, what stress it would have spared the soul! He turned out the palms of his hands and stared at them. Love was both a sword to pierce and a shield to protect.

And the work to which he had dedicated his life now lay in ruins around him. How swiftly the façade, already honeycombed with his own doubts and reservations, had crumbled. Yet he knew that belief and faith as frail as his had borne many of his fellows to the close of their days, both honoured and mourned. But they had steered clear of the shattering rock that he had run upon. He who had so often realised that all his sermons, all his counsel, could be cancelled by one deed, now saw with equal clearness that one deed could not be erased by a thousand words. 'How beggarly all arguments appear before a defiant deed,' he quoted bitterly.

He arose and went slowly down to the road. As he walked home he met a farmer and his wife, members of his congregation, driving towards him in their trap. With shame and embarrassment he saw the little stir that passed over them as they recognised his figure. When they approached him he saluted them and bowed his head so that they had no choice but to bid him the time of day and drive on. He didn't avoid the little cloud of dust that rose from their wheels. It fell on his clothes but he walked on, unheeding.

CHAPTER EIGHT

★

THE MEN CAME home from the timber auction, tired and out-of-sorts. They had gone there, Hamilton looking for some sawn timber to build a turf-house and Frank for trimmed saplings to renew gateposts. Hamilton had seen nothing to please him, and had been equally dissatisfied with the green wood that Frank wanted to take. 'They would be in mush in a twelvemonth; we'll face up the ould stone pillars and make do,' he said. So they came jogging home in the cart, silent and half asleep in the sun.

They ate a heavy supper and afterwards sat round the fire for a while, Frank shaking his sunburnt head and blowing violently through his nostrils which always felt clogged up after a day in the sun. The dusk was seeping into the close and the hens had gone to roost. 'I'm away t'my bed,' said the younger man, yawning and rubbing his face. Hamilton pulled on his boots and shuffled out to lock up the animals. When he came back Sarah was winding the clock. 'Was there anything stirring with ye, the day?' he asked.

She replaced the clock on the mantelboard. 'Not a sowl,' she answered. He sat down, kicked off his boots again, hung his socks over the crane, and went down to bed.

The next morning Sarah was early afoot. The windows

were still squares of watered darkness when Frank was awakened by the thudding of the poker against the back of the hearth. He heard the wooden doorbar being withdrawn and the swish of emptied water on the close. Curtains billowed and lamps swung gently as the early morning air rushed through the house. He strained his ears to catch the time. But no birds chirped among the trees in the rath and away in the distance he heard the faint trumpet-note of a cock. 'It's still the scraitch o' dawn,' he grumbled, pulling the blankets over his head. 'What does she want to be moving about at this hour for?' He peered over at Hamilton's bed and saw that it was empty.

He was awakened again by Hamilton coming into the room to dress. 'Ye may rise,' he said, 'for Sarah's wanting to get away to Ardpatrick this morning, on an errand.'

'Who's driving her in?'

'She'll drive the wee pony herself. Rise now, like a good man, and no be detaining her.' Frank yawned, swung his legs out of bed, pulled down his shirt, and rubbed his face vigorously with his hand. 'I'm glad we didnae buy them bits o' posts, yesterday,' he said. Hamilton smiled and nodded. 'We were well guided to let them be,' he answered.

When Frank went down to the kitchen he found that Sarah was already dressed in her Sabbath clothes. 'Will ye bring back two or three packets o' fegs wi' ye?' he asked, laying some money on the table. 'Oh, and a bit o' plug for Petie.' Then Hamilton remembered a few things that he wanted, and as Sarah supped her porridge and buttermilk she scribbled down the purchases she had to make.

Immediately the meal was finished she washed up, brushed the floor and tended the fire. There was an air of urgency and decision in her movements as she hurried about the house, pushing the men aside and knocking the brush against their chair legs as they sat for their brief after-breakfast smoke. Unable to bear it any longer they went out into the close to finish their pipes. A few minutes later Hamilton came to the door. 'I've yoked the pony. What'll ye do with the wean?'

Sarah turned from the mirror where she was arranging her hair under her hat. 'I'll leave him off at Agnes's till I get back.'

'Aye. He'll be all right there, I don't doubt,' said Hamilton rather reluctantly as he withdrew.

Sarah lifted the boy from his crib, pulled a woollen cap on his head, pinned a large shawl around him, and after bolting the halfdoor behind her, carried him out to the trap. Frank had already gone to the fields and Hamilton was in the byre from where he appeared when he heard the click of the pony's hooves as it moved off.

'Will ye be back afore dark?' he called.

'Aye, long afore dark!'

'Well, I might take a dander up to Agnes's and meet ye. Heh! my bold boy,' he cried to the baby, 'So long now!' Sarah jerked the reins, clicked her tongue at the pony, who set off with stiff carefully placed forelegs down the steep rocky descent.

It was a glorious autumn morning with a faint tang of frost in the air, and the climbing sun promised heat later in the day. As they drove along the road a vermilion leaf or two came fluttering down from the trees, and high above the swallows sped and circled with their flittering crescent wings.

As the pony wound up Knocknadreemally, Sarah saw Agnes and Bridie Dineen standing on the road at the top of the hill. Agnes had a hen under her arm, and the other woman, around whose skirts two or three children swung and played, had a tin basin in her hand, that gleamed and waned as it was struck by one of the shouting children.

The faint clip-clop of the pony's hooves reached the women on the hilltop. In a moment Bridie Dineen had gathered her children into her, and after a few hurried words to Agnes, swept them and herself out of the sun into the shadowy firelit depths of her cottage.

Agnes waited until the trap drew up beside her. 'How are ye, Sarah?' she asked, and then as she saw the small shawled figure in the crook of Sarah's arm, she cried 'Ah, did ye bring the wee fella! Give us him down here.' Sarah climbed down with the baby in her arms. 'I'm going on an errand to Ardpatrick, and I was wondering would ye look after him till I get back?'

'Aye, God bless him, I'll dae it with a heart and a half.'

Two or three of the children had crept out again from Bridie's cottage and now stood blinking at Sarah and the handsome trap. Sarah glanced at them. 'Tell me, Agnes, why did the Dineen woman go indoors when she saw me? She went off like a clockin hen when it hears a magpie!'

'Och, don't heed her. She said she smelt a pot boiling over.'

'It was a quare pot boiling over! Look at her now,

keeking at us through the window. Heth, but she's a sleeked one, that.'

Agnes cuffed the hen that was pecking listlessly at her hard freckled arm. 'Och, she's like many another. She was learned as a child tae stick tae the highroad for this,' and here she nodded at Bridie's children, 'and she's irked when she finds another has ta'en a short cut through the dykes, and arrived wi' as much honour and more ease.'

Sarah did not know what to make of this. She searched Agnes's face carefully. 'Is she envious o' me, then?'

The old woman chuckled mirthlessly. 'Aye, ye could say that—if ye take any pride in short cuts in the matter o' bearing weans.'

Sarah thrust the child abruptly into the other woman's free arm. 'I'll be back afore dark. Hamilton said he might take a walk up.'

'Whenever suits ye,' answered Agnes, and went into her cottage with the child in one arm and the truant hen in the other.

As Sarah lifted the reins she remembered that she had meant to ask Agnes if she wanted anything brought from Ardpatrick, but she was so bitten into a fury by the old woman's remarks and by her apparent sympathy with the Dineen woman, that instead of drawing up and going back, she cut at the horse with the whip and set him cantering recklessly down the hill.

She was in the mood of knowing that she was criticised by a standard which she herself accepted, and was being rightfully blamed for falling below it. And while there was something furtive and cowardly in the manner of the criticism, it was not sufficient to cancel out the justice of it. So, as the horse drew her swiftly towards Ardpatrick, she thought bitterly of the Dineen woman, hating her for her pharisaical pride in her lawful wedlock, despising her for her poverty, detesting her for her papishness; all by turn, and none with any feeling of sincerity.

The sun was almost overhead when she reached Ardpatrick, and the old market cross, aslant in the middle of the cobbled square, cast a blunt deep shadow over two of its four ancient watering troughs. She drove slowly round the square, peering at the name-plates beside the doors and clicking her tongue impatiently at the pony when he shied at the geese he disturbed in their warm dust-beds. Except for the geese and two old women nodding in the sun at the watering-troughs and a man leaning against a sunny wall, the square was deserted. As Sarah came up to the man she brought the pony to a standstill.

He was occupied in squirting long slivers of tobacco-juice in the shape of a fan on the flags, an occupation which promised some hours of amusement, as the sun always dried up the first one or two spittles by the time the design was completed.

'My good man,' said Sarah, leaning out of the trap, 'would ye kindly move a weethin till I read that board behind ye?'

'There's no call for me to move,' responded the man raising his eyes from the pavement. 'The board says "Ardpatrick Registry of Births, Marriages and Deaths—Registrar, Dr P. O. Furphy—In attendance 10 till 11 an' 3 till 5." And the ould boy is in there, himself, bating about like a hen in nettles.'

Sarah glanced at the church clock at the bottom of the square. The hands pointed to a quarter to eleven. Nodding to the man, she urged the pony towards the market cross. There she dismounted, eased the bit, and fastened the reins to one of the sunken stone posts around the cross. When she left him the pony moved towards the troughs, blowing on the surface of the water till his thick black lips quivered.

The Registrar's office was situated in what had once been the parlour of a dwelling-house, and although it was but a few feet along the hall from the front door, Sarah had to go up and down several steps before she reached it. The lounger's description of Dr Furphy suited that gentleman admirably. When Sarah entered he was moving aimlessly around the large dark room peering at paper-littered chairs, scratching at documents impaled on wire hooks hanging from the walls and advancing and retreating between tables and cabinets with irritated grunts. He was a short, stout, bald-headed man, dressed in a tweed jacket and shooting breeches, and on the wall behind his desk hung a tweed hat tufted with trout flies.

When Sarah entered he retreated to a swivel chair and sat down with his back to her, and then with a flick of his foot, swung round until she saw his red bulbous profile. This time there was a note of interrogation in his grunt. 'I want to put down a child's name,' said Sarah.

'Sit down, then,' said the doctor, spurning the floor again and being carried round to his desk, a tall mahogany affair with mirrors and brasswork, which, when he slid back the lid revealed a tangled bank of papers reaching up to overflowing pigeon-holes. He pushed some of the papers aside, drew out a book and opened it on the leaf of the desk. He dipped his pen, adjusted his spectacles, and without looking at Sarah began to question her.

'And what's your name——full name?'

'Sarah Gomartin.'

'Your husband's name?'

Sarah, seated on the edge of the chair, remained silent. The doctor looked up. Although her head was averted she flushed and touched her lips nervously with her fingers. Furphy raised his brows encouragingly and smiled. 'The father's name?'

'I don't know.'

A change came over the doctor. His glance which had been kind, encouraging, slightly condescending, narrowed into a stare of curiosity. He noted her decent Sabbath clothes, her well-gloved hands, and her face, which although darkened now with shame and embarrassment, bore the habitual traces of firmness, independence and even arrogance. With a feeling of surprise he recalled the sound of wheels in the square and the clear voice of the woman. How could this decent prosperous young woman be a libertine?

But suddenly, as though it flowed into the room, he saw the placid dimpled trout-stream waiting for him three miles away. He grunted impatiently and drew his pen through the column that should have shewn the father's name.

'Is it a boy or a girl?'

'A boy.'

'What name do you wish to call him?'

'Andrew.'

The doctor looked up again. 'You realise that, legally, his name will be Andrew Gomartin?'

Sarah nodded.

Furphy's pen scratched on until he had filled in all the details. 'Do you want a certificate?'

'How much is that?'

'Two shillings and sevenpence.'

She sat considering this, then took the money from her purse and laid it on the desk.

When he had completed the certificate, he folded it neatly, handed it to her, and then held the door open as she went out. 'Good day to you,' he said.

'Good day to ye, doctor.'

He watched her cross the square, adjust the horse's harness and wheel him round on the cobbles. 'B'God it's a strange world,' he mused, plucking at his lip. He stood there until she was out of sight, still plucking at his lip. 'It's a bit bright,' he said aloud, but now he was thinking of the sun on the stream.

CHAPTER NINE

★

MR SORLEYSON SAT at his study table. He pushed away the books before him and one fell unheeded on the floor, spilling loose sheets of paper over the carpet. His open hands, twitching a little, were laid on the space that he had cleared. He stared unseeingly at Madame Lebrun and her Daughter on the opposite wall. Slowly a change came over his whole appearance. He drew himself upright in his chair, his body rigid and erect. Unexpected lines and ridges marred the curve of his smooth pleasant cheeks. His habitual expression of kindliness and irresolution gave way to one of turmoil and distress. He pressed his hands on the table until the polished mahogany around his fingers misted with sweat. He sat like that for a long time then suddenly he slumped back in his chair, and on his face there was the look of a man who had awakened from a long and restless sleep. He had come to a decision. For a moment a faint moisture of self-pity rose in his eyes. He plucked his spectacles off, wiped them, and forced them on again, springing the legs painfully behind his ears in exasperation.

He rose and went down to the sitting-room. His wife, her pretty feet drawn under her chair, sat at the fire, knitting. As he entered she laid her knitting in her lap, and smiled up at him with tired sweetness. 'I was just longing for a cup of tea, dear. Will you stay and have one with me?'

'Yes,' he replied, sitting down opposite her.

In a short time she was back with a tray on which sat two cups and saucers, buttered barmbrack, and their intimate little supper teapot in its wollen cosy. He cleared the leather pouffe of scissors and needles and the evening paper so that she could set down the tray.

He didn't speak to her as he sat there, eating his bread and sipping his tea and staring into the fire. But there was nothing unusual about that, she never expected him to speak to her, much. He is thinking of his sermon she re-assured herself, in accordance with the pitiable game of make-believe that she had played for years. Then suddenly he looked across at her. 'Victoria, I've decided to—to ask for a transfer to Belfast.' The last six words came in a rush. For once she was startled. 'But—I thought you were happy, Edwin. Don't you remember you said you had a sense of *fulfilment* here?'

He beat his hand impatiently on the arm of his chair. 'Yes, yes, but there's no scope here! I feel that I could be of more use in Belfast. Anyway, it's time I had a change in the city.' He was quite irritable by now, not so much with her as with himself. What he had meant to say, calmly and with no further discussion, was, 'Victoria, I've decided to leave the church and take up teaching, perhaps.' But his courage had failed at the enormity of that, and he had retreated even further in the reason he had given for leaving Ravara.

But she understood him so perfectly. Had she not dedicated herself for just such as this, to be the pastor's

160

helpmeet; the shepherd's staff as she once laughingly described herself at a women's meeting? (an old illiterate peasant woman had rebuked her by quoting the fourth verse of the twenty-third Psalm).

How she had loved those early days! On Saturday afternoons they walked far out of the city, and there, as she sat on his handkerchief on a grassy bank, Edwin would deliver his virgin sermons. How she had clasped her hands in ecstasy at some particularly felicitous phrase; how the tears had risen to her eyes as he dwelt on the love and agony of our Saviour; how her flowerlike face had contracted in little pangs of anguish as he spoke of the erring soul and the Judgement to come. And then Edwin would suddenly crush the sheets in his hand and run to her and take her face in his hands and kiss the shadows away. Ah, happy happy days!

Then as he became moody and irritable and discontented with her, what marvels of ingenuity and self-deception she practised on herself! Were not these moods and silences and brief displays of temper the human frailties that had marked every great man? But slowly and reluctantly, and not without much self-reproach, she began to admit to herself that Edwin might not be the great divine they both so fondly imagined he would be, in their courtship and early marriage.

When Sorleyson arrived at his decision in his study that evening he experienced a sense of relief far outweighing any fear of what the future held. For the first time he had admitted to himself, openly and frankly, his incapability and distaste for the life of a clergyman. But when he went to tell his wife his courage failed him, and he left her with the idea that he would grace a pulpit elsewhere. The same idea got abroad in the townlands and among his brethren and friends in the city. With growing horror he realised that he had merely escaped from one plight into another which was becoming equally unbearable. Time after time the truth trembled on his lips. And time after time, as he looked on the patient questioning face of his wife or met the bland glances of his fellow-ministers, he swallowed his words.

On his last evening in Ravara Manse he sat in his study endeavouring to parcel up his manuscripts. His wife appeared in the doorway with a small plaster figure in her arms. 'Shall we take this?' she asked, holding out her burden like a child. Sorleyson felt a fresh paroxysm of self-reproach. That she should follow him so uncomplainingly! He threw himself at her feet and putting his arms around her, buried his face in her dress. Suddenly the small woman shook him from her skirts and looking up he saw her face pink with anger. 'Get up, you foolish man!' she cried. 'You nearly made me drop it on your head!' After she had gone he sat down again and began to laugh in a shamefaced way. He stood up and looked at himself in the mirror over the fireplace. 'I'm a sick man,' he said, nodding dejectedly to his image.

CHAPTER TEN

★

THE DEPARTURE OF the Reverend Mr Sorleyson and his wife was hardly spoken of in Rathard. So far as Hamilton and Frank were concerned, any thought they had on the matter was one of relief, and as the Echlins had by this time completely severed themselves from Ravara Church, they did not expect a renewed effort on the part of Sorleyson's successor to interfere in the relationship between them and Sarah.

When she first heard the news, Sarah dimly associated the minister's departure with the afternoon that he had come up to the farm. But as she had already thrust the memory from her mind, (in some way that she could not explain, it was associated with the memory of her mother) and because she was incapable of understanding what a disturbance the encounter had created in the more sensitive mind of the man, the news roused little interest in her, and was soon forgotten.

Isolated though they were, situated high on the hill-farm and almost sufficient to themselves, the inhabitants of Rathard were not unaware of the criticism of their conduct by the people of the townlands. The irregular *ménage* of Rathard might have been rectified by the intervention of someone with the moral authority of a clergyman. But the people knew as well as he did, that his power to bring about a more normal relationship in any home was limited to counsel and warning. And the warning was, in the last extreme, limited to such incorporeal things as the displeasure of Providence. Having no economic hold over his flock, the minister could not go beyond that.

And how potent was this warning of the displeasure of God? Men or women determined to pursue some selfish course, hardened their hearts with an ancient knowledge that the world did not behave as the clergy wanted it to do, or worse still, said it did. In a drought the peasants might flock to church with every mark of fervour to pray for rain, but they knew that when the rain did come, it would come vast, rolling, drenching the world from horizon to horizon and not seeking out, with scrupulous justice, the meadows of the pious.

For some months after the birth of the child the Echlin brothers kept as close to the farm as possible, but some traffic with their neighbours was unavoidable, and it was these few visitors to Rathard who spread the story that Sarah Gomartin was now the master as well as the mistress of the farm. They found that when they bought potatoes in the field or straw in the haggard, it was in the house they paid the money. And it was Sarah who took it.

'And are those pachels of brothers going to put their hearth and bread into the fists of that creature!' cried the women in exasperation. 'Ah, fair's fair,' pleaded the storyteller. 'Fair's fair. She'll never take a penny too much, or give ye a penny less, to my knowing.'

But the women, those shapers of opinion and prejudice, would hear nothing in Sarah's favour, and the men for peace's sake, agreed that she was a shameless bisom and worth the watching. Yet, among themselves, as they gathered at the crossroads, there could be detected a tickled humour at the idea of this matriarchal household set up among them, and one man expressed the opinion that if there was any truth in the old saying that 'a man maun ask his wife's leave to thrive' then the Echlins would do rightly with Martha Gomartin's girl.

While the neighbours greatly exaggerated Sarah's position in Rathard, there was no doubt that a subtle change in relationship had come about between the men and the woman. Sarah was indeed, as she had told Sorleyson, behaving with strict impartiality to the brothers, and because of this she had unobtrusively taken control of the house. Yet, she had not done it designedly.

Hamilton and Frank, for different reasons, encouraged her towards this end. For all the different, even antagonistic traits in their characters, they were both men of a fibre who did not willingly repudiate a deed whether it proved to be profitable or otherwise. Now that the child was born and the brothers realised the disrepute into which they had fallen, they felt the necessity to achieve some unity among themselves. For that, an equilibrium was necessary so they accepted Sarah's management of the economy of the farm.

It would have been unnatural if the woman had not felt some triumph at this turn of circumstance. But soon it became a matter of acceptance. It is the men and women who are unsure of themselves who are for ever triumphing over their work. But Sarah stood above, and accomplished every task with ease. She had the prudence, the

165

physical persistence, the eternal patience of the peasant. With Hamilton, she felt a deep sense of understanding, of being cherished, but with Frank she knew that the truce was only temporary. She shared herself between them both, in body and in mind, and so disarmed the younger brother.

CHAPTER ELEVEN

*

B Y SLOW DEGREES the boy Andrew learned to walk. He was over fourteen months old before he made his first stumbling journey, one Sunday afternoon, from the hands of his mother over a good three yards of the kitchen floor to the safe haven between Frank's knees. Hamilton was brought up from the parlour by the excited and gleeful laughter, and the three adults squatted round the child as he sat on his creepy stool. 'Again, son, again,' pleaded Sarah, holding up a muscatel raisin. But the child sat gazing at his pink feet in solemn wonder. He was raised up and unleashed a dozen times from the hands of his mother or the men. All possible combinations of propulsion and attraction were tried but Andrew walked no more that day. The next day, at the midday meal, he clambered down from his high chair and went staggering after the dog. Half-way across he lost his balance, spun round slowly and sat down on the tiles. From then on, his progress was speedy and each day saw him venture further and further from the hearth until his tiny figure, dressed in shawl and petticoats, was to be seen daily among the dogs, pigeons and fowl that inhabited the close.

One night Sarah was awakened by the coughing of the boy. Rising, she lighted a candle, and crossed over to his cradle. Shading the candle with her hand she looked down into the face of her son. He lay on his back and as she bent over him his mouth gathered into an O, and a cough, followed by a peculiar indrawn whoop shook him violently. Then he was seized by a paroxysm of coughing until he lay weak and trembling, a skein of spittle on his cheek.

The coughing began again and the young mother raised the child in her arms in an effort to ease him, but this seemed only to aggravate the attack. Hurrying down to the kitchen she blew up the dying fire and heated a little milk. When she gave it to the boy it seemed to soothe him and he lay back in her arms with his eyes closed. Then he retched the milk up which had curdled in his stomach, and the cough came again with greater violence. The child's face darkened, and he grasped Sarah's nightdress convulsively while he drew breath in great whoops of sound that terrified the woman. Looking towards the inner door distractedly, the mother heard noises beyond the wall, and first Hamilton and then Frank appeared, blinking and screwing up their eyes. 'What ails him, Sarah?' asked Frank, padding forward on his bare feet and peering down at the boy. 'I'm feard it's the whooping-cough,' answered the mother. 'One of ye may go and fetch Agnes.' Hamilton had already left the room and in a few minutes he reappeared, with jacket and trousers pulled on and unlaced boots on his feet. He brought a hurricane lamp with him which he proceeded to trim and light. 'If you're going, don't delay, Hami,' pleaded Sarah, as he closed the globe. He left the house and went out into the close which was bathed in keen white moonlight. Under the moon the lamp became a pallid globe of light. He extinguished it, and setting it on the ditch, hurried down the loanen.

It seemed hours before Frank and Sarah heard the measured clack of feet ascending the loanen. The old woman came in and lifted the boy from his cradle. 'Aye, it's the whooping-cough,' she said. She told Sarah to heat some water while she held the child's wrists to ease the strain on the little body. When the water was heated she mixed a draught that she had brought with her, and made the boy drink it. The coughing eased considerably, the vomiting ceased, and as the first light of day crept into the sky, the boy fell asleep. Agnes stood up and shook herself. 'The wean will be as right as rain in a day or two,' she said. 'And hold your tongue like a good woman,' she continued, when Sarah tried to thank her. She smiled and shook her head as she looked at the woman and the two men gathered round the cradle. 'It's a quare world,' was her last remark as she left the house.

CHAPTER TWELVE

*

TIME, AND AGNES'S ipecacuanha wine rid little Andrew of his whooping-cough and the only reminder he had of his illness was a peculiar singing note in his ears, which remained with him when he had recovered. Sarah would discover him lying in some out-of-the-way corner with a strange rapt look on his face as he listened to the rushing noise, like a tiny waterfall in his head. 'Water, mammy,' he would say, 'water,' and press his fresh young cheek against hers, but his mother could never hear the water, and eventually as he became used to it, he ceased to mention it any more.

He was a swift inquisitive child, strong limbed, with fair reddish hair and dark eyes. He had Frank's short square fingers, and in those unguarded moments when the initiated claim to perceive the parentage, he showed a resemblance to the younger brother. He spent most of his time with Hamilton in the outhouses among the animals or in the fields, and sometimes, as he considered some childish task, his face would take the same pondering look, and he would splay his tiny legs as the man splayed his.

It was a great day in Rathard when his third birthday arrived and he discarded his petticoats for ever and was buttoned into his first knee-breeches. Sarah invited Agnes and Petie for the great occasion, and Hamilton, who carried the message to Knocknadreemally, suggested to Agnes that she might bring young Con Dineen with her, now a boy of four. But when the old couple arrived they were alone. 'Did ye no fetch Owen's wean?' asked Hamilton as they came into the kitchen.

Agnes shook her head impatiently. 'I did not.'

'And why for not?' persisted Hamilton, as she lifted up Andrew.

'I went into Bridie's and told her that ye bid Con to Rathard for Andra's birthday. "That's kindly o' Mr Echlin," says she, "but I'm no sure he can go. His da's no at home." And then she goes lilting round the house and making no shift to wipe the wean's face. "Bridie," says I, "leave over your fooling like a good woman, and answer me—is the wean coming or no?" "Ach, Agnes," says she, "sure I havena a clean jersey to put on the cratur." But I could see by the look o' her that it was only a put-off. "Peh," says I and left her.'

'Maybe you're satisfied now!' cried Sarah, her eyes bright with anger.

'Maybe the wean hadna a clean jersey for all my knowing or your knowing,' returned Hamilton calmly, and said no more about it.

But this initial unpleasantness was soon forgotten, and they sat down to the birthday tea. The young Andrew sat at the head of the table in his grandfather's great rope-bottomed chair and had three slices of deil's bun, a dark rich bread flavoured with treacle, spice and fruit, and usually kept for Hallowe'en.

After the tea, the gifts. Agnes brought him an old silver caddy spoon with which to sup his porridge; Petie gave him a money-box made from a cow's horn; Sarah hanselled him by dropping a brand new shilling into his breek's pocket; Hamilton gave him a carved boretree whistle, and Frank, slipping out mysteriously amid all the gift-giving, came back again leading a black-nosed, delicate-footed kid.

'What d'ye say to that now, son?' asked Sarah.

'Thank ye,' answered the boy, lifting his shy flushed face from the kid's neck.

Then, when he had gone to bed, the older folk gathered round the fire. The shadows were creeping up from the lough when at last Agnes stood up. 'I hope the Good Man looks down on the wean and sends him many another birthday,' she said. 'Aye, indeed,' said the others. Sarah took the shilling from the boy's breeches pocket and put it into the cowhorn money-box on the mantel-shelf.

CHAPTER THIRTEEN

★

NOW THAT ANDREW was a man of breeks, with a dog and a goat of his own, he willingly permitted curiosity to lead him into the fields and dykes around the hill of Rathard. The terrier, a fat and genial braggart, and the boy, as yet as innocent and merry as the dog, could play for hours beside the little stream that trundled round the hill to the lough. Politely they broke their play for a moment to applaud each other; the dog to stand with trembling legs, stiff ears, and panting mouth, as a boat was launched and slipped away lying over to a full press of feathers, the boy to kneel fearfully beside the dog as he tore with savage intent at an otter's den until the ravager tired of it and scampered off unabashed, revealing a shallow muddy groove in the bank.

So, as they ranged the land, Andrew came upon the road. It ran away on either hand, rising and falling, curving between its hedges, and smooth to the finger and eye with a white floury dust. Then one day he saw Petie descending Knocknadreemally, and ran to meet him. From then on he was allowed to walk with his dog to the Sampson's house, it being agreed that he should start at set times and that Petie would watch for him from the top of the hill, so that he was passing out of the range of one watchful eye to come under the view of another.

He loved going to Petie's house. Agnes made toffee in

the shape of little boys and he experienced a fearful pleasure in biting off their heads and feet. She held great pink shells to his ears, but though he laughed he knew that it was the insistent, ever-present singing in his own ears that he heard. In the heart of a tiny rock-fringed knowe she taught him to plant a garden with cowslips and marigolds. Then, in the evening, when Petie came in, and before his mother came to fetch him home, he would sit with the old man on the long stone before the door, and Petie would play his flute or whistle below his breath while he beat out the rhythm of a lambeg drum with two twigs on the legs of his moleskin trousers, and the dogs, stretched in the warm dust, snapped at flies and cuffed each other lazily.

He never spoke to Con Dineen. One afternoon as he climbed Knocknadreemally he saw the red-headed boy sitting with Petie on the low wall that separated the little pebbled closes before the cottages. Fingering the marbles in his pocket, Andrew quickened his step, but as he appeared in sight of Dineen's window he heard Mrs Dineen call 'Co-o-on! Con, come in at onct, I'm needing you!' and the boy with a long reluctant look at Andrew, went indoors with hanging head.

'What happened to the other wee fella?' asked Andrew of Petie.

'Didn't ye hear his ma calling on him?'

'Will he be let out tae play marlies wi' me?'

'Son, Con's a papish.'

'Aye. Will he be let out tae play marlies wi' me?'

'Did ye hear what I telt ye, Andra?'

But the simple child, ignorant of the wisdom of his

elders persisted in his question until Petie led him away to watch the waterhens on the linthole behind the cottages.

That evening when his mother came for him he was sitting on the road sifting the warm white dust through his toes. He jumped up when he saw her, and taking her hand led her to Agnes's cottage.

'I saw ye with Petie at the linthole,' she said, smiling down at him, 'were ye swimming a boat?'

'No. We were watching the wee black birds dooking in the water. Ma,' he said as they were passing Dineen's cottage, Sarah looking straight ahead, 'I was going to play marlies wi' the wee fella that lives in there, but his ma called on him to come in.'

Sarah stopped abruptly, her face flushing with anger. 'Andra,' she said, shaking his hand to give her words emphasis, 'if I ever catch ye speaking to one of that breed, I'll draw my hand across the side of your head. D'ye hear me?'

'Aye.'

'I'll no let ye come back to Petie and Agnes,' a threat that had much greater effect on the child.

The boys were to see each other again that evening, for the last time. It was the evening hour, between darkness and light, when blue wraiths creep over the fields, the white dust seems for a moment to be luminous, and dark little winds come to roost in the hedges. This is the time when country children, reprieved from bed for another minute, dart round the houses in their bare feet, their hearts full of a delicious terror of the dusk.

Andrew, tiring of the talk, went out and sat on the wall. Con was kneeling disconsolately in the window of his house, staring out at the glowing twilight. The eyes of the boys met in a long searching stare. Each was searching the other for that longed-for acknowledgement. When both of them, with poisoned words still percolating through their young minds, withheld it, there could be only one result. Andrew screwed his face into a horrible grimace and Con stuck out his tongue as far as the roots would permit. Then, feeling the smooth and pleasant coolness of the glass, Con flattened out his tongue on the pane. It stuck there, like a poppy petal, between his face and the window, and the boy outside forgot his enmity, and laughed, and edged forward a little the better to see. Con winked, and as he winked he was suddenly plucked backward into the darkness of the kitchen and his place was taken by his mother, angrily wiping the damp mark from the pane, and avoiding the questioning eyes of the child outside.

Meanwhile, in the cottage, Sarah, Agnes and Petie sat round the fire drinking tea. Suddenly Petie said 'I heard tell that the Bourkes are selling out all the land beyont the road to the lough.' Agnes paused with her cup half-way to her mouth, waiting for her husband to continue, but as he did not, she asked with some asperity, 'Does that mean the cottages, too?'

'Aye, it'll mean the cottages, too,' said Petie, in a tone of patient explanation. 'Considering that the cottages sit twixt the road and the lough, it'll mean the cottages, too, woman dear.'

'And did it dawn on ye that we're living in one of them?' demanded Agnes, annoyed by her husband's reiterative reply. 'Where did ye hear this story?'

'Stewartie Purdie heard tell of it at McIlveen's auction rooms yesterday, and he told me the-day.'

Agnes turned to Sarah. 'Did ye ever see the match of that man? The roof might be sold over our heads and he would never think o' going up to see Mr Bourke and making sure that we're no moved! I declare to God, Sarah, there's not his equal between here and Cork!'

But Sarah did not appear to be very interested in the sale of the cottages, and when Andrew appeared again, she bade him get ready to go home.

The boy's horizons widened slowly. In those summer days he saw cattle moving over the fields other than the cattle of Rathard, dogs other than his own dog, and men other than Hamilton and Frank. One evening as he played on the road, dipping along the cool cloisters of the hedge for wild strawberries, he came upon several young farm-labourers stretched out in the late sunshine at the mouth of a loanen opposite to Echlins'. As he passed them, one of the young men raised himself on his elbow and spoke in a soft lazy voice to the boy. He was a handsome fellow with a smooth olive skin and dark eyes. 'There's the wee by-blow,' he said. 'Son, you're a wee by-blow, you're a wee bastard.' Andrew, shy but delighted at being spoken to by the man, smiled at him as he passed. One of the loungers laughed and the dark-skinned fellow raised his voice softly and called after the boy, 'You're a wee by-blow, son, ye don't know who your da is!' The boy, warmed by the man's soft voice and smile, turned and laughed gleefully. Then he hurried homeward, skipping occasionally on the dusty loanen as he dipped into the hedges like a blackbird.

CHAPTER FOURTEEN

★

THE THREE OF THEM sat round the hearth. Sarah was flowering a piece of linen, Frank was filling the tobacco pipe which of late he was affecting, and Hamilton sat with his thumbs hooked in his belt, gazing at the rafters. The fire, subdued after its daylong struggle with the sun, was falling down in feathery puffs of ash. From the window opening out on to the garden came the spicy odour of carnations and the piping of homing bees.

The woman and the men were silent and yet there was a feeling in the room as if a voice had but ceased and all three were weighing what had been said. Hamilton rose, and going a few steps into the open air, stood scratching his chin and gazing at the fields between Knockna-dreemally and the lough. He came in and sat down without speaking and again took up his contemplation of the rafters, occasionally rasping his unshaven chin with his hand. Frank rose and sidled towards the door. He walked out beyond the rowans, scarcely glancing at the fields that had held his brother's attention. He strolled round the farmhouse, aimlessly kicking stones and twigs across the floor of the rath. What ailed him that he had always to be suspecting the woman? She had told them about Bourke selling the cottages and the land as if she thought they had a right to know. And she had done right there, he had to admit. Bourke's land lay into theirs from the road to the lough. And yet he had a notion that there was more behind her words than that. Was she thinking of her son that would come after Hamilton and himself? At that thought there arose uppermost in his mind something that had been irking him for weeks. He was growing away from this house. He was tiring of Sarah and her calm pale looks and her love in which there was neither passion nor endearment. Perhaps these lands might be a means of escape. He hurried round to the front of the house again and stood looking over the fields with even more attention than Hamilton had done. Potatoes and corn there, he noted, a bit o' flax along the side of that planting, grazing at the lough where the cattle could water. He regretted there wasn't a decent farmhouse on the land, and for a moment raised envious eyes to Quinn's-o'-the-Hill, a snug homestead that crowned the opposite hill, a twin to Rathard.

He went back into the kitchen and sat down again. Sarah glanced at his face and then dropped her eyes to her embroidery. Hamilton was grunting a little as he tugged at his boots. 'I think we might see your man Bourke, and lay him a reserve offer afore the auction,' said the young man looking at his brother. There was silence as Hamilton methodically drew the laces out of the holes. 'I'll sleep on it till the morn,' he answered at last.

His brother looked up sharply. 'I'm for it,' he said.

'And I'm neither for it or against it, till the morn,' replied the other, dropping his boots in the corner. 'Sarah, get us a bite o' supper, there's a good woman.'

But in the morning when Hamilton had walked round the fields, he was for it. At the dinner table the two men argued and calculated, going out half a dozen times to look at the fields, and between them, Sarah sat eating her dinner, as demure as a mouse.

At last a bid was decided upon, safe, but not too extravagant. At the last moment it was increased as a result of Sarah's casual remark that they should expect to offer a bit more than the bidders whose farms lay some distance from the auctioned land. This opinion met with the approval of the brothers and the offer was raised by twenty-five pounds. After dinner, Frank drove over to Bourke's to make the offer. He came back dissatisfied and excited, like a gambler, to say that they were too late, by a day, to buy the land by private deal, that it was now in the hands of Messrs Gomm and Bean, Ardpatrick, and that Mr Bourke had agreed to write to these gentlemen, conveying the brothers' offer. There was an air of restlessness about Frank that evening and during the next two or three days, and even Sarah found it difficult to conceal her excitement and apprehension. But the moment the offer had been decided upon, Hamilton seemed to have forgotten the matter, and went about his work without as much as glancing at the fields that might soon be his.

At eleven o'clock on the morning of the auction Sarah climbed on to the roof of the carthouse. A long procession of traps and carts crawled slowly up Knocknadreemally and down the other side until they were balanced, as it were, over the brow of the hill. There they halted, and the drivers got out and clustered round the auctioneer where he stood between the two cottages and at the head of the fields. She could almost imagine she saw the pale bewildered face of Bridie Dineen peering from the tiny window at the back of the cottage. Was the red-haired woman wondering now which of these men, tall or short shouting noisily or bidding in dry silent nods, would be her new landlord? Sarah, for a moment, shared the other woman's anxiety. Perhaps, for all she knew, the brothers had been outbid long ago. But Frank was there to raise the offer another twenty-five pounds. After what seemed a long time, but was really only fifteen minutes, the crowd of men dispersed slowly and went back to their vehicles. She descended from the roof, and drawing a shawl over her head, hurried down the loanen to the road.

Speeding down Knocknadreemally towards her with its slender spokes quivering in the sunlight, came a sulkie, drawn by a nutbrown high-stepping pony with yellow bandaged fetlocks. In it sat Frank and a man with a yellow vest. At a word from Frank the driver slackened as they approached the loanen-mouth where Sarah stood, withdrawn into the shade of the hedge. Frank did not dismount immediately but sat for a moment talking to his companion. Sarah, from the seclusion of the hedge, recognised the driver as Mr Lalor Burke, the owner of the cottages. He was a cheerful pouchy-faced young man rigged out in a tweed jacket, bedfords, and a yellow waistcoat with dark leather buttons. As he sat there, curbing the nervous animal that danced on the road, he did not seem to be downcast that still another part of his family lands, which, according to the old men, had once stretched as far as the eye could see from any hill in the three townlands, had been melted down into cash to be poured out on the race-courses of Leopardstown, the Curragh, or across the water in Aintree. At last, after shaking hands with Bourke, Frank got down and the pony and the sulkie shot away, the dapper driver touching his cap with his whip to Sarah.

The girl rushed out impatiently. 'Well, did ye come any speed?'

'Aye, girl dear, I did indeed! And with the first bid, too! We were ten pounds above the best call, but 'tis better to be safe nor sorry!'

The woman stopped and turned to look over the newly-purchased fields. 'And now it's all Echlin land as far as Quinn's-o'-the-Hill.'

'Aye, 'tis.'

'Ye know, Frank, I've been thinking. When you are lifting the praties from that lough field it'll be a long traich up to Rathard. Would it no be better to clear one o' the cottages on top o' the hill for a pratie-house?'

The young man scratched his head and looked at the cottages referred to. 'Ye know, Sarah, that's a brave good idea,' he said. 'Clear one o' the cottagers right away.'

'But no the Sampsons'.'

'No, we couldna clear the Sampsons.'

He looked at her but her eyes would not meet his. He knew now why she had told them about the sale of the land, and marvelled that spite against Bridie Dineen could drive this woman into such a tortuous plan of achieving her desire. 'Clear one o' the cottages,' he repeated, and laughed as though something had dawned on him.

They climbed the loanen together. The woman may

have seen the noisy, living, little home with its smoking chimney turned into a potato-house with shuttered windows and hay-auction bills plastered on its padlocked door. But Frank saw a different picture. For him the cottage had been swept away completely, and he saw there a tall white house with a slated roof, low pebble-dashed walls facing on the road, fuchsia at the gate, a green door, a shining knocker and a fanlight as handsome as the Bourkes'. And in the house? In the house he imagined a woman, dark, slim, light of foot, lighting up the rooms with her laughter. But she eluded him and he could not see her face.

Hamilton came into the house shortly before supper. 'Well, ye don't know what's happened here!' said Sarah, as she slid a hot plate on to the table. The dark man smiled. 'I know rightly. Stewartie yelled it at me ower the breadth o' three fields. Well, Frankie, how did we come out?' he continued, turning to his brother.

'Our first offer was ten pounds over the next best. But I suppose we canna reproach ourselves on that?'

Hamilton slapped him on the shoulder. 'Don't be blething, man dear. What's ten pounds when ye have to speak in hundreds?—ye did bravely.'

'There's another thing,' said Frank as they sat down at the table. 'Quinn was at me about letting the grazing at the lough.'

'Well, we won't say aye, yet, nor no to that, till we have time to look round us,' answered his brother. 'Our worry'll be the lifting o' the praties and corn from Bourke's fields. We may get another hand or two frae Banyil.'

'And there's the housing o' the crops.' said Sarah.

'Aye, there's the housing o' the crops. We couldna get the barn door closed on the last harvest, and the haggard's no grown any since last year.'

'Ye may clear one o' the cottages on the hill.'

Hamilton laid down his spoon and stared at her. 'In the name o' God, woman! We canna put the craturs out on the road for a wheen av bags o' corn and praties!'

'There's no talk of them going out on the road. There's more cottages nor one in the countryside.'

'We didna buy the Dineens wi' the land!' Frank burst out angrily. 'And we're no going to be held up by the likes o' them. This thing's twixt you and me,' he continued pointedly. 'And that's my say, flat and plain.'

'You've taken a very sudden scunner at the Dineens.'

'I've taken no scunner at the Dineens. But there's no good saying one thing and thinking another. We'll be looking that cottage afore the harvest, so what's the use of all this farting and fiddling around?' He paused, and then added, 'As Sarah says, there's more nor one place they can go to in the countryside.'

The three of them continued eating in silence. Not one of them honestly believed that it was necessary to turn the Dineens out. Had it been any other family the brothers would have put themselves to any inconvenience to find another storage house. Yet they, and even Sarah, liked Owen Dineen. But deep down in all three the centuries-old enmity against the papist stirred, and neighbourliness and a more ancient kinship were forgotten.

'Well, the both of ye seem to be set on this,' said Hamilton, rising. 'But we'll make no move till you've seen Mr Bourke, Frank, and got another place for Owen and his family. Are ye agreed to that?' Frank nodded without speaking.

And Frank found them a house. Two mornings later, when he had been over to Bourke's estate, he came in to say that Bourke had agreed to let a cottage on his land, and that he had gone up to Knocknadreemally and given Owen his notice.

'Where's the house?' asked Sarah.

The young man narrowed his eyes and smiled. 'Ye know it well. Ye were bred in it.'

'My mother's house!'

Hamilton laid his hand on her shoulder. 'There, Sarah, dinna take on. Things will aye be someway. Your mother wouldna hae minded. I'm sure o' that.' She shook his hand from her shoulder and turned her back on them. From that moment she began to hate Frank.

When the morning of Dineen's removal came she went to the door a score of times to look up at Knocknadreemally. She saw the smoke of the breakfast fire pluming up through the trees, and then at last it vanished. A short time later she hurried out and climbed up on the shed roof and gazed towards the distant road. A little procession was coming down the hill. First Owen leading a borrowed donkey and cart in which was piled the few furnishings of his house. On top of that were the two youngest babies. Then came the red-haired woman with a child at each hand. Before they had disappeared into the dip Sarah descended from the roof. Her face was grey and sullen. Now was the time of her triumph, and it had turned to ashes in her mouth.

CHAPTER FIFTEEN

*

DURING THE WARM grey days, Andrew was rarely indoors with his mother. At four years of age he was nearing the day when he would have to go to school, but now he was growing hardened and knowledgeable in the outside world. He was not very intimate with Frank. Of the two brothers, Frank might have been the more entertaining and instructive, for he had inherited his father's lore of the countryside. But when he and Andrew were together in the fields or the outhouses, the man always seemed shy or too voluble, until the boy, sensitive to the man's unrest, wandered away. At that time the vivid memorable threads of his young life were inserted by Frank. It was he who took Andrew with him when the boy's favourite heifer was driven off to be served by Purdie's bull. When Sarah heard of this jaunt, she was very angry, but she dare not speak of it to the boy himself and did not care to tell Hamilton, so that, unwittingly, she was restrained from tainting the boy's fresh unfolding curiosity. It was Frank who discovered the boy screaming with terror and anger in the rath, one afternoon. He was drawn up on the grassy wall, nursing his cheek, and before him danced a white cock, crowing boastfully. The man hurried away without speaking and came back with a broom. 'Here, go for him. Gie him a dunt wi' that!' he ordered. Slowly and fearfully the boy clambered down towards the fuming cock. He charged the bird, struck him on the breast and knocked him spurs over comb. The cock picked himself up and went scuttling out of the rath with his wings trailing and Andrew racing after him. Frank overtook him as he leant against the corner of the house, breathless, between laughter and tears.

But it was Hamilton who filled the weft of his life. With him he could walk the fields or sit for hours in the barn where Hamilton practised his hobby of basket-making. As the man bent and thumped the scobes the boy would patiently imitate him with lighter reeds until, his childish fancy tiring of the game, he would produce a knotty and cracked plait of grass. They sat together one day in the barn while Hamilton contrived an egg-basket for Sarah. The boy sat some little distance from the man, singing softly to himself, half-in and half-out of a beam of sunlight that slanted through the open door and set his hair gleaming every time he raised his head to watch a butterfly lurch across the sunlight, or a hen trot in, pause with upraised leg, and then retreat with a querulous mutter.

The boy, who was scooping the white pith from a piece of boretree, turned round to pick up a pretty speckled feather which he could use as a sail. For the first time the words of his song became audible to Hamilton:

> I'm a wee by-blow,
> I'm a wee bastard—

The man threw down the basket and springing across the barn plucked the child to his feet. 'What was that I

187

heard ye singing!' he shouted. Andrew, who had burst into a gleeful laugh at Hamilton's rush, was frozen into silence at the sight of the man's glowering face. 'What were those words ye were singing?' Hamilton shouted and shook him roughly. Frightened by the shaking and the angry persistent questions, Andrew burst into tears. Hamilton raised his hard cupped hand and then paused and looked down at the boy's face. Gathering him up under his arm he hurried into the house with him. At his repeated calls, Sarah appeared from the dairy. 'Ach, what's wrong wi' the wean?' she crooned, taking him on her lap. Realising that the boy was not hurt she looked up at Hamilton, and like Andrew was startled at what she saw there. 'What's wrong, Hami?' she demanded sharply.

'I heard him calling himsel' a bastard. Where did he hear that word? Who learned him to call himself that?'

Sarah raised the boy's head from her shoulder. 'Son, what was it ye said?'

In a voice broken by sobs, Andrew repeated the words to his mother. Hamilton knelt before him as he sat in Sarah's lap. 'Andra, who telt ye that? What body did ye hear saying that?'

Encouraged by his mother, the boy pointed out of the window in the direction of the road. 'A man down there. He said I had no Da.' The man and the woman gazed at each other dumbly. Slowly Hamilton rose to his feet and rested his arms and head against the mantelshelf. He spoke over his shoulder to Sarah. 'Tell him those are bad words. He mauna use them.' Without looking at Sarah and the boy again, he turned and left the kitchen, dragging his feet like an old man.

CHAPTER SIXTEEN

*

ON THE FOLLOWING morning Frank was
told what the child had said. There was something so ludicrous about the words as his brother
repeated them, that he burst out laughing. Then as the
realisation of what had happened dawned upon him, his
laughter ceased abruptly. He left the house and walked
aimlessly into the fields.

He was not surprised that someone had called the child
a bastard. For a moment, as he stood looking down at the
lough, he was filled with anger and contempt for the
creature who had taught the boy those words. But that
was no longer any concern of his. Hamilton could attend
to that. His brother loved the child and the woman.

He had been prepared for something like this to happen.
He had a prescience that a judgement had been slowly
forming at the hundreds of hearths around Rathard.
Sooner or later he knew it must become articulate. But he
had been preparing for it, like a man making ready to flee
from an approaching storm and yet lingering on in those
last few hours of stifling calm.

One by one the ties that bound him to Rathard had
broken. His desire for Sarah had dwindled long ago.
Throughout the past year their intimacy had become less
and less frequent. The separation had grown between
them, naturally and without reproach: on his part,

because he had wearied of her, and realised how empty and futile his life had become; on hers, because she needed him no longer, and he had alienated her by many of the things he had done such as setting the Dineens in her old home. He felt no jealousy when he knew Hamilton was with her. Indeed he was glad, for it made him feel free and innocent again.

And out of this weariness had risen a desire, the most powerful and seemingly worthwhile, he had ever known. He wanted a woman of his own choice, he wanted a home and children of his own. Many times recently he had felt impelled to break away from Rathard, but indolence, fear of a rebuff, and a reluctance to see Sarah step into his place in the household, had combined to frustrate him and keep him tied to his old home.

And all the time he knew that the people of the townlands were watching them, nodding, whispering, turning their eyes up at the hill farm, until that whispering and insinuation and obloquy had merged into a popular judgement. But he had always promised himself that he would always anticipate the actual word and render it harmless by some swift action, such as marriage. Now Andrew's misadventure had brought it very close to him, swiftly and without warning, and he had been unprepared, in his indolence and indecision.

Perhaps it was already too late? At that thought he stopped abruptly on the steep descent to the lough. Perhaps no woman would look at him now. He might never get the chance to show that he was wholesome and honest in heart and worthy of affection. That would mean going away from his own countryside. He almost cried out at that thought, for love of his own scene was very deep in him, and the house on Knocknadreemally was inextricably woven into his dreams.

His feet rattled on the loose stones of the beach as he crossed towards the boathouse. The keel rollers, like slow burrowing animals, had settled down into the shingle and sand. He tore them up and laid them close together under the bow of the dinghy. As he heaved the boat forward the top of the rudderboard crumbled to dust in his hands, and he saw how dried and sprung were the curving timbers of the skin. A faint squealing noise made him turn round. He had uncovered the nest of a brown rat in a fragment of rope under the boat. As he turned he saw the sinuous body of the bitch-rat disappear into the dry-stone wall of the shed. He trampled the blind puling creatures to death and kicked their bodies out on to the shingle.

The tide was high and by lifting the rollers and re-placing them under the prow he worked the boat down to the edge, climbed in, and drew out on the grey gently-breathing water. At first the water seeped heavily and he had to draw in his oars and bail. Then the timbers filled and he lengthened his stroke and sped out between the islands.

On his left hand he saw the soft green hummock where the boat had foundered and his father had been drowned. On that dark wind-torn evening it had appeared like a jagged, overhanging rock. It gave him courage to see it now, in the clear daylight, a small green mound of earth and grass with its crumbling feet lapped by the waves. Perhaps his own fear was nothing more than a green hillock, and the voice that threatened his peace nothing more than the voice of a frightened sheep.

The sky was filled with motionless goose-grey cloud, threadbare toward the east, where the sun pierced fitfully, striking an island alight with emerald fire or launching a swift glittering commotion in the channels as if a shoal of silver fish had broken water. Each little island was crowned by shrubs and plants, the fruits of bird-borne and aeolian seeds. The silver willow nodded in the water, and in the green gloom of ash, briar, and dwarfed beech, marigold and celandine glowed like clotted sunlight.

He rowed among the islands, peering into their secret glades and marking the thread-like tracks of birds and rats. Suddenly before him lay the stony beach of Pentland's island. He pulled vigorously on the oars three times, shipped them, and waited for the impact of the keel on the shingle. When the boat struck he took off his boots and socks and stepped out into the warm languid surf. He drew the boat up, put on his footwear again, and climbed up through the coarse grass towards the farm.

His path ran close to the broken walls of the monastery, upwards through a thicket of fuchsia and blossoming thorn, and then rose steeply about twenty yards to the plateau.

When he had climbed to the level ground he saw before him a man with two dogs walking slowly towards the farmhouse. He shouted, and the dogs came back and circled round him warily, their barks echoing and lingering in the hollow of the island. The man turned and looked back, and after a moment raised his hand in salute.

At that sign the dogs ceased to bark and fell in behind Frank as he approached his cousin.

As he took Pentland's hand he noticed that his cousin had changed considerably. His face had lost flesh and was darker and netted with little wrinkles at the jaw and eyes. His eyes and mouth were less mobile, and his smile seemed to disentangle itself from something within him. His vest and shirt were stained with clay and the top of his breeches gaped, disclosing his small ugly belly. As he looked at him, Echlin suddenly felt his old boyhood affection for his cousin. He stretched out his left hand also and grasped him by the forearm. 'Are ye bravely, Fergus?'

'I can't complain. It's many a long day since ye set your foot in these parts.'

'It is. But I just took the notion that I would pull across and see ye.'

'Well, you're welcome. Look, I've been out gathering these.' Pentland held out his cap and showed half a dozen eggs in the lining. 'I'm searching the nettle thickets like an ould wife these days.'

'Aye, I remember your mother miscalling the fowl. It was a bad blow when she went, Fergus.'

'It was that.'

'How are ye getting on now?'

'I've two men from the Ards stopping at the farm. One lays claim to be a sea-cook, but b'God ye could bate the fried eggs against the wall.'

'That's not a thing to persevere in, Fergus, for nothing murders a man like bad cooking. D'ye never think of getting yourself married?'

Pentland looked sharply at the other man. 'It could happen,' he said and hastened his step.

They entered the close and passed the two farmhands on their way to the house. 'Make us a drop o' tea,' said Fergus to one of them. The man followed them into the house and lowered the kettle on the fire.

When the men, with whom they had shared the meal, had gone out again, and Fergus and he were seated with their pipes alight, Frank ran his eye over the mellow-tiled floor that cast its bloom on the walls and varnished ceiling. But he noticed also the burst horsehair sofa, the smoked lamp-funnel and the grey dust of whin kindling littering the once shining range.

'It's time ye had a woman here, Fergus. Ye know,' he continued thoughtfully, gazing at the fire, 'I thought ye were set on Sarah Gomartin at one time?'

Pentland flushed angrily and stole a bitter glance at Frank's lowered head. But when his cousin looked up questioningly he saw no trace of derision in his candid eyes.

He took the pipe from his mouth. 'I was.'

'And what came betwixt ye?'

Pentland paused with his pipe half-way to his mouth, a look of angry amazement on his face. 'Are ye out o' your senses, man?' he shouted.

Frank nodded understandingly. 'Oh—that?'

'Aye, *that*—what else!'

'Well, b'God, Fergus, you're hardly the one to hold that against the woman—hadn't ye a hand in it yourself?'

Pentland went white. He sprang to his feet hurling his

chair against the wall. 'Damn ye, Echlin, ye know rightly I hadn't!'

Frank had risen swiftly, for he thought his cousin was going to strike him. He lowered his hands and sighed. 'I'm sorry, Fergus. I shouldna have asked ye that. I didn't know the right way o' things.'

Pentland had crossed over to the window and stood beating the tips of his fingers on the table. Suddenly he turned to his cousin and shouted: 'That woman near killed me! I was stooned for days after it!'

Frank laughed irritably. 'After what, man? Ye threw in your hand meekly enough. Your want for her wasna very big if ye couldna take her as she was.'

'As she was? Wi' another man's wean in her belly?' A shadow crossed Echlin's face at the coarseness and spite in the other's voice. Pentland turned again to the window, drumming his fingers on the table, his head jerking in peevish indignation, like a woman's.

Frank seated himself again and idly probed the glowing turf with a twig. When he spoke his voice was low, with a dreaming note in it. 'D'ye know what I think, Fergus? It's an ill thing for a man or woman to be aye looking behind them. Yesterday and the-morrow don't yoke over well at times.'

'Aye, and it's a worse thing to be standing betwixt them, as I was,' answered Pentland, as if he had caught a note of criticism in Echlin's remark.

'All men stand betwixt them,' said Frank rising and taking his cap from behind the door.

The two men left the house and took the path towards the beach. Fergus stopped when they came in sight of the water. 'Answer me one question, Frank. Are ye free?'

'As free as a swallow.'

Pentland smiled slowly. 'I thought that. There's a soirée at Ravara on Saturday's a week. D'ye think would ye go?'

'Like a swallow.'

'I'll pull over to Purdie's rock at seven in the evening. I'll see ye if you're there.'

'I'll be there at seven, Fergus, if we're spared.'

Pentland watched his cousin crunch over the shingly beach. When Frank had pushed off, he turned and climbed leisurely back towards his house. At the top of the rise he paused, and leaning his arms on the fence looked across at the dark clump of trees that shrouded Rathard. He stood there long enough to smoke a cigarette, and as he tossed the stump away he straightened up and spoke aloud. 'One man's enough for any woman.' He whistled lightly as he crossed the close.

CHAPTER SEVENTEEN

*

THE SOIRÉE OF which Fergus had spoken was really the 'treat' and sports that followed the yearly religious examination of the Presbyterian children of the townlands. But the event had, over many years, acquired a much greater significance than that. It was now known in the countryside as Ravara Fête to which the young men and women of all religious persuasions came. The afternoon was given up to the children with their scriptural examinations and 'treat'. At the treat great quantities of strong tea, currant bread, barmbrack and coarse wholesome cakes were consumed. Children of tender years had been known to drink four or five pints of dark scalding tea as well as gorging themselves with baker's bread. But relief was gained by a run round the field to 'joggle up their guts' and the surfeit of tea and currant-bread was ejected in a brown liquid stream, then a handful of sourleek was chewed to sweeten the mouth. After that the feaster, with a steady head and a clear eye, was ready for the games and trials of skill.

Later in the day, as the air grew cool, the young men and women dressed in their finery arrived, and the wearied children left them the field and wandered homeward. It was now that the fête took on its fuller significance as a communal gathering and a Puritan propitiation to amorous merrymaking. As the treble voices of the children dwindled, the clamour from the gathering became deeper, taking on an excited. passionate note. Every gesture and word seemed heightened and intensified. The foot races round the great tree in the field were fought out with clenched teeth, streaming hair, pounding bare feet, and vicious elbows. The games, taken over from the children, remained the same in name, but their nature changed to the pursuit of one sex by the other. Figures mingled together in bewildering confusion, the women running with breathless despairing laughter, the men pursuing silently with outstretched hands.

These young men and women burst away in chase of each other from slowly revolving rings of singers whose rhyme ended with a demand that the man should kiss his partner. Sometimes the girl entered into the climax with such ardour that the youth again took his place in the ring, tenderly feeling bruised lips; sometimes long after the round had ended they were still wrestling vigorously until the perspiring and wrathful face of the girl was drawn back by her hair, and lustily kissed. In other parts of the field races were being run, billets hurled at upright stakes, and in a hollow by the road some barefoot men were trying to leap over an osier wand resting on the shoulders of two of their companions.

There was no liquor at this merrymaking, for these people were sporting under the eye of their minister, their joy and ardour needed no enhancing, and even the wildest among them remembered that this day had been a festival of the children. There was no country dancing. Long ago they had lost the arts of the ballad and the dance, which, as kin, they had once shared with the ancient people of

Ireland. A solitary man sat in the hedge playing a melodeon, and the air was filled with the odour of bruised grass.

There were many people in the field when Frank and Fergus arrived. Fergus stopped to speak to several young men at the gate while Frank stood silently at his elbow. A ring circled erratically a few yards away, and suddenly, as it swerved towards them, two young girls caught Pentland by the arms and swept him away.

Frank smiled to himself as he observed the sudden change that came over his cousin's face. One moment he had been standing talking to his neighbours, his head bent to one side, his mouth slightly open and a frown on his forehead as he listened. He stood with his legs apart and his paunch drooping, so that he looked like a man of middle age. Now he was prancing round with a girl on each arm, throwing up his knees like a horse, his mouth wide open in laughter in his brick-red face and the black locks dancing on his brow. Frank hunched his shoulders and pushed further into the throng.

As he passed slowly over the crowded field, gazing into little groups of frolicking folk, he caught the glances of neighbours and old school-friends and nodded and smiled in reply to their greetings. But no one asked him to stop and join in the sport. Once, as if by accident, he looked back and saw that the people were watching him and whispering together.

He felt that he must turn and rush away from the field and never stop until he was back on the lonely slope overlooking the lough. But pride or obstinacy kept dragging him toward the great beech tree in the middle of the field.

When he reached it he turned and leant against its muscular trunk and studied the grey soil at his feet where neither the sun, nor the rain, ever fell.

After a time his attention was attracted to a little group of men who were following the minister through the crowd. At each game they would pause, and the minister, on the advice of the young man at his side, would call a man from his sport and ask him to join the party that he led. As they came closer to the tree, Frank heard his name called aloud. He looked up and saw Willie Gill, a boyhood companion, beckoning to him. 'Put down Frankie Echlin's name, Mr Hunter. He's the boy that can run.' The young clergyman approached Frank. 'Would you like to join in this?' he asked. 'It's a scarf game.' He put his arm in Frank's and drew him along with the others.

Mr Hunter stopped and turned to face the fifteen or twenty young men following him. 'I think we'll divide the sides into one from Ravara and one from Banyil. But first, we want seven scarves from the young ladies. Perhaps you would rather pick your own.' One or two of the men hastened away and brought back the scarves. Meanwhile, Gill, for Ravara had picked his ten men, and a great lumbering fellow, Robbie Art, nicknamed Moiley, because of his high bald forehead, had selected the men from Banyil. The two teams lined up, facing each other, and about forty paces apart. Mr Hunter walked down between the teams, dropping the scarves on the ground at equal distances. Gill numbered his men from one to ten and Frank was number seven. Art numbered his team and he himself was number seven.

When he got back to his place in the line, he took off his jacket and threw it behind him. He dragged his bare feet in the grass and smiled threateningly across at Frank.

The other games in the field had dispersed and most of the people were gathered in a great circle around the contestants in the scarf game, shouting encouragement to the men of their own townlands.

'Are you ready?' called Mr Hunter. At a nod from Gill and Art he trotted lightly down the row of scarves, paused at one, pointing to it with his toe, and then, when he was clear of the lines, called 'three!'. A man shot out from either side, racing for the scarf. The Ravara man was Willie Gill and he reached the prize first, braced himself over it for a fraction of a second, and then as his opponent rushed in, he suddenly lunged forward with his open hands striking the Banyil man on the chest and knocking him flat on the grass. Then he lifted the scarf and trotted back to his own line. Cheers and counter-cheers greeted this first score, and the Banyil men glared grimly at each other and poised themselves for the next call.

The next number called was nine and both men reached the scarf together, closed and wrestled over it, until Frank's team-mate feeling himself overborne, put out his foot and touched the scarf. 'Burnt!' cried the watchful crowd, and Mr Hunter waved both men back to their lines.

Another scarf was won by the Ravara men, and then in quick succession two were lost to their opponents. And in between these scores were always several 'burnts' or other infringements, until Frank, his number lost apparently in Mr Hunter's mind, allowed his attention to stray from the game and his eye to the crowd that pressed in on the contest.

He saw Fergus among the onlookers, his arms still encircling the two girls who had caught him up in the ring. Perhaps, he thought, if I wasn't tied to this foolishness, I might have met a woman in the crowd. A stranger perhaps, from a distant townland, who didn't know me, or didn't care about what had happened in the past. He imagined what she should be like; medium height, her eyes level with his shoulders, tawny hair darker than his own, her skin would take kindly to the sun with maybe a freckle or two, and there would be a smooth creamy hollow at her throat. That was the face that had eluded him in the tall house on Knocknadreemally. He was suddenly aware of Gill shouting angrily at him and the laughter of the onlookers. His eyes searched for Robbie Art. The big man had tossed a scarf on the grass behind him.

When Mr Hunter had the attention of the contestants again, he ran lightly up the line, tipped a scarf and called a number. One by one the scarves were lifted until there was but one left. Two men were running for it now. The Banyil man, much the faster, stooped as he ran, but he glanced at his opponent and missed his aim. The other man over-ran it and then they were wrestling until a foot kicked the scarf. 'Burnt!' cried Mr Hunter, and they went back to their places.

Again Frank allowed his eyes to wander to the crowd. Suddenly he straightened up from his runner's position, for there, looking over the shoulders of two youths, was the face of the girl he had pictured to himself. The cool evening breeze loosened a strand of hair over her brow. He saw her brush it back and then allow her hand to rest at her throat. Her scarf was a prize in the contest. He wondered had it already been won. Then he saw the little smile and frown as the wrestling men trod upon the piece of cloth on the grass. When he saw that, he marked where she stood and then crouched down waiting for his number. Four was called. Nine was called. But Frank knew that none of these men was to win the last scarf. He changed his position, standing further from the scarf and at an oblique angle so that he wouldn't meet Robbie head-on. The word had barely left Hunter's lips before Frank dropped like a stooping hawk from his place, swooped and picked up the scarf from under the hurtling shadow of Art, sped on, circled behind the bewildered man, and was back among his team-mates. 'Like a bird!' shouted Gill, thumping his back.

The contestants, after putting on their jackets and shoes, mingled with the crowd. Some hurried away to join in the games that had started again, some sat on the grass among their admirers, those who had won scarves searched for their owners.

Frank stood with the scarf drooping from his fingers. He saw Pentland moving in the crowd, still with his arms around the two girls. Hurrying towards him he caught him by the elbow and held up the piece of coloured cloth. 'Whose would this be, Fergus?' The other man threw back his head and laughed. 'How would I know, man? Sure, there's girls galore here wi' scarves like that! Put it in your pocket and you'll find the owner soon enough!'

and still laughing, his cousin rushed off across the field dragging the two girls with him.

At a loss, Frank turned away and found himself face to face with a group of girls who seemed to be encouraging one of their number towards him with pushes and laughter. As he met her eyes he saw that she was the auburn-haired girl he had noticed in the crowd. At the moment her face was flushed in vexation, yet she could not bear to meet his gaze and looked away from him, half in shyness, half in anger. Then suddenly she turned her back on him. Her companions, aware now that the young man knew the owner of the scarf, ran off leaving the girl alone.

As he slowly approached her, he could see the nape of her neck, spangled with freckles under her gold-flecked hair, for her head was bent. 'Would this be yours?' he asked, dangling the scarf before her eyes. He was too quick for her and plucked it away as she snatched at it. 'I didn't get it easy to give it away easy,' he said, putting it behind his back.

She swung round on him. 'Give me my scarf, Frankie Echlin!' she cried. She made another fruitless effort to grasp the scarf and he felt the faintest touch of her soft breast against him before she drew back.

'Oh, so ye know my name!' he laughed.

'I know who ye are, all right,' she replied, her lip curling slightly.

A shadow passed over the young man's face. He gazed at her until she raised her head and looked at him, and the pain and disappointment she saw there filled her young heart with pity. He held out the scarf in silence. She took it and folded it and put it around her neck. But she did not move away. In twos and threes the revellers were leaving the field. From the road the melancholy notes of a piper were heard as a band of merrymakers set out for a distant townland.

'Are ye going now?' asked Frank.

The girl turned and moved towards the gate. Suddenly she stopped and looked again into his face. There was doubt and perplexity in her eyes as they searched the face of the young man. Frank stood silent, anxiously watching her, unable to plead in his own defence. She moved away a few steps. Then, as though she were answering a question, she said 'But ye canna leave me home.' Yet in spite of this decision—perhaps because he felt that her mind had dwelt on the unspoken request, perhaps because of the faint shade of regret in her voice, Frank's heart leapt.

So, when they came out on to the road both turned away from Ravara towards the townland of Banyil. Here and there in the hedges could be seen the dim outlines of courting couples, half-hidden in the lush grass. The murmurous sound of their words and their stifled laughter came to Frank and the girl as they walked along the dusky road. The dew felt chill on the young man's face, white moths flitted silently under the trees and against the silver-green light of the sky, bats fled like polished stones. Once, as they approached a dark gateway, he touched her arm, but he felt it withdrawn under his fingers, and they passed the place in silence.

At last, at the head of a loanen where several men sat, she paused. A voice from the blackness of the hedge bade her good night. She answered, and then hastened her steps and drew the young man further up the loanen. 'Well, good night, now,' she said.

'But wait, I don't know your name!' cried Frank, reaching out to touch her.

She withdrew a little. 'Molly McFirbis. That was my father and my brothers wi' those men at the head o' the loanen.'

' "Molly McFirbis" ' he repeated. 'And I didn't get my reward for the scarf.'

She said nothing.

'Molly,' he asked, bending towards her, 'will ye go to Lusky Woods dance wi' me?' Again he felt the girl's eyes trying to read his face in the dark. 'I'll be going anyway,' she said at last.

'Aye, but will ye go wi' me? Molly, will ye go wi' me?' She came close to him. 'Yes. I'll meet ye here at eight in the evening.'

He bent swiftly and kissed her. She stood there for a moment and he could hear the soft catch of her breath. Then turning she ran from him into the gloom of the loanen.

Not until her steps had died away did Frank go down to the road. As he passed the men at the corner he spoke. He saw a head, silhouetted against the green afterglow, wag silently in response, and down in the blackness of the hedge a cigarette glowed suddenly and viciously.

CHAPTER EIGHTEEN

*

THE ROAD THAT ran from the scene of the
fête across the townland of Ravara and past
Rathard, lay silent. Then, in the distance, was
heard the chanting of pipes and a harmonious murmur of
voices. In the owl-light there appeared over a rise in the
road the piper followed by twenty or thirty lads and girls.
Some of them, arm-in-arm, were prancing before him
as he played, others, weary-footed, trailed behind him,
and the rest, on wavering slowly-moving bicycles,
brought up the rear. When they reached the cross formed
by Echlin's loanen and the loanen on the opposite side of
the road, where the banks were gently sloping and
smooth, they stopped and laid themselves and their
bicycles on the grass. The piper stepped into the middle
of the road and fingered a jig, *Tomelty's Verdant
Breeks*.

High above them in Rathard close, Hamilton heard the
piping and shouting on the road. He went indoors and
called on Andrew. 'Come on down to the road wi' me,
son, and see the fêters coming home.' Andrew, turning a
deaf ear to his mother's demur that the night was dropping, twisted restively in her hands as she pinned a shawl
around. Then he hastened out to Hamilton who was
trimming a hurricane lamp before the door and tapping
a foot to the distant music.

They descended the loanen hand-in-hand, the noise of the revellers becoming clearer as they neared the road. The piping had brought out the old men from their cottages in the fields and now they were seated with the young folk enjoying the music, the laughter, and the air. Petie had brought his flute and sat tapping it impatiently as he waited for the piper to tire. Hamilton and Andrew joined him on the roadside as several young men and women, Roman Catholics from a townland beyond Ravara, set themselves to dance to the piper's music. The others fell silent, not quite sure what to make of this, watching shyly and with pleasure, and nodding and smiling to each other in the dusk. And when the dancers ceased the people on the roadside applauded with shouts and handclaps.

Andrew watched the shuttling dancers with a smile of delight. When they had finished he looked up with a laugh at the men. Then his interest seemed to be distracted by something else. He sat very silent between Hamilton's knees, peering through the gloom at the people on the other side of the road. Suddenly he raised his finger and turning to Petie said, 'I know that man laughing wi' Eileen Purdie.' 'Dae ye, son?' nodded Petie, absently, and turned again to Hamilton. But the boy felt Hamilton's knees grow hard and rigid and suddenly he felt afraid. The man behind him raised his eyes under his hanging brows and examined the faces of the men opposite them. He put his hand on the boy's shoulder and said 'was that the man ye heard them words frae, Andra?' The boy was silent, but Hamilton raised him up and turned him round so that he could see his face. He did not need to ask again. The crestfallen and frightened face of the child answered him.

He thrust the boy into Petie's arms and stood up. His action was so abrupt that it escaped none of the people seated opposite him. The brown-faced laughing young man saw it too, and his glance shifted for a moment to Andrew. He withdrew his arm from Eileen's waist and eased himself up on the grass, his eyes fixed on the man clambering slowly down the opposite bank towards him. Several of the younger men had applauded ironically when Hamilton stood up, as though he were about to sing. But there was such an impression of malignance about that slow groping step and out-thrust head that they fell silent. Everyone watched him as he stepped slowly over the verge. 'What's wrong wi' Echlin? What's biting the baste?' they whispered to each other. Suddenly his foot sounded on the naked road. The young man sprang up, raced along the ditch and disappeared up the loanen that lay opposite Echlin's.

Hamilton, heavier and slower of foot, started after him and was immediately swallowed up in the gloom. The pursuit had started so unexpectedly that for a moment the crowd, sprawled at ease on the roadside, stared at each other open-mouthed. Then two or three youths sprang up with a whoop and raced after the two men whose footsteps could be heard receding on the stony track. The rest clattered after them according to their age and pace.

Petie, who had been as astonished as the others, tucked his flute into the breast of his jacket, took Andrew's hand, and hurried up the loanen after his neighbours. They were soon left far behind and the old man paused for breath. 'What came over Hami to go hunting after that man, son?' he asked. The boy looked up and shook his small pale face in silence. Then suddenly, ahead of them, they heard the shattering roar of a gun. The boy, whose hand was pressed close to Petie's leg felt the man's thigh quiver at the sound. For a moment a silence more frightful than the explosion flooded the darkness, and then the cries and counter-cries of the country-folk broke out again.

Petie hurried on again dragging the child after him. They arrived at the low cottage that stood at the head of the loanen, where several men and women stood at the doorway gesticulating and talking excitedly. Peering through the men's legs, Andrew saw Hamilton leaning back in a chair while two women bent over him. The lamp, swinging from the rafters, had been lit hurriedly with the funnel awry, and it threw a waving smoky light over the crowded room. In a corner, on a settle, sat the dark young man who had run away. Two candles were touched into life on the mantelshelf and by the added light Petie saw his wife raising a stained cloth from Hamilton's shoulder. An old woman sat rocking herself at the fire while little moaning noises came from her lips. 'What happened, wife?' asked Petie. 'I heard the clap o' a gun as I came up the loanen.'

'Ye can see what happened. Tammie Gilmore tried tae blow Hami's head off, and Hami got him by the thrapple. Look at that child! Bring him up tae the fire and not hae him catching his death at the door!'

Petie brought Andrew to the fire where the child stared in fear at the crooning woman with the silver loops of spittle on her chin. There was a stir in the room as Hamilton rose. The man on the settle sat up too, fingering his throat. Several men came forward, tucking their pipes into their waistcoat pockets. Disregarding Hamilton's protests they raised his arms on their shoulders and helped him towards the door. The wounded man paused. 'Did I see wee Andra here?' he asked.

'Ye did,' answered Agnes. 'He's as right as rain. He's wi' Petie.'

'How's Gilmore?' asked Hamilton, looking back into the room. The man on the bed felt his throat and swallowed painfully. One of Hamilton's helpers stepped forward into the open pulling the wounded man so that he winced. 'Bugger Gilmore,' he said brusquely, 'I'm sorry I pulled ye aff him.'

Someone with a lamp led them across the close. As Hamilton and the men who were assisting him went down the loanen, they passed women with their shawls drawn over their heads, whispering in the hedge. When they came to the road, the men and women who had been in Gilmore's kitchen parted from the few people who continued their way up towards Rathard. First went Agnes with the boy, then Hamilton on the shoulders of the men, and then close on their heels, Petie with a lamp that threw grotesque staggering shadows up the dark tunnel of the loanen. The boy was reeling against Agnes with fatigue and excitement so she picked him up and carried him in her arms. As they started to climb the last ascent to the farm, Petie heard quick footsteps behind him and the lilting whistle of a man. In a few seconds Frank overtook them. Petie explained in a whisper what had happened. The strange glow that had lighted up the young man's face died away as he listened. He strode ahead, turning as he passed, to look into Hamilton's face, and then he took the wearied boy from Agnes, telling her to go on and prepare Sarah for their homecoming.

When they were still some distance from the farm they saw Sarah hurrying down the hill towards them. She pushed one of the men aside, and drawing Hamilton's arm over her shoulder, put her strong arm around his waist.

They lowered Hamilton into a chair in the kitchen and then the two neighbour-men stood around, twisting their caps in their hands, unable to keep their eyes from wandering round the kitchen. 'Is there anything more we can do?' asked the man with the lantern. Agnes touched his arm. 'Say no more of this business than you can help,' she whispered. 'Now go, men, before ye have to refuse a sup o' tea, for the poor woman will have enough to do.' The men needed no second bidding, and pulling on their caps and waving aside Hamilton's thanks, they left the house.

Sarah, who had rushed Andrew off to bed, returned with towels and a basin. Agnes had cut away the torn shirt from the wound, and when Frank saw the mangled shoulder he drew in his breath with a hiss. 'God's curse on Gilmore!' he said in a low voice. 'I'll fix him—I'll put him where he'll never lift a gun again!'

'Behave yourself, man!' retorted Agnes sharply. 'D'ye want the countryside filled wi' polis, nebbing intae everybody's business? Tammie Gilmore's suffered enough thenight—this near kilt his old mother.'

'Aye, but he near kilt Hami!' cried Sarah.

'Now, Sarah, take my word. Let the thing rest, for the

mair ye tramp in dung, the mair ye spread it around. Let there be no more said about it, like a good woman, and fetch me a knitting-needle.'

When the knitting-needle was brought the old woman reddened it in the fire and then, with skilful fingers, she coaxed out the pickles of shot from the wounded flesh. At last she straightened herself, and Hamilton opened his eyes. 'Is it all out?' he asked.

'Aye, it's all out. We'll put a clean clout on it tae keep it from festering.' She patted Hamilton's cheek. 'Ye bore it like a kiltie, son. Hae ye nothing in the house tae give the man?' she asked, turning to Frank.

He smiled suddenly. 'Yes,' he said, 'I have.' He left them and went down to the parlour. They heard him fumbling in the sideboard, and then he appeared again, with an untouched half-bottle of whiskey in his hand. 'Ye remember the day I bought this?' he asked, drawing the cork.

He offered some whiskey in a cup to his brother, which Hamilton drank. As he handed back the cup Hamilton winked slowly at Frank and the younger brother turned away, the tears rising in his eyes. Easily stirred as he was to either love or anger, and still glowing with the happiness of the evening, this added emotion was too great to be borne by the young man, and he went out into the dark close and remained there until he felt calm again.

When he came back he found that Hamilton had been undressed and laid on the trestle bed in the kitchen. 'Let him bide there,' said Agnes, 'and I'll be up to see him in the morn.' Frank slipped his arm fondly round the old woman's waist. 'I'll see ye down to the road,' he said.

CHAPTER NINETEEN

★

HAMILTON'S SHOULDER MENDED rapidly under the hands of Agnes with her herbs and clouts. But during those days of his enforced idleness a change came over the people of Rathard. It was nothing dramatic, but more a subtle slide and shift in the pattern they wove ceaselessly and unwittingly as a background to their lives.

The weight of the farm-work had fallen on Frank. The young man found himself immersed once more in those duties that he had relinquished, in his despondency, to Hamilton. Now he undertook them so cheerfully and painstakingly that a suspicion naturally entered Sarah's mind. Naturally, that is to say, because having the clay of avarice in her own heart, she assumed that Hamilton's brother was now seizing this chance to reinstate himself as master of the Echlin farm. Yet she knew that her suspicion was foolish. In a week or two Hamilton would be well again. And Frank himself had never been so considerate in his attitude to his brother, so genial and yet non-committal with herself.

But she could not rid herself of the impression that something of great importance had happened to Frank on the evening that Hamilton had been wounded. As she watched she realised that Frank's happiness had no connection with his brother's mishap. Once more she went over the events of that evening. Frank had been to the school fête. Already she had thought of him meeting a girl there but had thrust the idea out of her mind for reasons that she declined to examine too closely. But now, the more she pondered on it, the more she realised that this was the only explanation.

A week after the attack Hamilton could raise his arm stiffly from his side. 'Gie the whangs o' your shoulder time to supple up,' counselled Petie when he brought up another dressing from his cottage. But Hamilton was in a hurry to be well again. He hadn't missed the brisk and light-hearted manner of his brother in the house, nor his light step as he went about the labour of the farm. Nor had he missed the shrewd and hostile expression that came on Sarah's face, as she looked at Frank.

One evening Frank came up from his bedroom clad in his Sunday clothes. 'Are ye away, the-night?' asked Hamilton, as his brother passed through the kitchen. Frank paused uncertainly for a moment. 'Aye, I'm going over to Lusky Orange Hall t' the dance.'

Hamilton nodded absently. 'Aye, just so,' he said.

Unwillingly Frank looked at Sarah. The glance that passed between pierced and dissolved the geniality of the past week. There was a question in Sarah's eyes, held in check by angry disdain, and in response the young man's eyes dilated in anger. Then the woman pulled her knitting back into her lap with a movement that seemed a shrug of the shoulders. Frank went down into the parlour and came up with his best cap in his hand. He drew it on and left the house without speaking again.

The evening sky was still suffused with light as he set off towards McFirbis's farm. The warmth of the day, drawn down from the hills, still lingered in the deep road, and for that reason and also that he wanted to meet his sweetheart unobserved, he walked slowly, so that he might not overtake any of his neighbours who were going to the dance.

He walked between hedgerows from behind which came the clink and rattle of tired horses being released from reapers. And, as he loitered along, hearing it seemed for the first time, the full lazy serenade of a thrush, gilded on a branch by the reddening sun, he tasted the sweetness of lover's meeting.

As he approached the loanen that led up to the McFirbis farm, he heard men's voices from somewhere close at hand. He looked up the loanen; it was deserted and the voices had fallen silent. He knew it was early yet for Molly to arrive so he leant over a gate on the opposite side of the road and drew out his pipe and tobacco. As he pressed the first few shreds into his pipe he heard someone breaking through the hedge, and glancing over his shoulder saw a young man whom he recognised as Greer McFirbis, free himself from the bushes and spring on to the road. He carried a heavy stick in his hand. As Frank watched the young man, he heard footsteps behind him. Turning round he saw old Sam McFirbis, Molly's father, and a youth of about seventeen years come out of the loanen. They also carried cudgels. For a moment the three men stood looking at Frank in silence. 'What's your business here, Echlin?' asked old McFirbis, taking a step forward. His sons closed in with him. 'D'ye hear me speaking, Echlin? What d'ye want here?' 'I'm waiting on Molly,' answered Frank stepping back towards the gate as McFirbis advanced. 'Ye bloody whore-monger,' said the old man: 'so ye wanted tae foul another decent home?' 'No, no,' said Frank: 'No—ye don't understand—' He was close to the gate, his hand fumbling behind him for the hasp. McFirbis saw the movement. 'Watch him, the whelp!' he shouted and poked at Frank with his stick. The abrupt gesture was all that was necessary to release the savagery in the McFirbis men. As Frank drew his hands from behind him to ward the blow, the elder son struck him on the forearm. With a shout of pain the trapped man turned and swung his fist at his assailant and as he did so old McFirbis struck down fiercely at his unprotected head. Frank stumbled out on to the road with his hand to his split ear. Then young McFirbis who had been convulsively grasping his stick struck him across the belly. With a sucking whoop Echlin fought for breath, and actually caught two of the descending cudgels and clung to them for a moment in agony. They shook him loose and closing in began to thrash him in a dull savage rhythm of blows. Yet he did not fall, but staggered over the dusty road, his arms raised unavailingly over his head, while tears and blood streamed down his face and neck. The blows of his assailants became less cruel. They caught glimpses of each other's faces now filled with fear and a realisation of what they were doing. As the others drew back the youth, who watched his father and brother beat the defenceless man, now rushed in and smashed his club across Echlin's back. Echlin drew himself up, stretched his open hands to the sky, and gave a loud scream of pain. At this, young McFirbis threw his shattered club away and turning, ran blindly down the road, his hands over his face. For a moment Echlin stood drawn up in agony, then he crumpled and fell face forward on the road.

CHAPTER TWENTY

*

I N TEACHING LITTLE Andrew to say his prayers, Sarah revealed one of those inconsistencies in her behaviour, which, when considered sympathetically, showed plainly that her estrangement from her church was not one of conviction, but of fear and shame. Fear of her neighbours partly, but also, let it be said, shame and remorse when she thought of the life that she was unrolling, day by day, before the sight of God and her mother in Heaven. So she knelt beside the child and prompted him when he faltered and in this way garnered some grains of solace for herself.

But to-night as she knelt at the bed, helping the boy as he laboured through the Lord's Prayer, her attention was divided. She was thinking of Frank, for she was now fully convinced that whether he had gone to the dance in Lusky Woods or not, he had gone out to meet a girl. And all the tragic possibilities for herself and her child that might arise out of that were quite clear in her mind. She knew that it would be impossible to live with another woman—a married woman—in Rathard. And there gathered slowly in her mind the intention to ask Hamilton that evening to marry her. She had no doubt about how *that* request would be received by the man who now sat at the kitchen fire, listening unconsciously for her returning step.

Andrew finished his prayers and sprang into bed. As Sarah bent to touch his head she heard the slow heavy tread of men in the close. Running to the window she saw four men carrying a door between them and on it lay the figure of a man with a horse-rug thrown over him.

CHAPTER TWENTY-ONE

*

FOR THE NEXT few days there was a numbness among the people in Rathard. Frank did not tell the full story of how he had received his injuries, and Hamilton and Sarah did not press him to tell. Meantime, little Andrew, with wide wondering eyes, crept silently among his maimed and downcast elders. The swift series of blows dealt at the inhabitants of his little world planted in the child a fear of everyone beyond the shadow of the farmhouse. If, from his eyrie on the rath wall, he saw a cart crawling on the road below, the driver, perhaps some jolly country youth, was to him a malignant creature eager to shoot, kick or beat any member of the Rathard household unlucky enough to cross his path. Even the company of old Petie could not entice him to Knocknadreemally again. His whole day was spent like a tethered goat, circling close to the dwelling-house of the farm.

Then came the sleepy afternoon when he was playing in the rath. Suddenly he heard a high wavering cry of pain from his mother's window that overlooked him. As he paused, crouched on his hunkers, he heard Hamilton calling on him again and again. As he raced round the corner into the close Hamilton caught him roughly by the shoulder. 'Damn ye, where were ye! Stay in the kitchen till I come back, and listen if you're called by your mother!' Hamilton ran to the trap-shed and through the window the child saw him swing out the springcart and yoke in the horse.

When the cart had bumped out of the close, Andrew crept down to his mother's door and listened. He heard her laboured painful breathing and a stifled groan which filled him with fear. Silently he tip-toed back to the kitchen, afraid that his mother might hear him, and call on him. Several times he stole backwards and forwards between the fire and the passage to his mother's room. Then at last he heard the wheels of the cart on the close, and running to the door saw Agnes Sampson clambering down from the cart. She came into the kitchen, and pausing only to tell Andrew to fill the kettle and lower it on the crane, hurried down the house to Sarah's room. That evening Sarah gave birth to a daughter.

PART III

CHAPTER ONE

*

RAVARA NATIONAL SCHOOL, presided over by Master Herriot, was a one-storeyed, white-washed building, rather like a long cottage, separated from the road by a bald pebbled close. An engraved stone above the door bore the words 'Ravara National School 1832' and the building, both inside and out, showed little evidence of change in its eighty years. The school itself was one large room in the middle of which sat an American stove, thrusting its sooty tail like a petrified monster through the raftered ceiling. A large map of Ireland, as yellow and glossy as a pippin, hung at the head of the room, and the other walls were hidden under a foliage of biblical pictures, charts showing the innards of people who drank alcohol, calendars, and fluttering specimens of 'copperplate', all held together by branches and running tendrils of finger marks, imprinted there by scholars who now husbanded the fields in the townlands or were incised names in the graveyards.

Around the stove the various groups of scholars clustered in circles, hollow squares and rows, receiving in turn the attention of Mr Herriot or his assistant, generally an older scholar, who, for some reason or other had been permitted to stay another few months at the school. Here, from nine o'clock in the morning until three o'clock in the afternoon, the children were instructed in the rudiments of reading, writing and arithmetic, and a system of geography that still contained some pleasant echoes of myth. But these bare essentials of an articulate animal were considered sufficient for the life of an agricultural community.

At noon the school broke for lunch, which, for most of the scholars, was the large buttered farl of wheaten or soda bread that they carried with their books in their oilcloth satchels. Master Herriot left the school to walk to his lodgings in a neighbouring farm and as he walked through the shouting, tumbling children he would playfully ruffle a little girl's hair here, or there hook the ball off a boy's toe and dribble it skilfully up the road followed by a rabble of gleeful boys shouting 'Hi, Mester! Here, Mester!'

Half an hour later he would come down the road again and this was a signal for the children to make their way into the close before the school and form into a straggling line. Then to the muted beat of a bell they would stamp noisily into their classes for the second period of the day.

At half-past two the 'infants' were released from school to be followed by the older children. Ravara School, catering as it did for a large area of the surrounding countryside, contained scholars from a number of townlands, and these gathered in neighbourly clans and parted from each other amid shouts and counter-shouts until they lost sight of each other on the white dusty road.

Among the children who turned down into the heart of Ravara townland was a tall fair-headed boy of about twelve who was among the leaders of those who went rambling off the road on various escapades, hunting goats in the paddocks, or stealing beans and sweet red carrots from the fields. Now and then he would throw a word or two to a girl about five years his junior and from the way in which he slewed her satchel round and rummaged in it for a ball, it was plain that there was a relationship between them, although neither in colouring nor cast of features was there any resemblance.

As they reached the brow of a hill, the drumming of a heavy engine vibrated in the air, and rising above the trees about half a mile away, the children saw a dark feather of smoke. 'The thresher's up at your place, Andra Echlin!' a boy cried. The fairhaired boy strained his ears to catch the sound. 'Aye, so it is!' he said. 'Come on Martha, hurry up!' and he thrust the ball into his sister's satchel, caught her by the hand, and hurried her along the road.

To those of his companions who had kept up with him, young Echlin pointed to where the loanen bank had been broken down by the tread of the tractor's wheel. Then he ran down the loanen, dragging his sister by the hand, until they came in sight of the thresher. Painted red, blue and gold, with ornate scrolls carved in its frame, it sat at right angles to the last stretch of the loanen that led uphill to the farm.

A great load of gleaming straw which clouded out over the cart and the hindquarters of the horse was just drawing away from the noisy dusty scene. The driver, his feet braced on the shafts, was half-hidden in the straw. Andrew waved his hand excitedly to him. 'Hello, Frank!' he shouted. The driver turned his yellow, wasted face slowly and looked at the boy in a vacant way before he nodded. Then he lashed the horse up the field track, leaving a free passage for the carts laden with sheaves that came rumbling down the loanen.

Petie Sampson was forking up sheaves to Sarah who stood on the thresher platform. She loosed the bands and handed the corn to Hamilton who splayed it out expertly on the rollers until it vanished into the rumbling puffing interior. The shrill cries of the children failed to penetrate the uproar of the machinery, and it was not until Sarah caught Hamilton's wink and nod that she knew they were there. She leaned down and funnelled her mouth with her hands. 'Away up and Agnes'll get ye your dinner—and then ye can come down and give a hand here!' The boy nodded, but delayed to thrust his foot into the rising pile of grain below the machine. Martha stood back in the hedge with her hands over her ears, gazing at the panting monster, and watching the patched ancient belt bouncing between the wheels. The boy glanced up to see his mother's angry face, and although her words were inaudible, he grasped his sister's hand again, and hurried up the loanen. Sarah, in answer to the shout of the man beside her, tore off another band hastily and thrust the sheaf towards him. The machine gave a dry empty roar until again it felt the golden straw and heavy heads among its rollers.

Martha and Andrew paid little attention to their dinner, and in less than ten minute's time they were back among the threshers. Andrew was quickly absorbed into the work, and his sister, much to his jealous anger, immediately began to play with the cone of grain rising on a canvas sheet below the machine. But he attracted his mother's attention to the girl and she was driven away.

By speeding up they managed to thresh two of the stacks by nightfall, and then the tired band of workers with ropes, bags and baskets on their arms, went up to the farm. Martha had been sent to bed long ago, but Andrew rode up the soft bumping field track with Petie. Agnes had supper ready for them when they arrived. Seven spoons, four silver, three horn, lay at equal distance on the scrubbed table. When the men and the boy were seated, Sarah and Agnes filled out plates of thick tripe soup with whole potatoes floating in it.

Andrew sat listening drowsily to the engine-man telling Hamilton and Frank about their neighbours' threshing, and the difficulty he had moving the cumbersome machinery from one farm to another. The boy crumbled his buttered farl while he watched the others lift the white cushions of bread between their dark, work-stained fingers, caught the glimpse of teeth as they opened their mouths and engulfed the bread, and fell asleep, lulled by their blurred and floury speech.

It was the signal for everyone to go. Petie and Agnes left with the engine-man who was to sleep in the loft over the potato-house. 'We've an early day the morra,' said Hamilton, standing up and stretching himself with a yawn. He turned out the lamp and ran it up to the polished ceiling.

CHAPTER TWO

★

THE NEXT MORNING, when the children awoke, the thresher was already at work, and the heavy beat of the engine came to them through the clear morning air. They arose quickly and in a few minutes were padding around barefoot in the kitchen.

Sarah smiled to herself as she noticed that Andrew ate his porridge slowly, staring into the fire, and twirling his bare toes together. 'Come on, Andra,' she said. 'You'll be late for school.' 'I'm no going to school,' answered the boy, raising his head in a surprised manner, as though his mother should have understood that he must stay at home, to-day of all days. 'And me too!' cried Martha beating her plate with her porridge spoon. 'You're baith going to school,' said Sarah. 'Now, no nonsense,' she added sharply, as she saw her son's face darken. 'Ye were kept at home for the hay and the praties. Ye canna afford to miss any more schooling—or ye'll no be able to read ava. That's enough from you, miss!' continued the mother, stifling a protest from the little girl. 'If you've finished your tea, go and put on your boots. It's time ye were out o' here.'

Reluctantly the children left the table, but now that they knew there was no further chance of a holiday the fear of another authority and the punishment for being late urged them to hurry. Sarah had made up their lunch parcels and as she tucked one into each satchel she said 'the threshing'll be done by the time you're back.' Andrew ran down to the corner of the house. The sight of the two empty stack-stands and the third stack with its head broken to the eaves, confirmed his mother's words. Slowly he returned to where his mother and sister stood. Sarah kissed both the children before they left. As she bent over Andrew she said 'Get all the school-ing ye can, son. Some day you'll get mair threshing than ye want.' The boy looked into her face gloomily, as if doubting her word.

As the children approached the thresher everyone around it seemed to be serving it feverishly. Even the hedges of the loanen they walked between were hung with straw, as if they wore aprons to help with the work. Martha ran ahead to stare at the dancing belt and the tireless piston of the steam engine. Andrew followed slowly, kicking at the stones on the loanen. He thrust a leg into the rising cone of grain until his boot and stocking were covered and he was standing knee-deep in the hard white corn. He heard Martha calling him, and turning saw her, feet pressed together, standing at some distance from the thresher. 'Stand here,' she said, 'close.' He put his feet close to hers and felt a tremor run up his back. They were standing on a spine of whinstone on which the tractor was set, and it pulsated like a piece of the engine. Martha's red cheeks were vibrating, and she opened her mouth small to let her teeth chatter. 'I'm a chitty-wren!' she shouted. 'You're daft,' said Andrew, and without another look at the machine he turned and ran down the loanen to the road.

That day the boy's deafness seemed to grow worse. It may have been the unusual volume of noise at the threshing, or because he had slept uneasily the night before. That always made him deaf the following day. By the midday break the voices of his schoolmates had become high-pitched notes without meaning to his ear. When he went back into school he kept his head close to his work so that none of his neighbours could talk to him. But as the school hummed and drowsed through the warm autumn afternoon, Master Herriot grew thirsty. He looked over the class before him and his eye rested on Andrew the nearest boy. 'Andrew,' he said, 'go into the Master's house and bring me a glass of water.' As he tossed Andrew the key his eyes wandered away from the boy's face to the window. The thud of the key on his copy book roused Andrew. The words that Herriot had spoken had been meaningless to him but he knew that he had been ordered to do something. His eyes followed Herriot's to the window as he struggled desperately to interpret the words. Below the window was a press that held a pile of unframed slates used by the older boys and girls for dictation and arithmetic. Andrew got up and went over to the press and tried to insert the heavy key in the lock of the press. At that, a wave of laughter rose behind him in a shrill squeal. He turned and found Mr Herriot's eyes fixed on him. 'Were you dozing, boy?' asked the Master. Again Andrew strained madly to catch what the man was saying. 'Yes,' he replied. Another squeal of laughter rose from the class and a puzzled and angry frown came on Herriot's face. He stepped down from the little platform behind his desk, cane in hand. 'Go in now, like a good lad, and bring the water from the house,' he said slowly.

Andrew stared at him for a moment, his face white with fear and desperation. Suddenly he threw down the key and raising his clenched fists beat them against his ears. 'I'm deef!' he shouted, 'deef, deef, deef!' He turned and ran out of the school and the startled and silent children heard the thud of his feet receding over the pebbled close. At a slower pace Herriot followed the runaway. The faint breeze lifted his tired sandy hair as he stood on the step, looking up and down the road. Beyond the school wall he glimpsed a blue jersey passing a gap in the hedge. He hurried down to the road and called on the boy, but he did not look back and soon disappeared from the schoolmaster's view.

That evening, after six-o'clock tea, Herriot put on his hat and set out for Rathard. The soft still evening light lay gently on the fields and Herriot noted with pleasure that the last of the corn was being moved to the stackyards as he ascended and descended the little hills on the white road.

As he turned up the loanen leading to Rathard he noted the banks torn and stamped by the toothed wheels of the tractor, and that the new ruts in the loanen had been already metalled. He was curious to see the strange household about which he had heard so many rumours. Under his arm he carried Andrew's tattered school bag. As he approached the farm he heard the boy's voice call 'wheet-wheet! wheet-wheet!' and saw the bobbing line of ducks come at his bidding, but the boy himself was hidden by the rowans at the mouth of the close.

Herriot slowed his pace so that he wouldn't overtake the ducks, and following behind them, came suddenly face to face with Andrew. He saw the look of sullen fear that came on the boy's face but he smiled pleasantly as he handed over the schoolbag. 'There you are, Andrew, you forgot that in your hurry to-day.' Then the schoolmaster pushed his tweed hat back on his head and took out his pipe. He nodded across the loanen. 'Your ducks'll be wandering again,' he said. At that moment the little girl Martha burst out of the house, followed by a dog. She stopped short when she saw Herriot, and stood with her finger to her mouth, eyeing him warily.

Herriot welcomed the interruption. 'Hello, Martha,' he called. 'So this is where you live?' Attracted by the sound of the strange voice Sarah appeared in the doorway of the dwelling-house, wiping her hands on her apron. Martha backed towards her, still watching Mr Herriot, and Andrew, realising that the trouble ahead could not be averted, went off after his truant ducks.

Herriot touched his hat and went forward. 'I'm the master—Mr Herriot. You're Andrew's mother?' Sarah nodded, watching him carefully as her daughter had done. 'You're welcome,' she said. 'Won't ye come in?' Herriot thanked her and entered the kitchen.

'I brought back Andrew's schoolbag. He left it behind him.' As the woman did not speak he continued: 'I asked Martha if this was where she lived—but she's lost her tongue.' The master smiled. 'You wouldn't think it was the same girl at school.'

Sarah glanced at her daughter and entered into Herriot's jocular mood. 'I'm sure she's a right nuisance at times to ye.'

The man demurred and then said: 'I'd like a word with you, Mrs Echlin.'

'Martha,' said her mother, 'away out and help Andrew house the ducks.' When the girl had left the house Sarah turned inquiringly to the schoolmaster. 'Please sit down,' she said, drawing forward a chair.

'Mrs Echlin,' began Herriot, 'do you know that Andrew ran away from school to-day? No,' he added, as he noticed the expression on her face, 'the blame doesn't lie with the boy.'

'Oh, who's to blame then?' asked Sarah, bridling at his words.

'I don't know—perhaps no one. But Andrew's going deaf. Did you know that?'

She wound her hands in her apron, a habit of hers when she was worried. 'I knew he was a bit deef at times. Still and all, he can hear well enough when he wants.'

'Maybe,' said the master. 'But there was no pretence to-day. He broke down—and I was wondering were you doing anything about it.'

'Ach, he gets hummings and drummings in his ears, but they come and go wi' the weather. Anyway, what can ye do about things like that?'

'Well, you could take him to a doctor, and if his hearing is really threatened, there's a special school in Belfast to treat children like that.'

'He doesn't need any more schooling. He's near

thirteen now, and Mr Echlin was just saying t'other day that it was time the lad was brought home—'

'I don't think you understand me, Mrs Echlin,' Herriot said, interrupting her. 'I know Andrew will soon be staying at home, but it was his ear trouble I was thinking about. Believe me,' he continued earnestly, 'there's nothing more tragic than the loss of hearing. We look on blind people and dumb people with pity and admiration when they make the best of their disability, but a deaf man is a dead man, for we always leave him out of our reckoning.' He stood up and lifted his hat. 'I hope you'll see your way to doing something about Andrew, anyway.'

Sarah appeared to be considering his words. 'Well,' she said, 'I'll see what Mr Echlin says.' As she followed Herriot to the door she added. 'But the boy'll soon be leaving school, and deafness will be no hindrance to him working on the land. But thank ye all the same, Mr Herriot.'

'That's all right. I just thought I'd better let you know,' and touching his hat to her, the master left the farm.

Later that evening, when they had all gathered in, Andrew watched his mother apprehensively. She laid his schoolbag on the dresser and crossing to the fireplace, lifted down the tea-caddy. She busied herself with infusing the tea before she spoke. 'Master Herriot was here the-day,' she said at last.

Hamilton lowered his paper. 'Aye, and what did he want?'

'He was here to tell us that Andra was going deef.'

'And what does he want us to do?' queried the man.

'Buy him new lugs?' Little Martha giggled and Andrew smiled and lowered his eyes timidly.

But although the schoolmaster's visit had been dismissed in this manner, when bedtime came Sarah called the boy to her when he had undressed. She examined his ears and then heated a little oil in a spoon and ran it into each ear. For several seconds the lad stood with his head tilted to one side, his eyes moving from his mother to Hamilton, and there was such an expression of anxious hope in his look that it arrested Hamilton's attention.

'Well? Well?' burst from Sarah, sharply, impatiently.

The timid unhappy smile came on the boy's face again. He shook his head. 'The bizzing's still there,' he said. Hamilton slouched back in his chair, lit his cold pipe and spat in the fire. 'Go tae your bed, son,' said Sarah. When the boy had left them the couple by the fire sat silent for a time. Then Hamilton knocked out his pipe and stood up. 'It's a quare thing the deafness,' he said, 'ye canna see it tae get at it.'

CHAPTER THREE

*

THE APPARENT INDIFFERENCE of Sarah and Hamilton to Andrew's deafness, and the scant regard they gave to Mr Herriot's advice, arose from neither indifference nor miserliness. Sarah had voiced the real reason when she told the schoolmaster that it was high time that Andrew left school and started his life work on the farm. A man can till and scatter the seed and reap even though his ears are dulled. Wasn't Frank with his twisted body and slow stumbling step a greater man now, than any creature who could only win a few rags from his tiny fields to cover his ox-like body?

The original farm of Rathard had spread in a series of swift outrushes. By judicious purchases, several small neighbouring farms had been absorbed, and the Echlin property had moved forward and spread out like a pool that overflows and gathers at some small impediment, only waiting to gather strength and flood into another little man's few acres. When Sarah went out in those grey unwakened mornings, scratching herself and yawning, there was nothing she loved better than to isolate those fields, trees, loanens and roofs that had passed into the hands of her and her men. When she had released the fowl, she would lean on the eave of the henhouse, indifferent to the river of eager feathered creatures that swirled past her ankles, and con the familiar fields again.

'All ours—all ours!' Ah, there were strong men and women wanted now in Rathard!

Strong men and women. Not men with twisted backs. But that had solved something too. Something of great importance. Frank was slipping further and further back into the shadows of Rathard. Everything was silent and blind about him now, except his groans at night as he lay in his single bed, and the implacable hostility of his eyes when he watched Sarah. But on her side was the strong unbroken man and the growing lad. No one could dispute Hamilton as her husband and as father to the children. He would have been the better man of the two, even if Frank had not wandered away from her and got himself broken. When a woman is forty and the faint colour that time has left on her face and bones is burned into her body like enamel, what does it matter if a man is clumsy and uncouth when they were alone? Time had solved many problems for her, it would solve that one too.

CHAPTER FOUR

*

IN THE FARM-HOUSES scattered through the townlands, Sarah was known as Mrs Echlin. To the older generation her story had lost its savour; and what profit was there in retelling an old story against a strong family like the Echlins? There may have been little change among the names of the old-established families. The Ogles, Bourkes, Pentlands, Gomartins, Arts, Gilmores, Purdies were still thriving, but an old residenter was cut down with each harvest, and birth, marriage and litigation had changed the families in the farms.

One of the last threads that bound Sarah to her past was Agnes Sampson. Since those early unhappy days at Rathard Sarah had discussed all her problems with the woman on Knocknadreemally hill. But a day came when she lost her old friend.

It happened about six months after Andrew had left school. One grey March afternoon as he was brerding a gap in the hedge near the road, he saw Petie trotting down the hill as fast as his old legs would carry him. When he heard the boy chopping in the hedge he stopped and called on him. 'Andra, Andra, son! Run for your mother and tell her Agnes is gey ill!'

'Is she very badly, Petie?'

'Aye, she's very badly. Now don't delay, like a good lad, but fetch Sarah.'

'Will I yoke the pony and go to the dispensary for the doctor, Petie?' the boy asked eagerly.

'Ach, you know what Agnes is about doctors! Now, like a good son—or will I hae to go mysel'?'

The boy did not wait for a second bidding, but fled up the hill to Rathard. Old Petie turned and hurried back to his cottage.

Agnes lay on the horsehair sofa her breath coming heavily from between her dark lips. Petie raised her head and wiped her mouth with a cloth. 'Sarah'll be here in a minute,' he said. 'Is there anything I can get ye?' At the sound of his voice, she raised her eyes to him, her lips moving soundlessly. At the sight of the woman who had nursed and protected him for so many years, now unable to help herself, Petie broke into sobs, and falling on his knees, buried his face in her skirt. The dying woman groped blindly until she found, and laid her hands comfortingly, on his bowed head. The effort seemed to calm her, for she lay still, until her husband, gently disengaging her hand, arose, and went out to see if Sarah was coming. But the glimmering bowl of the road lay grey and silent.

A sudden March shower had fallen, and then swept away across the darkening hills. From every twig the sullen little drops crept down to feed the tumbling trinket that suddenly found voice in the roots of the hedge. Slowly the old man entered the house and lowered the kettle on the crane to bring it to the boil, as though there would come some moment when water would be called for, to bring relief to Agnes. Then he dragged a cutty-stool to the side of the sofa and taking his dying wife's hand between his own, sat with his back turned stubbornly to the silent door and the waning light.

Then suddenly he heard the quick step of Sarah on the flat stones outside the door. She entered hurriedly, peering into the gloom of the cottage. 'What's ailing her, Petie?' she asked. The old man stood up, shaking his head helplessly. 'Andra's away in the cart for the doctor,' continued Sarah, as she raised Agnes's head to place a cushion under it. The grey hair of the woman, unloosed from its fastening, streamed down on to the floor. At the sight of it, Petie turned away, wringing his hands. 'Come on now, Petie, like a good man,' said Sarah drawing a small bottle from her pocket, 'get me a clean spoon till I give her a sup o' this whiskey.' As she spoke the woman on the sofa gave a great sigh. Petie stumbled across the room and bent over her. 'She's dead!' he cried. 'Oh, Agnes, Agnes, don't leave me!' He fell on the floor beside the sofa saying over and over again: 'Oh, my God, what'll become o' me now—what'll become o' me now?'

After she had raised the old man to a chair, Sarah got out linen, and as she was binding Agnes's head, Andrew arrived with the doctor. The doctor was familiar with the dead woman's reputation and he gave a gesture of impatience as he brushed aside a bunch of herbs dangling from the rafters, but he laid his hand sympathetically enough on Petie's drooping shoulder. There was little he could do, and after a word or two with Sarah, he left, Andrew driving him away.

With the tottering help of old Petie, Sarah carried the dead woman into the bedroom, where she washed her and laid her out. She finished alone, for Petie had sunk into his rope-bottomed chair, and sat staring into the fire. She tidied the room and went up into the kitchen. 'I'll send Andra down to bide wi' ye the-night, Petie,' she said. The old man shook his head. 'I'll stay alone wi' her the-night,' he replied.

Bidding him good night, Sarah left the cottage and set off wearily for Rathard. At the top of the loanen she turned and looked down on the countryside. The spring dusk was thickening on the fields, and in the hollows of the little hills the trees stood like grey pencil strokes. Here and there over the townlands lights winked up in the darkness but she could see no light gleaming from Knocknadreemally.

CHAPTER FIVE

★

AS ANDREW AND Martha grew up, Frank
found less work to do in the fields, and spent
most of his waking day in the barns and byres
but rarely in the house, for he was obsessed with the idea
that Sarah wanted him out of the way. And so he made
jobs for himself, that he might still claim some part in the
life of the farm. Many times Hamilton had asked him to
relinquish his work, assuring him that he, more than
anyone, could rest and take it easy.

'D'ye say rest?' Frank turned his face up to his brother
who leaned over the half-door of the meal-shed, watching
him draw a waxend through a broken fragment of harness. 'Rest, and let that witch fault me for doing no work
about the place?' He rose and shambled over to the door.
Putting his face close to his brother's he whispered:
'That's where she wants me, ye know.' He pointed to the
ground, winked, put a finger to his lips, and shambled
back to his stool. Hamilton stood silent for a moment.
'What the hell are ye blethering about, man?' he said.
Frank looked up, smiled twistedly, and nodded. 'I'm
telling you,' he added. Hamilton kicked the half-door
open, strode in, and stood over his brother. 'What witch
—what d'ye mean?' Frank dropped the harness from his
hands, hands still lean and brown and finely shaped. He
raised his face to his brother with a child-like smile.

Slowly Hamilton laid his hands on the misshapen shoulders and sank down on his knees beside Frank. 'Frankie boy, are we bad to ye? Are we hasty in the tongue wi' ye, at times? God knows, Frankie, but we don't mean to be, we don't mean to be.'

Frank laid a finger gently on his brother's cheek. Some of the tenderness of his young manhood shone in his eyes. 'We? You're close knit, aren't ye, Hami? There's no splitting ye.'

'The three o' us, Frankie,' Hamilton mumbled. 'The three o' us is woven throughother.' He felt Frank draw away from him and saw the sidelong furtive glance of his eyes. 'That's a lie. I'm no part of ye now. I'm not woven intae this place. I'm the broken reed wi' the withered pith.'

Hamilton tried to draw his brother to him again, but Frank held him off, turning his face away from the man kneeling beside him. 'I'll have none o' ye. I sinned onct, and God chastised me. Now I know I maun save another from sinning.' Hamilton stood up and pulled the crippled man round to face him. 'Who'll ye save, Frank?' he asked harshly. 'I'll say no more,' answered the other, pushing his hand from his shoulder.

For some time Hamilton stood gazing at his brother's back. Frank had lifted the piece of harness on to the top of some bags of Indian corn at the end wall, and was fumbling at it in the gloom of the shed. Hamilton knew that his brother couldn't see what was in his hands, and for some reason the thought made him afraid. 'Come out into the light, Frank,' he said. 'Come out into the light, man.'

'I want no light for what I'm doing,' answered the man in the gloom. Hamilton retreated to the door, and lifting a straw, drew it thoughtfully through his teeth. 'Aye, by God, maybe you're speaking an honest word at that,' he said at last, and left the shed, closing the half-door after him.

He saw Sarah coming up from the well in the lough field, her body straight and taut between the two lipping buckets held away from her skirt by a wooden hoop. As she stepped unsteadily on the rutted track little silver fringes of water leapt out from the buckets and fell on the earth. He walked slowly across the close and down the track and seated himself on the stone dyke. Sarah put down the buckets with a sigh of relief and rubbed her numb fingers. 'It's fine to see the gentry taking the air on a summer's day,' she said. Hamilton's lips curved in a smile, then he crooked his finger for her to come nearer. 'Sarah, tell me, have ye noticed Frank talking ower much to Andra or the wee girl?'

'For why?'

Hamilton raised his hand. 'I only asked ye a question. Have ye, or have ye no?'

'Nothing more nor ordinary.'

'All right, then. Now, there's nothing to be feard of,' he added, noticing the uneasiness on the woman's face. 'Frank has just been acting a wee bit odd, of late.'

'Aye, odder than ye think. He attended Ravara Meeting-House last Sunday. That's where he was in the trap.'

Hamilton's face lit up. 'B'God, I'm glad to hear that!

246

He's welcome to it, if it gives him any comfort, for the cratur has had a wicked time of it, wi' that back o' his. Aye, he's welcome to it.'

'Aye,' echoed Sarah, but her expression was not one of agreement. Hamilton stepped into the hoop and swung the buckets up lightly in his fingers. But he was silent as they made their way towards the farmhouse. He hadn't told Sarah what was uppermost in his mind, and now his loyalty to his brother was struggling with his loyalty to Sarah and the children. When they reached the gate into the close he put down the buckets and turned to the woman. 'Sarah, I want no more said about this—but, if ye see Frank—kind of—telling the weans things—I don't mean wicked things—but things that might scald their hearts—'

Sarah laughed, but there was a tender note in her voice when she spoke: 'Hami, why do ye say one thing and think another? You're feard that now Frank has got the religion he might take the notion to tell Andrew or Martha about—us?'

'Aye! Aye, that's it!' burst out Hamilton more stirred and troubled when he heard his innermost fear spoken aloud. 'Sarah, we've been good to the wee ones, haven't we? They've naught tae reproach us wi' have they?' He watched her with fear and anxiety.

At that moment Martha jumped from the corner of the barn and shouted loudly to frighten them. Sarah opened her arms and cried: 'Come, my wee lamb!' The girl flew across the close, nutbrown, lithe, beautiful, and sprang into her mother's arms. 'I scairt ye, didn't I? I scairt ye!' she shouted, hiding her face in her mother's neck. 'Aye, dearie, ye scairt us,' answered Sarah, folding her arms passionately around the child. Hamilton lifted the buckets and followed them into the house.

One evening later, Sarah was weeding in the rath garden. A hush lay on the farm disturbed only by the belling of a dog on the shore and the thud of Andrew's spade beyond the earthwork where he widened a trinket of water to make another pond for the ducks. His elders had advised him against it, but he was unheeding, and the rich-smelling soil, the fragrance of the garden, and the calmness of the evening, bred in Sarah a lazy contentment with whatever her son did. Suddenly she heard a low sibilant whistle from beyond the blackthorn hedge to her left, and then Frank's voice calling quietly 'Andra! Hi, Andra!' She raised her head over the screen of daisies and saw Andrew looking over his shoulder expectantly. Frank called again and she watched the boy drop his spade and walk round the rig of the field beyond the rath. Creeping stealthily across the garden she peered through the hedge. Frank had climbed up through the young corn and was seated on a tumbled mound of the rath in such a way that she could clearly see his face. The boy stood before him, waiting for the man to speak.

'Aye, Frank? Ye called me?'

'I called ye, son, I wanted a word wi' ye.' The boy waited obediently before the man, but as the seconds dragged past in silence, stirred and glanced impatiently over his shoulder. 'I wanted tae—' Frank halted again and Sarah saw the mounting resolve in his eyes. She tensed herself to break through the hedge when to her amazement Frank caught the boy to him and burst into tears.

'My wee son!' he cried. 'My wee son!' She saw Andrew look round in distress, and then lay a soothing hand on the bowed head of the cripple. She crept down from the hedge, and stole back across the garden, as silently as she had come.

CHAPTER SIX

★

A GIRL OF ABOUT sixteen years of age wheeled her bicycle out of the loanen leading to Rathard, and crossing carefully to the other side of the road, pointed the front wheel to Knocknadreemally Hill. She didn't mount immediately but stood looking at the bicycle with obvious satisfaction. It was brand-new. The spokes and rims twinkled in the sunlight as she let it run forward, and the black and yellow strings of the dress-guard were as taut and clean as harp-strings. She pushed it a little faster and put on the front brake. When the back wheel rose slightly from the road at this sudden check, the girl chuckled in delight with a note as sweet as the bell on the handlebars. It was a lovely bicycle.

She mounted, and after a few preliminary wobbles picked up speed to thrust swiftly down the slope before the ascent of Knocknadreemally. The impetus of her flight carried her half-way up the hill, then she raised herself over the bars, her bare shapely legs thrusting strongly on the pedals, her red lips open as she breathed. She defeated and completely subdued the hill under her twinkling wheels, and shook back her brown curls to the cool air when she reached the level. On her right were two small cottages, one shuttered, with a beard of grass on its thatch, now used by her family as a potato-house.

At the second, as she sped past it, she saw a bent old man clad only in a nightshirt, standing at the door. For the briefest moment she saw him reach out a clawed finger at her, saw a smile break on his dirty stubbled face, heard him cry, 'wee Martha! wee Martha!' But she was safely past, rushing down the hill away from the old fool and the stench that neighbours said came from his dark untended home since his wife died.

At the bottom of the hill a flock of hens lay on the road murmuring to each other, yawning and fluffing dust on their feathers. She bore down on them laughing and trilling her bell madly. They fled before her spinning wheel, searching holes in the hedges, and when she was far away she could still hear their indignant abuse and the angry stutter of the cock.

She cycled along the undulating road that ran through Banyil Moss, and after pushing up a hill dismounted at the door of Skillen's grocery store. The shop was a continuation of Skillen's dwelling-house, a pretentious pebble-dashed house, with a fringe of nasturtiums running along the base of the wall.

The shop itself was large and dark and the air heavy with the varied odours that rose from the merchandise that the store displayed. From the left of the door the heavy dusty smell of meals, crushed corn and maize mingled with the smells of bacon, red cheese, onions, candles, camphor and agricultural medicines. A large red oil-drum, with a copper measure dangling from the spigot, sat in a dark circle of paraffin soaked into the floor. At the ping of the doorbell a young man's head rose from behind a round red cheese that sat on the counter. He hurried forward wiping his fingers on his apron. 'Hello, Martha,' he said grinning bashfully. The girl held out the string shopping bag she carried. 'I want half a pound o' tea, and two pounds o' sugar, and my mother says'll ye get the van to leave up four gallons o' paraffin the next time its near our place?' The youth unwound his fingers from his apron and took the bag. 'I suppose you're letting on ye don't remember me going to Ravara School?' 'Of course I remember ye! Didn't ye go to school with our Andrew?' retorted the girl, scornful at such puerile raillery. 'Then what do they call me?' he demanded. 'They call ye Joe Skillen.' 'Ah, then ye *do* remember me!' cried Joe triumphantly. 'Of course I remember ye. D'ye think I'm as daft as all that!'

Joe, chivalrously acknowledging defeat, retreated behind the counter and put the tea and sugar in the string bag. 'Ye won't forget the paraffin?' asked the girl as she accepted her purchases. 'I'll bring it up meself. I can't say fairer nor that!' cried the youth, rubbing his hands together briskly. The girl looked at him gravely. 'No, I suppose ye can't,' she agreed.

He opened the door for her and followed her out on to the road. As she stepped across the bicycle and stood poised, Joe rearranged the string bag that she had hung on the handlebars. 'It might catch on the brakes,' he warned. Suddenly he slid his hand along the bar until it closed on hers. He felt her warm brown hand quiver under his like a bird. 'I'll be up wi' the paraffin one of these evenings, soon,' he said in a quick unsteady voice. He bent his head down to see her face under her tumbled hair. Her mouth was curved in laughter, and his heart raced again. Without a word she shook her hand loose, and pushing vigorously on the pedals sped away from him.

When he went back into the shop his father was cutting tobacco at the counter. 'Who was that ye were ushering out?' he demanded. 'Martha Echlin from Rathard.' 'Oh, it was, was it?' said his father putting down the tobacco knife and turning his red moon face on his son. 'Well, you've damned little to do wi' your time, helping that daughter o' Jezebel t'load a pickle o' tea and sugar on her bislick. Damned little to do.' And tucking the plug of tobacco into his waistpocket, he left the shop by the door leading to the dwelling-house.

CHAPTER SEVEN

★

FAR AWAY, ON a neighbouring hill, a cock clapt his fiery wings and lifted his trumpet to the sky. In the bog below Knocknadreemally a cow crooned patiently. A bronze shape stirred in a corner of Petie Sampson's kitchen, shook itself, stepped into the middle of the floor and stretched its long body. The prying light that filtered through the window glowed on the warm colouring of the dog and lit up the miserable kitchen, with its spider-linked roots and dusty jars. The dog trotted over to the sofa and nosed Petie where he lay in his cocoon of blankets. The old man turned over muttering but didn't rise until Kipper (the seventh in a line of Irish setters of that name) laid his forepaws over his chest with a resounding thump. Petie shook him off. 'Damn-it-skin, you're a right pest,' he mumbled. After a few seconds of groaning, stretching and scratching his belly under his shirt, he lowered his bent naked legs to the floor. Still scratching himself he hobbled across the earth floor to the chair where he had thrown his trousers the night before.

He drew them on, and a pair of socks as stiff as boards, and clumped into his boots. His toilet was as brief and simple as his dog's—a rubbing of his eyes with a soiled cloth and phlegmy spittle shot into the back of the smouldering fire, and he was ready for breakfast and the day's work. He drew the bolt of the door and went out to relieve himself at the gable of the house. When he came in again he prodded the fire, threw a fresh turf on it, and pushed the porridge-pot and the soot-crusted kettle into the embers. When a languid bubble burst on the surface of the porridge he stirred the skin into the steaming mess. 'Gie's it a bit o' body,' he explained to Kipper, who sat on his haunches watching expectantly his master's preparations.

When the porridge was warm enough to be spooned into two dishes the kettle shot a splutter of steam and water from its spout. Petie took a canister from the mantelboard and shook a handful of tea into his palm. He emptied this into the kettle and poured out another handful from the canister. Before he added this to the water he poured some of the brew into the back of the fire, observing critically its strength and colour. 'Strong enough,' he said, emptying the handful back into the canister. 'That'll gie us a fresh cup when we get back frae Belfast.' The tea and the porridge and a few dried crusts were mixed up on a dish for Kipper; Petie lifted his own plate on to his knee, and master and dog ate their break-fast.

The daylight had broadened when Petie went out again. He lifted his nose and sniffed appreciatively at the marbled sky. 'We'll get a dry run the-day, Kipper boy, if that sky houlds. 'Tis time them boyos were showing signs,' he added, looking down the silent road towards Ravara. But he had scarcely gone back into the cottage again before faint shouts came filtering up the hill, and an undertone of many hooves. Pulling on his jacket and cramming a battered hat on his head, Petie trod down the fire, lifted an ashplant from the corner, drove Kipper out before him, and closed the door.

Stretching from hedge to hedge a solid herd of cattle was advancing up the hill. A man carrying a now useless hurricane lamp strode before them. As he approached Petie he threw back his head and roared 'Are ye up yet, Petie, my ould dragoon!' 'Aye, I'm up, and waiting for ye this past hour,' answered Petie. 'Well, put this lamp somewhere, and get in ahint wi' the brother.' Obediently Petie took the lamp and put it in the small lean-to at the end of the cottage.

The herd had passed him by this time and he had to run to catch up with the young man who followed the animals. He nodded to Petie and then turned his attention to a little black bitch that snarled and bristled as Kipper gambolled playfully around her. The young man slapped his stick on his moleskin leg. 'Quit that, Molly, or I'll cut the tripes out o' ye!' he shouted, politely ignoring Petie's dog. He turned and again nodded amiably to Petie. 'Doesna know a gentleman when she meets one— bad wee baste.' 'But powerful at the herding,' answered Petie, not to be outdone in politeness. With a few further words between them the three men settled down to driving the cattle on the long road to Ardpatrick and the cattle train.

The two brothers who had offered Petie a day's work in helping with the cattle to Belfast, were Hugh and Peter Ogle, young farmers from the townland of Lusky Woods. They were Catholics, which might have deterred Petie in his younger and more obstreporous days. But beggars can't be choosers, and Petie's life was now as near a beggarly one as made no difference. He was wanted no more at Bourke's farm where young Mr Bourke had done all the byres up in tiles and cement with a new-fangled milking machine. At Rathard he could still get a meal and a spell of light work, but Sarah had made it clear to him that he was a nuisance when he went up too often, and had a way of tossing him a pair of done boots or a tattered jacket that hurt the old man's pride. Forgotten was the glib resolution to give old Petie the means to live out a decent old age, and only Hamilton had returned the old man his half-crown rent for the cottage one day, and told him not to worry about it again.

But not even Petie could eke out life with the help of thirty pence a week. So Peter Ogle, moved to pity perhaps by having seen old Petie working round his cottage, or perhaps by some casual association of name, had cycled over a few days ago to ask him to help with the cattle with a promise that there would be a shilling or two in it, at the end of the day. Anyway, here were Petie and Kipper on their way to Belfast, the lovely animal circling the cattle effortlessly at the men's bidding, and Petie trotting from side to side, shouting, blattering rumps with his stick, his wizened face scarlet with excitement and pleasure.

The bullocks were loaded into the cattle wagons and the three men and the two dogs climbed into a third class carriage. On the way to Belfast Hugh Ogle produced a pack of broken cards and in front of Petie's staring eyes proceeded to lose fifteen shillings to his brother. 'Made o'

money, that's what ye are—made o' money.' whispered
the old man gazing at the brothers in dismay and awe.
Peter Ogle gave him a slap on the chest that sent him into
his corner. 'Tits, man!' he shouted, 'sure it's all coming
out o' one pocket!' And the brothers lay back and roared
with laughter.

At Belfast they got the cattle safely out of the station
and turned on Queen's Bridge for the Sand Quay.
Among the thundering traffic of the city Petie's confidence ebbed, and he kept close to the cattle, so close
indeed that sometimes he was walking between the
steaming flanks of the beasts, and his eyes were as wide
and bewildered as those of the cattle he drove. But the
Ogles were experienced drovers and soon the cattle were
trotting briskly down the Sand Quay, past the church of
St John's and into the cattle market. When their business
was settled Peter, Petie and Hugh crossed over the bridge
to Cromac Square, turned down towards the city centre,
entered a public-house and ordered drinks.

They lifted their pints from the counter and carried
them over to a snug. When they were seated Peter Ogle
lifted his glass, closed his eyes, and slugged down the
porter in one long draught. He set down his glass and
shook his head appreciatively at his brother and Petie.
'That clears the cow-clap out o' your throat, all right' he
said. When the others had finished their drink Peter
beckoned to the barman. 'Three more pints, will ye? And
bring a couple o' tin lids or something for the dogs.' The
pints came, bland as milk, and a chipped enamel basin for
the dogs. The three men each poured a little of their
porter into the basin, and Kipper and Ogles' bitch

approached it warily and dipped their tongues in the freckled umber liquid.

Hugh Ogle glanced at Petie who sat beside him and then nodded briefly to his brother. 'Damn-it-sowl, I near forgot!' cried the man opposite, and fishing with his finger and thumb in his waistpocket, drew out a pound note and pushed it down into the breast pocket of Petie's jacket. The old man fumbled at the note and drew it out. An expression of surprise and dismay came on his face when he saw the magnitude of his wages. 'Dammit, men, there's no call for that, no call at all. Quarter o' it would have been more'n enough—'

'Not a word out o' ye, now—not a word!' cried Peter. 'Come on Hugh boy, dip the hand afore we choke wi' thirst!' The barman was summoned again, and when that round was consumed Petie insisted on standing his whack. As the drink mounted in them the brothers found the porter slow and the pints gave way to bottles of stout and the stout to 'half-uns' and 'balls o' malt'. They were big robust men, the Ogles, living a hard vigorous life, and the whiskey only fired them and loosened their tongues. And Petie, who had drunk more in the past two hours than he had in the past ten years, hung grimly on to the discourse, and the table. The brothers held out their arms for him to feel and boasted about their strength and skill at gaelic football.

'And I tell ye what, Petie, me bould cock,' said Hugh, 'you'll see the day when we'll all be playing the ould Irish games—all creeds and persuasions o' us!'

This generous piece of heterodoxy was matched by Petie raising himself uncertainly at the table and singing:

Ireland was a Nation
When England was a pup
And Ireland will be Ireland
When England's buggered up.
I'm as good a Roman Cath-o-lick
As ever went to Mass
And all you English gentlemen
Can kiss me Irish Ass!

A tremendous uproar broke out from the snug at this. Hugh Ogle thumped the partition with his fist, and Peter, tears of laughter running down his face, raised old Petie's hat and clapped it back on his head. 'Oh-ho, ye black-mouthed ould Presbyterian! We'll have ye in wi' us yet, before ye die!' he roared. The bartender had to shout before he could make himself heard. 'Come on you men, pack it up. Ye saw that sign up there—"No Party Songs". You've had enough—more'n enough by the look o' your da,' and he jerked his thumb at Petie.

'One more for the road, manager,' said Hugh, raising his hand. 'Not a damn drop—you've got all you're gonna get in this house.' He held the door open invitingly. 'Now, any time ye like—gentlemen.'

'Ye can go t'hell,' said Hugh, settling further back in his corner of the snug. But the barman was experienced in the ways of drunks. He opened the door and stared coldly at Petie until the old man, unable to bear his scrutiny any longer, stumbled to his feet and came out of the snug followed slowly by the brothers and the two dogs. The barman followed them politely and distantly to the street door and held it open for them to pass out.

'I could go back and clip that boyo one,' said Hugh. 'Ah, come on,' said his brother. 'It's time we had something to eat any way. M'belly thinks my throat's cut.' Petie stood with Kipper pressed closely against his leg, bewildered by the hurrying city crowd that streamed past them. 'Would there be a place close at hand here where we could get a bite?' he asked. 'And a bit o' steak,' he added, jingling the half-crowns in his pocket.

'And a spud for the dogs,' said Peter. 'Come on, men. we'll hae to go up the middle o' the town I'm fear'd. There's no eating-places about here. Here's a tram coming,' he added, halting at a tram-stop where a crowd of shipyard workers had gathered. Petie stared fearfully at the red clanging vehicle as it bore down on them. 'Could we no walk a bit, Peter? A mouthful o' air will do us good—'

'Not at all, man! Ye never walk anywhere in the city.'

'They'll no take the dogs on her,' said Petie without much hope as the tramcar grinded to a stop before them.

'Oh aye, they will!' retorted Peter. 'Upstairs wi' ye now!' he shouted, herding his brother and Petie and the dogs off the pavement.

By vigorous use of their shoulders the Ogles gained a foothold on the platform. Behind them came the dogs and Petie, buffeted and tossed by the men pressing behind him. Just as he got his foot on the step, a youth came clattering down the stairs and leapt from the tram, knocking him staggering back on to the street. The conductor, open-mouthed, craned his neck over a mass of oil-stained caps to see if everyone was safely on. 'All aboard!' someone sang out. The bell pinged and the tram, gathering speed, snored into the brown city murk. Just before it disappeared, Petie saw a sudden upheaval among the men crushed on the platform. A lithe golden shape wriggled out from the moving tram, slithered along the road for a few feet and then turned and came bounding joyfully back to Petie. It was Kipper.

Further up the road a mill suddenly released hundreds upon hundreds of men and women. They came surging down the pavement, sweeping all before them, so that pedestrians moving in the opposite direction had to hug the wall or step off on to the street. In a fumbling darting run Petie and Kipper crossed the street to the quieter side. What little sense of direction the old man once had was now lost. Hunger, weariness, and too much drink had left him in a befuddled condition ready to be swept along by any force outside himself.

He had crossed at the opposite tram-stop, and now, when a tram drew up before him, he moved forward automatically with the other waiting people, clinging desperately to Kipper's scruff. 'Upstairs with that dog,' ordered the conductor and Petie stumbled upstairs. He held out two pennies when the conductor came along. 'One for me and one for the dog,' he said. The people who overheard him, laughed, but the conductor snatched a penny from his hand and thrust a ticket into the crook of his thumb. A kindly woman leant over to Petie. 'They take dogs free,' she said. She smelt the reek of whiskey from him and turned her head abruptly away.

The tram lurched and sang up the road, climbing out of the city. To Petie it was a confused blur of hurrying people, the lighted windows of huckster shops, hoardings, dirty brick walls, street lamps, and people; people scurrying blindly along the pavements or moving forward in patient droves as the tram stopped.

'Penny stage!' The tram came to a stop, then laboriously began to pick up speed again, only to be halted by a fierce tang of the bell. The conductor came clattering up the stairs. 'Hi you! Penny stage!' and he plucked Petie's sleeve. Petie gaped at him and then turned to the man who shared his seat. The man caught his eye. 'Your penny's up. Are ye getting off?' Petie grasped at the only phrase he understood. He nodded eagerly. 'Aye aye, getting off.' He rose, dragging Kipper from among the passengers' feet and crawled downstairs after the conductor. As he stepped down on to the street he could see the passengers in the lower saloon staring angrily at him.

There was a public-house at the corner of the street where he alighted. After looking round him helplessly the old man pushed the door open and went in. There were already several men drinking at the counter, some having a quick one before they went home, some who had no intention of going home until their money was done or they were turned out. At the end of the pub, with his back to the fire, stood a young Irish Guardsman surrounded by three or four other men, his relations or neighbours. A shining receptacle filled with tiers of pies spouted steam on the counter. Petie's breath whistled through his lips as the warm odours of food and drink came to his nose. He herded Kipper into a snug and sat down, waiting for the barman. When he came the old man ordered a pint and two pies. He tossed a pie to the dog, bit ravenously into the other one, and gulped down a draught of porter. When he had finished he stood up and called over the partition for two more pies. He threw one on the floor for the dog, but he ate his own more slowly, for his hunger was blunted.

The bar was filling up quickly. Men who had been drinking since knocking-off time in the mills found a new thirst as workmates arrived. The hum of talk, the ring of glasses, and the thud of cork-drawers grew louder. People trickled into the snugs on either side of Petie and at last his snug door was opened and a man and woman, after glancing at him, slipped in and sat down. Petie moved back into the corner and pushed the dog under the seat, but the man and woman hadn't a word for him, and he began to feel lonely.

Then over the din of the pub rose a voice singing *The Bold Fenian Men:*

> ... all who love foreign law
> Native or Sassanach,
> Must out and make way for the bold Fenian men!

Petie's eyes brightened; he got up and the woman without ceasing her talk or taking her eyes from her companion's face, swung her knees aside to let him pass. It was the young Irish Guardsman who was singing while his friends good-humouredly shielded him from a distracted barman who ran round them like a terrier round a herd of bullocks. Petie, smiling and eager for company edged his way down the bar. The boss of the pub, taking a sour eye off the singer and his helpless barman for a moment, saw Kipper. 'Who's bloody cur is that?' he asked a man who was drinking a pint at the counter. The man glanced down at the dog. 'Never saw it in me puff,' he said. 'There's a good man,' said the boss, 'wheek it out for us, will ye?' The man looked at the boss for a moment, then set down his pint and catching Kipper by the scruff threw him out through a side door into the dark street.

Petie had wormed his way into the inner ring around the singer. As the soldier ended amid the applause of his friends, Petie laid a hand on his chest. 'Soldier—soldier, would ye sing us the Ould Orange Flute?' A silence fell on the pub. The claque stood frozen with their hands stretched out in the act of clapping. Men put their pints down on the counter silently without tasting them. From a dark snug at the top of the pub an old crone peered out, wiping the tony wine from her mouth with her shawl.

The barman turned a frightened face to the boss. 'Jasus, boss,' he whispered, 'I ast him to sing no party songs!' The Guardsman stared down at Petie with a hard menacing frown. But as he searched the drunken wrinkled face of the old man the frown slowly cleared. He bent his knees until his face was level with Petie's. 'No offence meant, old one?' he asked. He spoke in the clipped voice of an Ulsterman who had served overseas. Petie turned with a helpless gesture to the silent crowd around him. 'Sure, what offence would I mean?' he asked. No one answered him. 'Well,' said the soldier loudly, drawing himself up, 'You'll get your song.' But he saw that he must placate his friends. 'The ould cod means no harm,' he laughed. The men lifted their drinks, turning their backs on him and Petie. With an air of bravado the soldier started to sing the Orange song. He sang it in a comic manner to purge it of offence, his eyes searching vainly for an answering smile among his friends. After a couple of verses he gave in easily, with a laugh, to the barman's pleading.

Then, inconstantly, the soldier's cronies pressed round Petie; somebody bought him a drink, another warned him it was a mad dangerous thing to call for a Party song before you knew the colour of your pub, a third congratulated him on not meeting a bunch of boys that would have given him his head in his hand, a fourth bought him a drink.

'But sure m'grandfather was hanged in the '98 Rising!' cried Petie. 'T'hell wi' that for a tale,' said an old man with a round intelligent face. 'Sure, I've never met a Presbyterian wi' drink on him yet, whose grandfather wasn't hanged in the '98!' They laughed at this, and drinks were brought for Petie and the old man. It was the last hurried round, for the bar counter had been mopped down, the cork-drawers stood erect, silent and motionless, and the boss and his curates leaned against the back of the bar with folded arms, shaking their heads silently to each wheedling appeal from the other side of the counter.

The publican straightened himself. 'Come on now, gentlemen, come on now! D'ye want the sergeant in on us? Time now, everybody!' The Guardsman and his friends and Petie were urged out of the bar on to the lamplit street. The soldier and some of the younger men wanted to continue the drinking in a nearby club. Some of the more temperate wanted to go home. As the men swayed against each other, shouting each other down, an old shawled crone came creeping out of the pub. She sidled up to the men her eyes searching among them. When she saw Petie she whipped a porter bottle out of her shawl. 'That's for *you*, ye ould Orange bastard!' she screamed, and struck him to the ground. She scuttled off at amazing speed and disappeared into the darkness of an entry. The soldier picked Petie up out of the gutter. His hat had broken the full force of the blow, but there was a trickle of blood starting from his forehead. 'Are you hurt, old boy?' asked the soldier. Petie clung to him, sick, stunned, dumb. Then he staggered away, and leaning against a lamp-post vomited heavily into the gutter. The men shuffled uneasily, peering sidewards at Petie. They had no sympathy with him now, he was a drunk who might attract the police. They began to laugh and jeer, moving away in little groups into the darkness. Only one or two friends of the soldier remained, trying to drag him away from the old man.

'Hell roast ye, Barney, the club'll be closed if we don't put an inch t'our step …' The soldier shook himself free. 'Well, on you go—I'm seeing the old one on his bus.' There was a shout of disapproval at this. 'Come on Barney, let the ould blirt be!' 'I tell you I'm seeing this man on his bus. Now on you go, the lot o' you. If I'm up in time I'll knock on the window—if I'm not I'll see you a the morn.' Still protesting, the soldier's friends moved away round the corner.

He half-lifted Petie on to a city-bound tram and on the slow journey pieced together his day's story and his destination. When the tram stopped in Donegall Place he helped the old man off and led him to Victoria Square.

There he propped him against a wall and went in search of the Ravara bus. When he found it he went back for Petie. He called the conductor and slipping his hand into the old man's pocket, held up the few coins he found there. 'Is that enough to take this man home?' he asked. The conductor laughed. 'Leave him to me, soldier. I know him well, and where he comes from.' 'Fair enough,' said the Guardsman. He placed Petie in a corner seat and peered down into his face. 'Good night, old one,' he said. Petie looked up at him silently, without understanding. The soldier grinned and nodded to the conductor as he left the bus. 'He's all right now?' 'As right as rain, mate,' answered the conductor, jerking the bell. As the bus moved off, a spark of intelligence came into the old man's eyes. He staggered to his feet and peered out of the bus window. 'Thank ye, son, thank ye!' he cried. On the other side of the street a tall figure in khaki passed under a street lamp and disappeared in the gloom without looking back.

As the bus crept up over the top of the Castlereagh Hills, a squall of rain struck it, slashing the windows with black and silver. Here and there along the road to Ardpatrick the bus stopped in the darkness and a man or woman entered or left. None of them gave more than a passing glance at the bowed figure of the old man who swayed weakly to the lurching of the bus, his hands grasping the seat in front of him. And slowly in Petie's mind a small black bud of terror grew and spread. He stretched down and groped blindly round his legs and feet. 'Oh, God, me dog! I've left me wee dog!' he cried out. He rose to his feet and blundered down the bus to the door. The conductor caught him and hurled him into another seat. 'Sit down ye ould fool!' he shouted. 'D'ye want to break your bloody neck!' 'But I've left me wee dog behind me! Oh God, he'll be kilt wi' all those people and motor-cars!'

'Ach, not at all, the police'll lift him and keep him for ye.'

'Oh, no, oh, no! I know he'll be beat and kilt among them. Oh, God, oh, God!' he leant his head on the seat in front of him and wept.

The bus bounced and jolted on, a speck of light crawling over the face of the dark countryside. The conductor shook Petie by the shoulder. 'Knocknadreemally Hill, next stop, Petie!' he shouted above the roar of the bus. The old man sat up, his face sober and quiet. 'I'm going on to Ravara crossroads, Sam,' he replied. 'But we're coming to your place now!' shouted the conductor. 'Ravara crossroads,' repeated Petie. 'You'll get no bus back the-night,' the man warned him. The old man was silent. 'Are ye staying wi' somebody there?' 'Aye,' said Petie, 'I'm staying wi' somebody there.'

As the bus passed his cottage he didn't look out of the window, but stared straight ahead at the empty seats in front. Once or twice the conductor who sat in front glanced back uneasily at him. Then at last he got up and sliding back the window behind the driver's head talked long and earnestly to his mate. When he had finished he stood aside so that the other man could look back into the bus. The driver screwed round in his seat and stared at Petie as long as he dared. Then he turned back to his wheel, spat into the darkness, and shouted something

269

over his shoulder with a note of finality. The conductor shut the window and sat down with his back to Petie.

At Ravara the bus came to a throbbing halt. The conductor stood over Petie, bracing himself by the handles of the seats. 'You're at the crossroads, Petie,' he said.

The old man looked up and smiled. 'Thank ye kindly, Sam. I know me way now.' He crawled out of his seat and walked slowly down the bus. The driver turned round to watch their last passenger descend. The force of the wind and the rain made the old man stagger when he stepped on to the road. He raised his hand in salute and the bus slowly picked up speed and went droning into the darkness.

Petie walked back a short distance to the gates of Ravara churchyard. They squealed as he pushed them open, and his feet crunched on the new gravel of the path. At a flat tombstone he turned off the path and pushed on through the seeping grass. He had almost reached the corner of the graveyard under the hedge before he stopped. The burying-place of the Sampsons was two graves wide and the family stone nodded over it, heavy with its tale of death. The top of one grave still rose in a gentle arch of new-healed earth. Here the old man fell on his knees, then stretched himself out, casting his arm over the grave. At first the rain struck him with a dry pattering noise, merging at last into the dull insistent murmur with which it fell on gravestones, grass, and trees.

CHAPTER EIGHT

*

SOME EVENINGS AFTER Martha's visit to the shop, Joe Skillen delivered the drum of paraffin to Rathard. The wheels of his light cart were not heard by the dogs of the farm so that when he suddenly appeared among the rowan trees they rose up in a clamorous outburst to hide their unwariness. Skillen had never been in Rathard before, and he looked with intense interest at the woman who came to the door of the dwelling-house and stared questioningly at him. He leapt lightly from the cart. 'The paraffin, ma'am,' he explained, touching his cap and smiling pleasantly. The woman relaxed a little. 'From—?'

'From Skillens. I'm Joe Skillen.'

She looked at him as though the addition of his name had been an impertinence. 'I'll send one o' the men,' she said, withdrawing into the house. The youth made no effort to roll the drum to the lip of the cart. He used every second to peer and probe with sharp eyes around the farmstead. Was the girl Martha out? Or was she sitting in the kitchen aware that he had come? Who would Sarah Echlin send to help him? Then his heart gave a great leap as the tall figure of Andrew appeared in the doorway. Skillen hurried towards him with outstretched hand. 'The bould Andra boy! What's the word with ye?'

Andrew took his hand in a shy fumbling manner. 'I'm rightly, Joe,' he replied.

'It's a long time since you and me kicked a hanky ball coming home from school!' continued Skillen, linking his arm in the other's and leading him towards the cart. Andrew laughed so loudly at this, that Skillen glanced at him in surprise. He did not understand that this was the first time in eight years that Echlin had seen one of his schoolmates in the close of Rathard, and that the young man had suddenly realised that people still remembered him, and would shake hands with him, as they would with any other farmer's son growing to manhood.

When Skillen had clambered up and moved the drum to the lip of the cart, Andrew pushed his hands away. 'I've ould clothes,' he said. 'You'll only muck yourself carrying it.' He put his arms around the drum and lifting it easily, carried it across the close and set it down in an outhouse. Skillen who had followed him, gripped his upper arm. 'B'god, there's pith there, Andra boy,' he said. Andrew smiled and lowered his head as he pulled down his sleeves. Then he looked Skillen straight in the face. 'Come on in and have a cup o' tea,' he said. He turned and walked with deliberate steps to the house door. 'I've brought Joe Skillen in for a drop o' tea,' he announced.

The four occupants of the kitchen looked up as Andrew spoke. Although he had never before seen any of the three older people, Skillen recognised them immediately. They were people from an old story come to life. That was Frank lying on the sofa, who got his back broke in a fight long ago, over some girl or other. That woman at the table who stared over her shoulder, not at him, but at her son, was Sarah Gomartin, and the big-boned man at the fire, of whom other men spoke with respect, was Hamilton Echlin. After a pause Hamilton pushed his chair back hospitably. 'Come in Mr—Skillen,' he said. And as he moved back the firelight that he had shrouded shot across the darkening room and Skillen saw her seated in the opposite corner, her small shy vivid face turned to him.

For the first time the assurance of the youth wavered. He smiled sheepishly and bobbed his head, 'Good evening,' he said. If she answered, her voice was so low that he did not hear it, but the smile she gave him was sufficient.

Slowly his cocksureness returned. After a few jocular remarks to Andrew he turned his attention to the older people, feeling warily for the most friendly one among them. He was no fool, young Skillen, and talked sensibly to Hamilton about tools and their cost, and crops and the prices they fetched. Now and again he threw a polite word to the woman at the table, but it was Frank who encouraged him and drew him out. It was the cripple lying back on the sofa who had realised the moment the young man entered the house why he was there, who had caught and interpreted the shy swift glance between Skillen and Martha. And as the conversation grew the man on the sofa flowered into wit and laughter, and his gaiety spread to the others. Sarah gave up her work at the table and drew a chair into the circle. Martha and Andrew, amid the talk and laughter, gazed with curiosity at this new Frank, they had never known before.

Hamilton sat quietly among them, except when a bark of laughter was drawn from him, his dark eyes fixed on his brother and a happy smile playing on his mouth. This was the Frank he remembered.

Then, as Sarah stretched forward to lower the kettle on the crane, Skillen stood up quickly. 'I must be away now,' he said. 'You'll stay for a cup o' tea, surely,' said Sarah. 'Ah, it's getting on,' he answered, buttoning his jacket, 'and I don't want to be giving you any bother.' 'It's no bother at all,' Andrew assured him. 'Sure this is our time for a cup o' tea, anyway.' 'Well now, if ye say that,' answered Joe, sitting down again.

When the tea was infused they took their seats at the table, for no one would have thought of drinking a cup of tea at the fireside with a guest present. The slight formality of the meal checked the spate of talk, but the feeling of cordiality still persisted after the cups were emptied. Joe had fallen silent for other reasons than having his mouth full of food. During the evening he hadn't exchanged more than half a dozen words with Martha. Now he was pondering on his next move. In his most optimistic moments he had never dreamt that he would make such progress with the girl's parents. But now, when he left, he feared that the curtain of insularity would fall on this household again, and all the ground that he had gained would be lost. He made up his mind to chance his luck further that evening.

When the men rose from the table and returned to their places at the fire, Joe declined to sit down again. 'No stopping this time, thank ye,' he replied. He peered out at the blue darkness of the evening. 'And it's going to be a sore job getting down that loanen of yours, seeing I don't know the way. I tell ye what—' he swung round with a tense little laugh to where Martha stood: 'You show me the way, will ye?' The girl flushed crimson, and the rest of the Echlins, with the exception of Frank, stared at Joe in surprise. Frank, who was stretched on the sofa again, lowered his head and picked idly at the fringe. My God, thought the lad, I've made a mistake. He drew back a little. 'Maybe it's too cold for ye to come out,' he murmured. There was silence for a moment. 'Put on your coat, Martha,' said Sarah slowly, 'and see Mr Skillen on his road.'

'Yes, mother,' said the girl, and taking her coat from behind the door, pulled it over her shoulders. 'Well, good night to you,' said Joe, putting his hand to his forehead and swivelling on his heel to include them all in his salute. Then he followed Martha out to the close.

His horse snickered when it felt the weight of feet on the shafts and stepped out readily when Joe lifted the reins.

There was silence between the two young people until the girl gave a low laugh and Joe caught the gleam of her eyes as she looked up at him. He slapped the reins lightly on the horse's rump. 'Well, what's so funny, eh?'

'You're a cool boyo, walking in just like that, and stealing me away from the fire.' Joe was no sluggard when it came to love-making. He was not one of those youths, who, after they have parted from their sweethearts, recall every word and gesture, and sink deeper and deeper into a cloud of self-reproach and despair, as they realise too late, the invitation hidden in the glance or word that held no significance at the time. Rather, he was a young man who not only seized the opportunity, but made it. He passed the reins into his right hand and clipped his left arm round the girl's slender waist.

'And what's this for, pray?' she cried, striving, but not too vigorously, to unclasp his fingers.

'That's to make up for the heat you're losing at the fire.' She murmured in protest, laughed, and leant back against his shoulder.

The horse edged carefully round the left-hand bend at the bottom of the steep incline and ambled slowly towards the road. When they reached it Joe pulled up at the verge. 'What do we do now?' he asked, looking down into Martha's face. She laughed timidly and withdrew from his arm. 'I mean, d'ye think your mother'll let me come up again?'

'Oh? Well, why shouldn't she, she's nothing against ye.'

'Do *you* want me to come up again?' He had to bend his head to catch her low-voiced answer. As he looked down at the young figure beside him a sudden wave of tenderness overcame him. 'Martha,' he said, in a husky uncertain voice, 'I want very dearly to marry you.'

She raised her face to look at him. 'But Joe, I don't know you.' Then as she lowered her head she added, 'And you don't know anything about me.'

He placed his fingers gently under her chin and raised her face again. 'The way I feel about you has nothing to do with knowing—or maybe it goes far beyont that. But you want to know about me? Ah, that's a different thing! Look at me.' He moved her round until they looked into each other's eyes. After a long grave unwinking moment she was trembling on the verge of laughter. 'Well, now you've seen me. There's nothing more about me to know. You've seen me as I'll always be, in youth and age, fair weather and foul.' And it seemed to Martha that this absurd statement was the truest thing she had ever heard. The light shining in his eyes transfigured the small nondescript face of the youth. She put her arms around his neck and pressed her fresh young mouth to his.

CHAPTER NINE

*

A COLD BITTER FOG crept out of Banyil Moss
and drifted slowly across the road. It was the
first black fog of the autumn and the smell of it
banished sunny harvest days from the memory. Blind
winter was groping for a hold on the earth; the silken
busbies of the thistles mustered for a last stand on the
dykes, and in the waste land the nettles pricked the mist
like a shattered army staggering away from the murk of
war. The fog muted the countryside and to the noises it
could not stifle it gave a strange unnatural resonance; the
flung bark of a dog, the booming of a cart's wheels, the
drumming feet of a man climbing Knocknadreemally.
He climbed steadily up out of the silent grey sea to the
crest of the hill where the mist drifted in thin ribbons in
the clearer air.

It was Joe Skillen. He passed the deserted cottages and
plunged down towards Rathard, lowering his head as he
entered the mist again. There were beads of moisture on
his hair, eyelashes and flushed cheeks.

At the bottom of the hill he paused in his rapid unseeing stride, and groping his way to a field-gate, leaned
his arms on the upper bar. Vast columns of mist, creeping
up from the lough and stirred by the air from the hilltop, shuttled and pirouetted and curtsied before him,
hiding in their flutings, trees, hedges and fields. But the

scene that Joe gazed on burned on his inner eye. He saw again his father, his ugly red face grown redder as he progressed from reproach to cajolery, from cajolery to threats, from threats to downright brutal rage at his son's stubbornness. 'Very well, ye cur ye!' he had shouted at last, running out to the hall door and throwing it violently open, 'Get out to your crew o' libertines and whores, and don't darken this house again till ye come back to beg pardon of me and your mother!' But his mother hadn't spoken a word during the scene between her husband and her white-faced son. She had sat on the sofa, moving her great heavy face from one to the other, endeavouring to piece out in her slow mind what the quarrel was about. And then as Joe left the kitchen realisation dawned on her and she had cried out in a voice sharp with pain, 'Joe, Joe my wee son!' When Joe turned back to her, his father had come slopping down the hall, and caught him by the hair just as he was about to put his arms around the pathetic creature on the sofa. And Joe, good-natured wee Joe, had turned and struck his father a clumsy blow on the forehead, but hard enough to set him on his backside on the floor. Then he had put his arms around his mother, pressed an awkward kiss on her flat white cheek, touched the scant grey hair drawn tightly back on her shapeless head, and left the house without a glance at the whimpering man on the floor.

As he went over the whole incident again, recalling the shame and stupidity of it, he ground his hands in his pockets. It was the culmination of a series of scenes mounting in passion and abuse, as the blustering man threw himself unavailingly against a determination which he never thought his son possessed, and which at times roused in him an articulate and murderous rage.

It's all over now, thought Joe, and yet he felt that he had lost more than he had gained, or rather, that stupidity and ill-reason had filched from him something that he valued. For Joe loved that slow-witted kindly woman, his mother, and even at this moment, while he deliberately reminded himself that his life with his father was broken, it was not the last stupid painful days he remembered, but all the happy times they had had together; at the markets, the trips to Belfast, and those days when the three of them had joined their neighbours cockle-raking on the beach at Castle Espie.

Joe was fond of telling Martha how free he was of fancy, an expression that became more popular with him in later life, as he grew more and more to resemble his father, but here, standing in the sunken gateway, half-way between his old home and Rathard, he felt with a brief clarity that he was standing at the gate opening to a new phase of his life. Behind him lay the house where he was born and the summer days of childhood, in front lay Rathard and the responsibilities of manhood.

He pushed the gate open, stepped through, and climbed up to Rathard through the drenched fields. As he neared the top of the loanen the mist fell away and he entered the clear air of the hilltop. He stopped and looked down on the silent coiling grey sea below him. Away towards his home the mist suddenly billowed and swirled as though it were disturbed by some creature floundering beneath it. He thought again of his mother and his heart constricted in pain.

But he had something more urgent to think about now. He had to face the Echlins and tell them that he had been turned out by his father, thrown out of his own home and heritage because of them. He knew that Martha would not be surprised, because he had already hinted several times of his father's opposition to their courtship. In this way he had explained why he could not take her to visit his mother. The men, he expected, had never thought this strange. But what of Sarah? Was it her guilty pride that restrained her so scrupulously from asking Martha or him what his parents thought of their relationship? If so, Joe reasoned, that spelt danger, for it could only spring from the knowledge that she and her daughter were still considered unworthy by the decent farming folk of the townlands, and that the woman who ruled Rathard had to solve a problem, which, for once, could not be solved by money or thrust aside by her energetic will. He turned his face towards the farm. Martha was his ally, his affianced wife, the men he could twist round his finger. But Sarah—Sarah was another matter.

The clamour of the dogs welcomed him as he entered the farm-close. First eager Martha, then Frank, then Sarah came to the door. Andrew came round the corner from the rath. He picked up a piece of wood and threw it for the dogs to retrieve. It fell near Joe's feet and he snatched it from them as they bounded towards him. Then, before he could get rid of it they were upon him, planting their forepaws on his chest and arms, wagging their tails and barking excitedly. Half-pinioned as he was, he tossed it to Martha, and then began a noisy, laughing,

three-cornered game between the young people, while
the dogs raced after the billet half-crazy with excitement.
'That's enough, that's enough!' shouted Frank, shuffling
down from the doorway. 'You'll have them dogs beside
themselves, if ye don't quit!' With a smile on his face, the
cripple adroitly caught the piece of wood in its last
erratic throw, and going indoors tossed it on the fire.
Andrew followed him, and Joe and Martha strolled
towards each other, laughing and mopping their faces.

'That's a terrible fog,' said Martha, looking down
towards the hidden fields. She saw the shadow that passed
over his face as he followed her glance. He did not reply
but stood brooding on the grey tumbling mist that
stretched as far as the eye could see.

'Is there anything wrong, Joe?' she asked at last.

He nodded briefly. 'Aye, plenty.'

Hamilton appeared at the gate leading to the field over
the lough. He had a swingletree on his shoulder and
waved his free hand to the young couple. 'You may tell
me after,' said Martha in a low hurried voice, as the man
approached them. 'You'll all hear it afore the night's out,'
answered Joe. He saw the look of anxiety in her eyes, and
pressed her arm reassuringly. 'It'll be all right,' he whispered. The boy and girl returned Hamilton's greeting
and followed him into the house.

As the men sat round the fire while Martha and Sarah
prepared the tea, Joe pondered on the best way to break
his news to the Echlins. He almost regretted that he
hadn't told Martha, knowing that she would have told
Sarah. But then again, it might be ill-advised to let Sarah
into the secret alone. He might yet need allies among the

men. He glanced around him: Hamilton, his ageing cadaverous face lit up by the fire; Frank lying on the sofa, staring patiently at the ceiling; Andrew playing idly with a floury goosewing and answering the older men in monosyllables. None of them had enough authority in this house to give a decision on the catastrophe that had befallen him and through him; Martha. He would have to tell them altogether, and he evolved a plan, some gesture that would make one of them question him.

Martha pushed her way among them, lifted the teapot from the fire, and carried it to the table. 'Tea's ready now,' she called. 'Come on and get it before it's cold.' The men moved clumsily around the table until each had settled into his familiar chair. The tea was poured out, the cups handed round, and everyone stretched forward for bread. The meal was half-way through before Frank noticed that Joe's egg was still unbroken. He tapped it with his spoon. 'Dammit, I thought ye had emptied it and turned it end up! What's wrong wi' it, man?' They were all looking at Joe now. 'And you've no bread on your plate,' cried Sarah. 'Have ye lost your appetite?' He pushed his plate away and studied the faces around the table before he spoke. 'To tell ye the truth,' he said at last, 'I don't feel like meat. I had a terrible thing happen to me to-day.' He paused again and looked at them. 'My father told me to leave the house.'

Sarah spoke first. 'For why?' she demanded curtly. But Joe knew that she knew before he answered her. 'He wanted me to give up going with Martha. When I said I wouldn't, he turned me out.'

'Your father turned ye out, eh?' repeated Sarah, with

283

a harsh edge to her voice. 'And why did he fault Martha?'

As Joe sought feverishly for an answer, Hamilton rapped the table with his hard fingers. 'It's no affair of ours, Sarah, why Mr Skillen doesna' want his son to keep company with Martha. What concerns us is that Joe has broken wi' his house, and its for us to decide what's best.' But when he had said that Hamilton fell silent, and it was plain to see by his face that what was best eluded him as widely as it did Joe, Andrew, and pale-faced Martha. But in Sarah's eyes a light slowly widened, and her full pale lips twitched. 'Have ye any money by ye, Joe?' she asked.

'About a hundred and eighty pounds. I did a bit at the fowl-dealing in the summer,' he added in explanation.

The older woman rose abruptly. 'Joe, I'm going to put another hundred and eighty to it, and set the both of ye up in a shop. What d'ye say?'

Joe stared up at her, his mouth loosened in astonishment. 'A shop? But what kind o' a shop, Mrs Echlin— and where?'

Sarah's eyes closed in a cold lingering smile. 'A grocer's shop. I was thinking there might be room in the townlands for two. Maybe another one about the top o' Knocknadreemally in what used to be Sampson's old cottage?'

For a moment the dying loyalty to his father flickered up in the boy. But the hard quizzical eyes of the woman standing at the table demanded an answer. He nodded silently in agreement.

CHAPTER TEN

*

THEY WOULD HAVE cleared the loft over the potato-house and put a bed in it for Joe, for though by some contriving room could have been made for him in the house, there was a reluctance among the older people to admit him so abruptly into the inner circle of their domestic life. Joe, quite unwittingly, saved them from embarrassment by going to live with an aunt, a sister of his mother in the townland of Darragh, only seven miles away. He hired an ass and cart and continued his dealing round the countryside, applying himself with even greater industry to the adding to the hundred and eighty pounds lying in the bank in Ardpatrick. In the evenings he cycled over to Ravara to see Martha and to lend a hand in the conversion of the old cottage on Knocknadreemally.

The new shop had been Sarah's idea; the money ventured in the scheme had been her's also, so it was only proper that she should choose which of the men should supervise the re-building. Her choice fell on Frank. There were a number of reasons for this, some deliberate, others of which she was only dimly aware. Frank was in many ways a better workman than Hamilton, he had that gift of craftmanship, of seeing the task in its entirety, and working towards that end. In some ways also, Sarah felt that she was compensating the crippled man. She realised that he was excited and joyful over the task, and for the first time for many years she did not have to probe behind his joy, seeking for some motive working against herself.

But indeed every member of the Rathard household was excited about the new shop. It was a sudden outlet for them. They were about to break through the social isolation that had parched their hearts and minds for years, and on Knocknadreemally there would arise a homestead bound by unbreakable bonds with Rathard, an outpost of their own kin.

Frank had many more suggestions to make and he outlined them to Joe one afternoon, sketching his plans on the doorpost of the old cottage. 'When things are going well wi' ye, Joe, ye can build a house for yourself on the plot o' land next to the shop. A decent house, two-storied wi' a slate roof, pebble-dashed walls facing on the road, a bit o' fuchsia at the gate, and a green door wi' a brass knocker.' The youth eyed the plot of land that Frank had pointed to, and nodded his head. 'It would look well there—and when it comes to the building, Frank, you'll be the man that'll draw it up!' Frank caught his arm. 'Don't forget that, Joe, I'll be the man that'll build it.' 'It's a promise, Frank, I won't forget!' and they both laughed.

Having learnt Frank's requirements for the shop, Hamilton himself supervised the buying of the heavy timber, sheeting, brackets and shelving. Andrew laboured manfully to cut a larger window in the ancient stone wall of the cottage, and Sarah, with Joe to advise her, applied her shrewd mind to the purchase of stock for the shop.

During the day, Frank had the help of Andrew when he was free from farm-work, and a labourer, Martin McSherry, who could put his hand to coarse carpentry. Hamilton rarely went near the cottage during the day-time, but in the evening, when his work was finished, he would take a stroll up Knocknadreemally to see what progress his brother was making. Joe Skillen hurried over as soon as he had cleared his cart and had a meal, but in these early November evenings it was usually dusk by the time he had arrived, and the men were tidying up to go home.

As they worked at the old cottage, the fields around them were stripped for the winter, the last ragged leaves were plucked by the wind, and already one or two mea-dows were barred with ever-widening strips of winter ploughing. Towards the end of the month they had days of warmth, as though the sun had furtively slipped back for one last look at the earth before winter exiled him.

Andrew and McSherry and Joe, who had arrived earlier than usual that evening, were lying on the grass bank opposite the cottage enjoying the glow if not the heat of the sinking sun. From where they lay they could hear the subdued chink of tools from the cottage where Frank was finishing his day's work. The work was going well, and Joe was expressing his satisfaction while Andrew and McSherry listened with modest pleasure, as all good workmen should.

It was McSherry who saw the ridge of the roof buckle and cave in, leisurely and without a sound. He watched it with staring eyes, too astounded to cry out to the other men. With a shout he sprang up and rushed across the road. Like a sigh, a gust of wind laden with the dust of centuries, met him as he ran through the doorway. Then all three of them were struggling through the falling ruin, blinded and choked by crumbling timber, thatch and mortar. They found Frank lying under the broken ridge rafter. Very gently they released him and carried him out to the open air. He was dead when they laid him down on the roadside.

CHAPTER ELEVEN

*

FRANK'S DEATH HAD a deep and lasting effect on the people of Rathard. Skillen's regret at the man's death was intertwined with his much more lively disappointment at the upsetting of his plans, for like many who enter on a project reluctantly, he had come to view the shop on Knocknadreemally with the greatest enthusiasm, seeing himself not only as a merchant, but as a miller and a strong farmer in the district. To Martha it was a passing shadow, a few tears as brief as a summer shower, and then the thought of her forthcoming marriage again flooded her young life. To Hamilton and Andrew it was the absence of a familiar voice and presence, for men who work and live together become part of each others' lives, for good or ill. It meant more to the elder man, for he had loved his brother, and their life together had been, as he had always understood it to be, and meant it to be, 'woven throughother'.

But Frank's death sounded deepest in Sarah's heart. As she stood in the close watching them carry the dead cripple into the house, she glimpsed for the second time in her life the inexorable pattern that they had ceaselessly spun behind their everyday lives, and realised that Frank's death could be traced back, step by step, to their early folly. And what frightened her and subdued her that evening, was the knowledge that she had brought much unhappiness into the life of the dead man. There was something drastically wrong with lives in which ambitions and passions were never disciplined nor checked except by external things that could be seen, weighed up, and overcome.

But a life-long preoccupation with other people's lives is not easily put aside, and that evening she discussed the future in whispers with Joe and Martha. If the youth revealed some bitterness, Sarah accepted it quietly, and when he warned her that he would never consider opening a shop or setting up a home anywhere in the townlands, she cried out 'No, no! My God, ye could never do that now!' with so much anger and distress, that Skillen, taken aback, mumbled something about having made other arrangements. In fact, he had come prepared for some shrewd and calculated plan on Sarah's part, but this time she had none to offer; nothing but an anxious and pathetic interest in what the two young people were going to do after they were married.

'After we're married,' said Joe, 'we're going to start up in Belfast. I could've rented a shop on the Newtownards Road six months ago, and I know it's still there for the asking.' He paused, but Sarah said nothing, so he continued: 'It's a good stand, and with the shipyards throwing a bit o' work this weather, the people have money among their fingers.'

'Aye,' said Sarah nodding, 'that would be a wise move.' She hesitated and then added: 'The money I offered ye is still there for ye.' When Joe bridled, she waved him aside with some of her old impatience. 'Maybe *you* don't want it, but it's Martha's due,' and the young man was silent.

At any other time Sarah would have got a sardonic pleasure from the letters that trickled in after Frank's death. Many had been laboured out by neighbours who would not have set a foot in Rathard but for the funeral. Now a few of the men appeared under the rowan trees, as sombre and stiff as their Sabbath clothes, refused refreshment, waited silently until the coffin appeared, and walked behind it the polite conventional distance, when they turned home again and left the relatives to convoy it to the graveyard. They had put in an appearance not so much to pay their respects to the dead man, as to Death itself.

But there had been one visitor to Rathard that afternoon, who entered the house without restraint or question. Sarah, who was watching the straggling group of neighbours from the window, was surprised to see a young clergyman entering the close. 'Andra!' she called, 'Andra, go and tell Hami a minister's coming up to the house!' Andrew came and looked over her shoulder. 'Ye needn't worry,' he said. 'Hamilton knows. He sent word to him yesterday. It's the new minister—but he was to meet us at the graveyard.'

As she heard the clergyman approaching the door, Sarah turned to meet him. He paused for a moment on the threshold and then came forward with outstretched hand. 'We haven't met, I know. But I've heard of you.' Sarah took his hand gropingly, her eyes fixed on his face. That they had met, was the thought uppermost in her mind, and it brought with it painful memories and echoes of the past. The round pleasant face of the young man beamed down on her. 'You think you remember me,

perhaps? Many people here do. My name is Sorleyson—
my father was minister at Ravara once.'

'Ah, I remember now,' said Sarah, releasing his hand.
'But you were never in this district afore, Mr Sorleyson?'

'No, I was born a year after my father left here.' He
looked around questioningly. 'Is Mr Echlin about?'

'Come wi' me,' said the woman, and led him towards
the lower room. 'Andra' she called to her son. 'You and
Martha and Joe may come, too.'

Isaac Sorleyson, standing on almost the identical place
where his father had stood years before, offered a brief
and simple prayer for the soul of the dead man, and a
word of compassion for those of the living. Then the lid
of the coffin was screwed down, and the bearers lifted it
to carry it out. It had always been a difficult task to carry
a coffin through the dark narrow passage between the
parlour and the kitchen of Rathard. But the men who
carried it were cunning in the handling of clumsy inanimate things. Sorleyson, standing in the doorway of the
tiny room where Frank had lain in delirium when his
father was carried out, heard the terse whispers from man
to man, each order as certain and precise as the movement
that followed. Take her round an inch at the butt—up a
handsbreadth at the jamb, Andra, and we're through. So
the strong living men carried their dead brother out into
the light, as they themselves would be carried out some
day, earlier or later.

Then, when the coffin was raised by the first relay of
bearers, the neighbouring-men coiled slowly after it,
none pressing forward for fear of usurping the place of
the relatives. So Frank Echlin was carried away from

Rathard, with the men of the townlands following him, and Sarah and Martha, standing among the rowan trees, watched his coffin and the dark-clad figures stumbling under it, until all disappeared into the folds of the little hills.

CHAPTER TWELVE

*

THEN FOLLOWED THOSE days when the memory closes over and subsides like a new grave, only for small insignificant things to thumb it open harshly. Sarah picking up the empty water bucket and calling 'Frank!' and then standing silent, fearful that the others might have heard. Hamilton and Andrew gloomily completing tasks that had been outside their ken. Martha rushing into the kitchen, trembling with laughter and shouting 'Didn't I tell ye —' and then sinking down on the sofa where there was now no man to tell.

But for all that, Martha laughed readily enough in those days of tarnished December skies over which great clouds crept, laden with snow. The shop in the city had been rented, and Joe had taken the girl to inspect the tiny rooms that seemed to have been pushed under the roof by the bustling shop downstairs. She had come back excited by it all; the shop, the tramcars, the picture palaces that promised delight, and the unbelievable number of neighbours she would have—a whole city-full, half a million souls!

Yet, there was some shadow on their happiness, some sunken log breaking the smooth stream of their lives. Sarah saw it in the silent troubled gaze with which her daughter watched her at times. She wondered why Joe, who had been so energetic and tireless in gathering his new home together, should be so tardy in making arrangements for his wedding. At last she spoke to him about it. He turned away from her, his face flushing red. 'Aye,' he muttered, 'there's still another thing to do— I've another matter to redd up.' And no matter how much she pressed him, he would say no more.

But a day or two later, the matter was made clear to her. A small blue car swept into the close, scattering the hens before it like foam, and the Reverend Mr Sorleyson climbed out and came up to the house. 'How are you all?' he said, smiling in at Sarah and Martha from the door. Sarah returned his smile, indeed, there was something so honest and pleasant about it, that it would have been difficult to resist. 'Come in, Mr Sorleyson. Would ye like a bite o' dinner—or maybe ye wanted to see Mr Echlin?'

'No, no. I wanted to see you, and I'll take a cup of tea with you, if you'll be so kind.' He turned to the girl and put his hand on her shoulder. 'Run away out, Martha, and come back in fifteen minutes, will you?' he smiled as he said it, but the hand that urged the girl forward was not to be contradicted.

Sorleyson took the cup of tea, stirred it, sipped it, and nodded his approval to Sarah. But his face was grave when he spoke. 'Miss Gomartin,' he began, and Sarah looked up sharply at the strange title, 'I've something to tell you, and I want to say it as briefly and—honestly, as I can contrive. You know, of course, that Joe Skillen and your daughter have completed their new home in Belfast, and all that remains to be done is get married?' Sarah nodded, and the minister continued: 'Right. Has it not seemed strange to you that there's been no headway made in the arrangements for the wedding?'

'I was wondering that myself, the other day, but when I asked Joe he said something about having another matter to redd up.'

'Aye. Well, I can tell you what that other matter is— it's you.' Sorleyson set his cup and saucer on the floor and leaned back in his chair to watch the woman on the other side of the hearth.

'Me? Have I done aught to hinder—' There was such a note of fear in her voice, that pity broke through Sorleyson's resolve to be stern, and the words came tumbling from him in response. 'No, no! You've been a very good mother to the girl! And yet, can't you see, she's never had a real father and mother? What has happened in this family in the past is bound to give your daughter a sense of shame when she thinks of her own marriage. And she has a responsibility to the future—to her own children, your grandchildren.' He paused and leaned forward in his chair. 'You would make her a very happy girl, if you marry Hamilton Echlin. That's the obstacle to your daughter's marriage, that's the matter to be redd up.'

Sarah, crouched in the chair opposite him, did not raise her head. 'You—think—that's what I maun do?'

'Of course I do! I'll say no word about the wrong you have done before God, to yourself, and to the men. Some day, perhaps, you may want to talk about that. But, for all your folly, I believe you've been a brave and courageous woman.' At this, Sarah straightened her back and looked the minister in the face. In a lower voice he continued: 'There are still many things I have to learn about the world, Sarah Gomartin, some maybe, that you can teach me, but this time you'll be guided by me, for the sake of your children.'

The woman stretched out her hand, groping towards the young man. As he caught it, she whispered 'I will, son, I'll marry him.'

When he stood up to go, Sorleyson said 'You'll want someone to be here when you're married—a witness, a best man, as it were.'

A reed of laughter shook in Sarah's voice as she answered 'Aye, we'll want a best man.' They passed through the doorway and stood in the open air. She nodded to where her son, a silhouette against the skyline, dragged a recalcitrant bullock across the lough field. 'Andra could come wi' us.'

My God, said Sorleyson to himself, and turned his mind from the thought as Sarah asked, 'And the sexton o' the church'll be there?'

'The sexton—of the church?'

'Aye. We'll be married in Ravara Church, and as soon as ye can manage it.' As if she guessed what was in his thoughts, she swept her eyes disdainfully over the countryside. 'I'm too old now to be caring what they think.'

'Well, I'll arrange it for you. Say a week from Wednesday. Good-bye, Sarah, I'm glad I came. I hope I've made a friend in you.' Sarah returned the pressure of his hand, her eyes smiling into his. 'Thank ye, thank ye,' she said, and she watched the old blue car until it had clattered out of sight.

That evening Sarah was restless. Half a dozen times

she picked up her flowering hoops, only to drop them again and wander aimlessly round the house, arranging and re-arranging the crockery on the dresser, the ornaments on the parlour mantelshelf, or to pluck the already lawn-smooth quilt on the spare bed. Then she lit a candle stealthily, and holding it up, examined her face in the parlour mirror. She got a brush and tried to arrange her still heavy hair over a white strand at her forehead. With a towel she rubbed her cheeks until they burned.

When Andrew had gone to bed, Hamilton realised that Sarah was not in the kitchen. He dragged his chair forward and gazed into the black mouth of the passage. 'What are ye doing down there in the dark, woman?' he called.

'Nothing, nothing!' cried Sarah from the room, and came running light-foot into the kitchen. Her eyes were wide and bright and a red glow pulsed on her pale cheeks. Hamilton stared reproachfully over his paper at her. 'Well, sit down here and close the door like a good woman. There's a powerful draught wi' ye leaving it open.'

Obediently she closed the door and sat down beside him. Then after a time she spoke. 'Hami, Mr Sorleyson, the minister, was here the-day.'

'Aye?' said Hamilton, without lowering his paper.

'He wants us to get married.'

Hamilton dropped his paper in concertina folds on his knees. 'He what?'

'He says we'll have to get married afore Martha can get married.'

'Ah,' said Hamilton, gazing into the fire. 'And when's this tae be done?'